T0077857

SEX SNOB

A LOVE LESSONS NOVEL

ELIZABETH HAYLEY

WATERHOUSE PRESS

To Amanda, for your unwavering love and support and for being our partner in hijinks.

We couldn't ask for a better namesake for our Sex Snob.

chapter one

We stumbled up the stairs, clinging to each other for support. We had gone for a few drinks after dinner, but we'd gotten a little carried away. The last few shots at the bar had done me in.

I always got horny when I was drunk, so I couldn't wait for Zach to get on top of me and give me the fucking I'd been hoping for. We laughed into each other's mouths, mingling the tastes of beer and tequila. When we entered his room, Zach immediately pulled his green T-shirt over his head and then lifted his feet clumsily, one by one, to take off his shoes.

Okay, I guess we're gonna take off our own clothes. That's a new one.

I followed Zach's lead and removed my shirt and bra. When I shimmied my skinny jeans down past my ass, Zach spun me around to face the bed and stood behind me, pressing his erection into my ass crack and pushing on the back of my neck to bend me over.

Oh, no. He's definitely not going to do this!

I pulled away, quickly collapsing to the bed as I removed the rest of my clothing and tossed it to the floor.

Zach followed me onto the bed and hovered above me. He began scooting his crotch up toward my mouth, making no effort to conceal his intentions. I closed my eyes, but as I felt the head of his penis slap me in the side of the face, my eyes shot back open.

Yeah, strike two, buddy. This shit isn't happening either.

I needed to find a way to change positions. Fast.

I pulled his hips down, and he took that as an invitation to penetrate me—if it could even be called that—without warning.

Ooookay, so we're skipping the whole foreplay thing, then. No problem, Zach. I rolled my eyes. *It's overrated anyway.*

I had to remind him to get a condom. So I waited, for far too long, while he fumbled with the wrapper.

Christ, has this guy ever had sex?

Condoms were the easiest things to open. They were made to be opened in the dark with slippery, frantic fingers. My three-year-old cousin opened one once when I was babysitting her. I was wrapped up in a *Dance Moms* marathon, and she somehow managed to find one in my purse. I couldn't even find my keys in that black hole most of the time, and that little fucker somehow found a condom. And opened it.

Zach finally did the same, and once it was on, he wasted no time picking up where he'd left off. As he entered me—*I think?*—he grunted into my ear, "I'm gonna make you feel so good."

Is he serious? Is that supposed to turn me on?

But he wasn't done talking. "You feel this rock-hard cock, baby?"

Um, no, actually. I don't feel much of anything. Well... except maybe regret.

"Your pussy feels so fucking wet," he said in between grunts. "You're so fucking tight." Had he been memorizing lines from poorly written romance novels in the hopes of compensating for his less-than-mediocre performance in bed?

First of all, the word pussy *is so not hot. Second of all, there is no way in hell that I'm wet. And he's clearly delusional if he thinks he's big enough for me to feel tight.*

He continued his awkward, monotonous movements. In. Out. In. Out. And when I started fantasizing about leaving to get a bacon, egg, and cheese from Dunkin' Donuts, I knew this was going nowhere—for me, anyway. It was time for whatever this was to end.

The only thing worse than bad sex was bad sex that lasted longer than it needed to. So I did something I rarely needed to do: I faked it. Badly. I thought I muttered an "Oh, God," and let out an unconvincing moan or two. Not my best performance, I'd admit. *But at least Zach and I have something in common.* I laughed silently to myself at my observation.

Further confirming my suspicions that he had no idea what it was actually like to get a woman off, Zach sped up and let out a loud "Uhhhh" within seconds. He either believed that he had given me an orgasm, or he didn't care if I got one or not. Then he stretched his sweaty head and chest up like he was in the cobra position at a hot yoga class, and yelled, "Fuck, I'm fucking coming inside you."

Well, not exactly, Zach. I'm pretty sure you're coming in a condom. But now's not really the time to split hairs.

He collapsed, a heavy, perspiring mass on top of me, and was asleep within seconds. When I finally found the strength to roll him off, I considered leaving. Breakfast sandwich? Vibrator? They both seemed like better options than sleeping next to Zach, but I couldn't drive in my inebriated state. So, I had no choice but to stay the night.

❤

My phone alarm sounded with LMFAO's "Sexy and I Know It." But as I felt the waterbed sway beneath me, my body reminded my brain where I was, and I felt anything but sexy. Rubbing my eyes, I quickly shut off the alarm and flipped over gently.

Thank God. Zach was still sleeping. The string of drool that connected the corner of his lips to his pillow was as good of an indication of this as any. I took note of his muscular physique, his squared jaw, his rumpled dark hair. He was gorgeous. Which only made what happened last night that much more disappointing. Finding out a hot guy was a train wreck in bed was even more devastating than finding out a hot guy was gay.

At least I could find out a guy was gay *before* I slept with him, so I didn't waste a few hours of my time. Or in Zach's case, a few minutes. Well, except for that one time with Johnathan. I internally scolded myself for not being more observant of his sexual orientation when he refused to let me shorten his name to John. But Christ, even *he* had been a better lay than Zach.

What happened to the good old days when drinking led to blacking out?

Slipping out from under the tan comforter, I couldn't help but lift it up to confirm my suspicions. Yup, he'd never taken the condom off. *Gross.* Nothing better than waking up with semen crusted to your skin. Better him than me.

Zach was exactly why I had Rule Number One: always sleep with a guy I'm interested in by the fourth date. In Zach's case, it had been our second, and I was glad I wouldn't be wasting any more time with him. I didn't want to get too invested in a guy and then find out he's awful in the sack. The attachment could make it sad when we had to part ways. And I couldn't have that. Yup, better to know early on.

"Always test drive before you buy, Amanda," my grandfather told me when I bought my first car at age sixteen: an '87 Nissan Sentra. Though I'm pretty sure he hadn't meant for his advice to apply to situations such as this one, I couldn't ignore the parallels. If Zach were a car, the Lemon Law would allow me to return him. He was rugged and beautiful on the outside, but once you took him for a ride, you'd realize there was something definitely wrong with the engine. Or the carburetor. Or maybe the transmission.

As I searched the room for my clothes, I couldn't help but remember the "sex"—and I used that term loosely—that transpired here after our date.

Now, as the morning sun streamed through the windows, I scanned the room, desperately trying to locate all my clothes so I could get the fuck out of here. How had I even managed to keep my buzz through that sexual nightmare? I guess miracles did happen. I smiled slyly as I wrote Zach a note and left it on the pillow where I had slept:

Dear Zach,

Last night was really something. We should do it again if I have time before I move to Holland next week.

Amanda

If he bought my pathetic *When Harry Met Sally* performance last night, he'd definitely buy that. I descended the stairs, still putting on articles of clothing as I exited the side door and began the half-mile walk back to the bar to pick up my car.

💙

As I entered the elevator in my office building in Center City, Philadelphia, at just after nine o'clock, my only thought was, *Thank God it's Friday.* I thought I had left Zach's in plenty of time to get myself ready for work, but after a night of horrendous sex and way too much alcohol, the walk back to my car had proven more treacherous than I had anticipated.

I knew a shower was a necessity, but I'd skimped on the makeup to save time. I'd opted for a little bronzer and tinted lip gloss to give my washed-out complexion some color and thrown my damp blond hair up loosely in a clip. By the time I actually made it to my office, I knew my new boss would have my ass, even if I *was* only ten minutes late.

Steve Bader was an arrogant dick. If the movie *Horrible Bosses* had been real, I would have hired Motherfucker Jones to help me kill him. He found fault in every*one* and every*thing*. And to add to his condescending personality, he insisted that no one call him by his first name. God forbid he lose any of the precious authority he bestowed upon himself. But little did he know that the entire office was laughing silently—and sometimes aloud—when they addressed him.

How our new boss had managed to go through half a century without noticing that "Mr. Bader" sounded almost exactly like "masturbator" was a miracle I'd never understand. But Mr. Bader didn't just make me think he was a dick. He looked like one too.

He was bald for the most part. And his wrinkly face

turned red—and sometimes a subtle shade of purple—when he was angry, which was often. He kept a few awkward strands of facial hair around his mouth and nose, creating what I was sure he thought was some sort of a trendy goatee but actually more closely resembled a prepubescent boy's first glimpse of manhood.

And even though the universe had played a cruel joke by inflicting Bader on me, at least some stars had aligned in my favor. Since I was a glass-half-full kind of girl, it was *my* idea to have the rest of the office staff address Mr. Bader directly as often as possible, simply for our own entertainment.

I'll have those files on your desk tomorrow, Mr. Bader, we'd assure him. Or, *I'll get right on it, Mr. Bader.* That last one proved to be exceptionally funny due to its double meaning and the frequency at which it could be used.

Of course, when Mr. Bader wasn't in earshot, we referred to him as *Master* Bader. Doing so allowed us to double our amusement: in addition to insinuating that our boss pleasured himself frequently, we could also point out his gratuitous abuse of authority.

Despite the fact that working at an accounting firm was a notoriously boring job, the people I worked with were amazing—other than Master Bader, obviously—and they got me through the day. It was like AA: one day at a time. And I couldn't even get through *one* of those days without my coworkers.

As the elevator doors opened and I stepped into the brightly lit waiting area of Riley & Maddox, Inc., for a moment I was thankful for my job. I obviously couldn't complain about the money, and the atmosphere was lively and inviting, with its natural light and contemporary blue and white decor. I

SEX SNOB

even had my own private office, complete with a comfy leather couch and a view of the city through the nearly floor-to-ceiling windows. I mean, I could have been working in an old middle school with no air conditioning and barely any heat like Lily.

"You're late, Mandi. And you look like hell. You *do* realize you're working in an office building and not a wholesale store, right? You look like you just rolled out of bed."

Aaand there goes my moment.

"Good morning, Mr. Bader," I replied with a sincere grin, courtesy of my getting to call him by name so early in the morning. I avoided acknowledging my lateness altogether. He wouldn't care if I apologized anyway. "And I actually prefer Amanda," I added. I had told him this on numerous occasions, but he refused to listen. Correcting him was futile, but I couldn't resist.

"I know, but I prefer Mandi," he said, as if that were an acceptable reason to call someone by a name they couldn't stand.

I also hated that Bader had a British accent. Under normal circumstances, I loved accents. Australian. English. Italian. They all had the effect of making guys seem significantly hotter. But in Bader's case, it just made him seem more pretentious than he already was.

"I met a beautiful girl named Mandi when I climbed Mt. Kilimanjaro years ago," he continued. "She was striking. It's been decades now, but I can still remember gazing longingly at what I could see of her golden skin and high cheekbones through her oxygen mask." He looked up past my shoulder as he . . . well, fantasized. "This was before the days of cell phones and My Face or whatever it's called."

Facebook? Myspace? What an asshat.

14

I nodded to feign my interest, which only encouraged him to continue.

"Anyway, we never spoke to each other after we returned home. We shared something on that mountain that could only be described as"—he paused for much too long to consider his word choice—"special."

Seriously? You stare into space for like fifteen seconds, and all you come up with is "special"?

"I've often thought about her on lonely nights and wondered what could have been."

I just couldn't resist. "I'm sure you have, Mr. Bader."

He awoke from his perverted daydream suddenly. "Anyway, Danielle and Steph are waiting for you in your office if you ever decide to start your day and actually get some work done." He pointed toward the closed door. "The LaPorte account still needs to be analyzed. I need it on my desk by the end of the day."

"Yes, Mr. Bader." As I turned in the direction of my office, I heard him mumble something about how he was sure a computer program or one of those "thingies" for your phone could do my job.

They're called apps, you arrogant dipshit.

I rolled my eyes as I turned to leave. Once Bader had you cornered, you'd be stuck with some boring-ass story until you either found an excuse to leave or he told you to go. And I was going to quickly take advantage of his abrupt dismissal.

Danielle and Steph had smirks on their faces when I walked through my office door. "What's goin' on with Master Bader this morning?" Danielle asked. "We saw him talkin' your ear off out there." She motioned to the glass wall that faced the common office space.

"Oh, you know. 'Mandi, you're late,'" I mocked, mimicking his British accent. "Then some bullshit about loving some girl he met on a mountaintop a hundred years ago." Steph handed me the files, and I flipped through them. "What do we still need to do here? I'd prefer not to work too late. I had a night from hell last night."

"Night from hell *good*? Or night from hell *bad*?" Danielle asked. "Judging by the looks of you, it could've been either one."

I looked at her curiously. "What does 'night from hell good' mean?" Only Danielle was capable of having a *good* night from hell.

"You know, like you were drinking all night, you danced with some gorgeous guy until after midnight, and you walked home from his apartment with one broken heel the next morning after a hot all-night fuckfest."

I raised one eyebrow to let her know I still didn't fully understand.

"Then you have to come *here*," she added. "That's where the 'hell' part comes in."

"So, basically like a typical Tuesday night for you, then?" I laughed so she wouldn't think I was serious, but I was really only half kidding. Danielle took the "living it up in your twenties" thing to another level. Too bad she was thirty.

When she sold her house a few months ago, the real estate agent had to tell her to take down the sex swing in her bedroom. So she hung a fake plant on the hook instead.

"No, not night from hell good, then," I added. "I'm missing the 'hot all-night' and 'broken heel' parts."

"Hmm, that's a damn shame. Guess you'll just have to try again. Surprisingly, I have no plans for Tuesday night yet," she said sarcastically. "How about the three of us go out?"

"Yeah, I could actually use a girls' night. That'll be fun," I said.

Steph nodded her assent too, though not as enthusiastically as I did.

"Okay, perfect," Danielle said. "Let me handle all the plans."

I was scared for what the night would involve, but I was also excited. Danielle knew how to have a good time. And despite her crazy stories, she always knew where to draw the line.

Finally, Steph was able to get us back on track by chiming in about what we were actually supposed to be doing: work. Without her as my assistant, I probably wouldn't get much done half the time. I'm intelligent and work efficiently—as long as someone's there to keep me focused.

With Steph's guidance, we were able to tie up the loose ends of the LaPorte account and have them to Mr. Bader by three o'clock, which was earlier than he'd requested.

"Ahh, what do ya know," he said as I placed the files in front of him. "You really *can* put a few women in a room together and have them produce more than just baked goods and meaningless gossip."

"I know, right?" I deliberately smacked my gum loudly and twirled a loose strand of blond hair around my finger. "Maybe one day, if we're *really* lucky, they'll let us become doctors." I opened my eyes wide to accentuate my excitement. *Fucking misogynist.*

"Good day, Mandi. That'll be all."

I turned to exit so he wouldn't see the smile I knew I wouldn't be able to suppress as I said my goodbye. "See you later, Mr. Bader."

♥

Two days later, as I pulled into a parking spot outside my gym, CrossFit Force, I looked disdainfully up at the building. I didn't feel like being here. I had a love-hate relationship with CrossFit. I loved what it was doing for my body. My five-foot-seven frame had always been thin, but I hadn't been toned like this since high school. I looked down at my legs as I sat in the car and admired my sculpted calf muscles. That was all the push I needed to haul my size-eight ass out of my Honda Civic.

As I walked, I put my hair up into a ponytail and pulled the front of my Nike spandex tank up to cover the girls a little better. I was thankful that all of this working out hadn't shrunk my D-cup breasts. They actually looked better than ever—perky, full, and firm. They provided some nice curvature to my otherwise slim physique.

I began to stretch as I watched the previous class finish up. From the look of the sweat-drenched participants, today was going to suck hardcore. As I watched the group strain to do their final round of burpees, my eyes fell on him.

Coach Shane. What a class-A prick. "Come on, chests on the floor," he yelled at the expiring exercisers.

This was what I hated most about this place. Shane Fucking Reed. He was a cocky son of a bitch who had made it his goal in life to irritate the hell out of me. In the three months I'd been a member here, he had never failed to make some flippant, antagonizing remark during my workouts with him.

My mind wandered as I thought about how lucky he was that he was so gorgeous, because his personality was really shitty. He was at least six feet tall, maybe taller, with light-blond hair and dazzling blue eyes. And he was fucking ripped.

Adonis himself would be jealous of Shane's body. He was lean, but every part of his body rippled with muscle. If he could only have been born a mute, he'd be absolutely perfect.

"You here to daydream, or are you going to actually try to keep up with the workout today?" Shane's words screeched through my fantasy like fingernails on a chalkboard.

"If you weren't so goddamn boring, maybe I'd be more attentive," I shot back.

"You talk a big game, Bishop. Too bad your body can't back all that smack up," Shane yelled over his shoulder as he headed for the gym's only office.

I shook my head as the previous class hobbled out the door.

"How was it?" I asked Lily, my roommate. She's a teacher, so she was always able to make the earlier classes during the summer.

"How does it look like it was?" she replied as she held out her hands and spun around. Her tank top was drenched in sweat. Since the gym was in an old warehouse, it didn't have air conditioning, and the late-August air was oppressive.

"Awesome," I muttered. Not only had I barely dragged myself here, but I hated when Shane saw me struggle. He got some sick, twisted satisfaction from it, I was sure.

"I'll see you at home," Lily said as she walked toward the cubbies where we stored our keys and other personal items. She took two steps and then turned back toward me. "By the way"—she motioned with her head toward the office—"he's an even bigger dick than usual today."

"Fantastic. He probably got shot down by a flock of sex-starved virgins last night or something," I replied.

Lily laughed loudly as Shane emerged from the office and

walked toward us.

"What's funny? Amanda's love handles?" Shane smirked as he stopped in front of me, blocking Lily from my view.

"Interesting. That brings up a question I've been pondering. Since you're in such great shape, what does your boyfriend hold on to when he's plowing into you from behind?" I asked, deadpan.

Lily leaned to the side, her mouth hanging open. She seemed surprised that I would say something like that. *Hmm, I thought she knew me better.*

I gazed curiously at him, as if I expected an answer.

Shane grunted out a harsh laugh. "Funny. We'll see how much you're laughing in an hour." Then he walked away as though I was no longer worthy of his company.

I turned to Lily. "Was it something I said?" I asked her as my lips began to twitch from trying to suppress a smile.

"Just remember, I warned ya. Good luck."

❤

"Okay, everybody, let's warm up. Kate, take them through it," Shane ordered.

Kate was also a coach, though she never actually ran any of the classes. She usually helped monitor us as we went through the workout to make sure we were completing the movements with the correct form and weren't fudging our counts.

She was tall, maybe five-ten, and beautiful. She had the body of a fitness model, with her shiny brown hair, flawless skin, and washboard stomach. I desperately wanted to hate her, but I couldn't. Truth was, she was incredibly personable and had a great sense of humor. And she often got stuck working with Shane. Poor girl. Though the way she looked at him sometimes made me wonder if there was something going on between them. And I can't lie. The thought made me a tad bit envious.

Despite his being a total asshole, I would still like to ride him like a fucking cowgirl. I mean, I couldn't ignore the fact that he was totally panty-dropping sexy. I had a very healthy libido, which kept my mind permanently in the gutter, and I wasn't ashamed of it in the least. I was ever on the prowl for prospective men who looked like they could give me a good dicking.

And if it weren't for the fact that I'd never be able to look at myself in the mirror again, Shane would be at the top of my list.

After the warm-up, Shane took us through the movements and told us to get our bars and find a suitable weight. Today would consist of as many rounds as we could complete in twenty-five minutes. We had to complete twenty burpees, twenty-five thrusters, and thirty box jumps per round.

Fuck. He really was in a bad mood.

I made my way back over to the bars and grabbed an Olympic women's. I added twenty pounds to both sides, which totaled seventy pounds to thrust. *Love handles my ass.* We practiced a few clean and jerks to wake our muscles up and make sure we could safely lift the weight we had chosen. Then we all grabbed a box for the box jumps. After about ten minutes, I heard him again.

"Okay, everybody ready?"

We all nodded and murmured our assent.

"Good. Time . . . starts . . . now!"

I hit the ground and began my burpees, trying like hell

to keep my form perfect. And as I pushed through them, I reminded myself that this was why I continued to come here. Because even though Shane was a condescending prick, he pushed me to perform better. I hated the smug look he got on his face when I struggled or he had to correct me on something, and I worked like hell to avoid it.

The burpees left me fatigued, but I grabbed my barbell and started the thrusters. And as I came down and shot back up, hoisting the bar over my head, I felt a welling of pride. *This is seventy pounds I'm pushing overhead. I'm a fucking beast.* But my pleasure was short-lived, as Shane squatted down in front of me.

"Drop your ass, Bishop. Lower!"

If looks could kill, he would have dropped dead on the spot. My ass was practically skimming the floor. There was no way I could get any lower. So I ignored him and kept my pace. When I finished, I dropped the bar onto the ground and trudged over to the box. I got two jumps in before my eyes registered Shane messing with my barbell.

"What the hell are you doing?" I yelled breathlessly at him as I continued to jump.

"This is clearly too heavy for you. You're barely squatting at the bottom. I'm taking twenty pounds off," he replied nonchalantly.

"Shane, I did them perfectly. Don't touch my bar," I warned.

But he didn't stop. He pulled a ten-pound weight off one side and then headed for the other. "I'm in charge here, Amanda." He overly enunciated my name, clearly mocking me. "If I say it's too much, it's too much."

I didn't have the breath to keep arguing with him and

continue my jumps, so I grumbled, "Fuck you," and kept going. "And square your hips at the top," he added.

"Get off my ass and go bother someone else," I hissed at him as I moved back to my open space for my second round of burpees.

"I would get off your ass if it weren't the size of a continent. Now either do the movements correctly or hit the road. I can't have you being reckless in here." He stared at me for a minute, challenging me to continue arguing with him.

His words stung me, though I'd never show it. I just looked back at him briefly before setting my jaw and saying, "Just go away, Shane." I think his face had softened slightly, but I didn't look at him long enough to be sure. Instead, I averted my eyes and focused on finishing the workout and getting the fuck out of here.

The twenty-five minutes seemed interminable, but finally, Kate called time, and everyone collapsed to the ground. Everyone except me. I paced like a wild animal. Kate called everyone's name to record how many rounds they had completed.

"Amanda?" she called.

"Five plus thirty-five," I replied, signaling that I had completed five full rounds, plus twenty burpees and fifteen thrusters. I kept my eyes on the floor as I continued to pace.

Once she had called everyone's name, I took apart my bar, returning everything to its rightful place, dropped my crate against the wall, and bolted toward my cubby to get my keys. I bent down, grabbed them, and turned as I stood. But as I came up, I ran smack into someone, knocking me off balance. Two strong hands reached out and grabbed my arms, steadying me. I looked up.

Fuck my life.

"Sorry," I muttered to Shane as I started around him before he could unleash a comment about how clumsy I was. But he didn't release me. His thumbs brushed the skin on my biceps gently. I looked down at his hands and then back up to his hypnotic blue eyes and was briefly lost in them. Electricity crackled at our touch, unlike any feeling I'd ever experienced between us before.

An "Excuse me" from another CrossFit member broke me from my trance. Pulling away from Shane abruptly, I side-stepped him and started for the exit. *Who does he think he is?*

"Hey, wait, Amanda," he uttered softly.

I stopped and took a deep breath before turning around and looking at him with the largest amount of hate in my eyes that I could muster.

"Uh..." He ran a hand through his short, rumpled hair. He was clearly uncomfortable, and I momentarily wondered why before I reminded myself that I didn't give a shit. I looked at him expectantly. "Uh, nice job today," he finished.

I scoffed. "Thanks," I said sardonically as I whipped around and stormed out of the building.

❤

I felt the tension radiating throughout my entire body. And anger. There was definitely anger. Though that anger was mostly directed at myself. Why did I let myself become so affected by Shane's comment? "Stupid," I growled through gritted teeth, smacking my palm on my steering wheel.

Because I had reacted like such a baby, he had taken pity on me and given me that lame compliment and placating touch. I blew out a long breath. Though I had to admit Shane's hands didn't exactly feel unwelcome, that was not the kind of shit I needed in my head right now.

But I know what I do need.

I quickly changed lanes and hung a sharp left. I needed Kyle.

❤

I pulled into the driveway of Kyle's condo. His car wasn't there; he must have still been at work. I glanced at the clock on my dashboard: seven fifteen. "Overachiever," I mumbled as I grabbed my workout bag and headed for the front door.

I sifted through the keys on my key ring, quickly selecting the right one. It was easy to pick out Kyle's. When he'd had it made for me, he'd chosen a key that had a picture of a giant cat on it. He'd handed it to me, and I'd looked at him, confused. I hated cats.

"If you keep fucking around, you're going to end up like one of those people on *Hoarders* who has fifty cats roaming around your house and shitting everywhere."

Such a sweetheart.

I had met Kyle about three years ago at a local bar. I was immediately drawn to him. His hazel eyes were known to change colors in different lighting. That night, they'd been deep brown with twinkling specks of bright green. And I'd felt them latch on to me from across the bar. In return, my own eyes had studied him from head to toe. His tall frame had easily towered over me, and with his dark hair clipped neatly on the sides and gelled up slightly longer on the top, he'd reminded me of Superman. I'd *had* to talk to him.

We'd struck up a conversation and, after asking what he did for a living to ensure that he met Rule Number Two—only date men who are as financially successful as I am—we'd headed back to his place. God, he was a great lay. We'd tried dating for a while, but we weren't compatible as a couple. We were both too . . . wild. But the sex was too good to walk away from, so we'd stayed friends and continued to have sex as long as neither of us was in a serious relationship.

I walked into Kyle's foyer, dropped my keys on a table by the door, and started down the hall toward the kitchen. Despite the fact that I had probably been here over a hundred times, I was always surprised by the place. Kyle put no effort into his house at all. The walls were all white, his kitchen still had the original linoleum it was built with twenty-five years ago, and his cabinets were worn.

He's a lawyer, for Christ's sake. Can't he do better than this?

I made over eighty grand and lived in a two-bedroom apartment with a roommate, so I had no room to judge, but I liked the company, and at least my apartment had some decorative flair. Plus, ever since Lily got back from Europe after her horrible guy problems last spring, we'd been closer than ever.

I grabbed a bottle of water from the fridge and headed upstairs to take a shower. I picked up my phone on the way and shot a text to Kyle.

*Hey, I'm at your place, so
don't bring any skanks home :)*

I walked into his bedroom and opened his drawers, pulling a pair of mesh shorts and a T-shirt out. The shorts were too long, since Kyle was about six-foot-two, but his clothes always fit well enough otherwise, thanks to his lanky runner's build. I kept telling myself that I should stash some clothes here so that I didn't always have to steal his, but that seemed weird. You didn't keep clothes at your best friend/fuck buddy's house. *Did you?*

Leaning into his walk-in shower in his master bathroom, I turned the knob all the way to the right so the hot water would steam up the room. I began to undress, when I caught sight of myself in the mirror. I sighed and stepped closer, placing my palms on the vanity and leaning on them. Staring intently at myself, I tried to understand what had happened tonight. I didn't even like Shane. Why had his comment upset me so much?

The reality was, even though I had a ton of self-confidence, no girl liked to hear negative comments about her body from any guy, let alone a hot one. He had made me feel self-conscious. And I was never self-conscious.

Was it because he was gorgeous? No, that couldn't be it. Zach had been gorgeous, and I couldn't have given a fuck less what *he* thought of me. What did it matter what Shane thought? I couldn't deny that the longer I knew him, the more his snipes bothered me. I just couldn't help it.

I stared into my eyes, trying to find the answer to my question, but the steam overtook the mirror before I reached any conclusions. Turning brusquely, I walked toward the shower, spun the knob to cool the water slightly, and stepped inside.

As the water cascaded over me, an unwelcome thought popped into my head. Only one other person had ever made me feel self-conscious: Nate.

I scrubbed my hands over my face trying to wipe the thoughts away, but they wouldn't budge. Nate was the best and worst thing to ever happen to me. He was why I had my rules.

I had met Nate right out of college. He was ruggedly handsome, with black hair that he kept buzzed short, honey-colored eyes, and perpetually tanned skin. He had played football in college, so he had the lithe, muscular build of a wide receiver. I'd fallen for him immediately.

We did everything together in the beginning. I didn't feel whole if I wasn't with Nate, and he seemed to feel the same way. We began working, and life started falling into place.

I had done an internship my senior year with an accounting firm in the city, and they had hired me on after graduation. I busted my ass, and it didn't go unnoticed. After about a year, I was entrusted with some larger clients, and I rose to the challenge. My salary increased exponentially, and I was making sixty grand a year by my second year with the firm.

Unfortunately, Nate's employment wasn't quite as thrilling. He had majored in business but had never done any internships because he was so focused on football. So he graduated with no experience and no connections. He finally landed an entry-level position at an insurance company. When he took the job, I had encouraged him, saying that if he put in the time and effort, he would build up a solid résumé and he could get in somewhere else. He was spurred on by this and worked hard. At first.

A year later, we decided to move in together. It seemed the next logical step. By this point, we had been dating for a year, then we'd live together, hopefully get engaged soon after, and live happily ever after. I had been really naïve.

It didn't take long for Nate to become resentful. He could

barely pay his half of the bills, so I took more of them on. I told him I didn't mind, and it was the truth. But he did. He grew sullen and withdrawn around me. He rarely took me out, always saying that he didn't have the money. I offered to pay a few times but stopped when he stormed out one night after berating me for an hour, telling me that he didn't need another mother to take care of him and that I rubbed my success in his face.

We lasted two more months. Then I came home one day to find all of his shit—and some of mine—gone. And a note:

I can't pretend that I love you anymore. Sorry.

That had broken me. I'd questioned everything that had happened between us for the past year and a half. Had he ever loved me? If so, why had he stopped? Could I have prevented this? Been a better girlfriend? Was there something wrong with me? Was I not good enough?

Finally, after a truckload of soggy tissues, countless cartons of ice cream, some texts to Nate begging him to come back—to which he never responded, the asshole—and an intervention by some of my girlfriends, I realized the issue wasn't with me.

Nate couldn't handle that I made more money than he did. This was what eventually led me to adopting Rule Number Two. I refused to date men who didn't earn at least as much money as I did. It only caused problems.

So, once I'd gotten my emotions back in check, I'd hit the dating scene. Hard. And as I got more sexually . . . experienced, I'd realized that Nate wasn't all that good in bed, either. He was selfish. Hence, Rule Number One. I could've spent my whole life with a guy whose idea of foreplay was telling me to get on top. That would've been utterly tragic.

I scrubbed shampoo into my hair as I thought about how far I'd come, yet how much of my life was still affected by my relationship with Nate. It had been nearly four years, and I still had wounds so deep it seemed as though they may never completely heal. The thought was depressing. Which was why I didn't often think of it. I'd had enough depression for one lifetime.

I dipped under the showerhead in an attempt to drown my melancholy mood away. And it actually did make me feel better, though not as good as it felt when Kyle slid into the shower behind me. I hadn't even heard him, the stealthy bastard.

"How long have you been home?" I asked quietly, relaxing into his embrace as he wrapped his arms around my belly and bent his knees slightly so he could push his erection into the meat of my ass.

"Five minutes. Thanks for the heads-up about the skanks. Things were almost super awkward," he said, and I could feel his smile against my neck.

I elbowed him playfully. "Please. You weren't with skanks. You were still at work like the geek you are."

"Did you just call me a geek?"

"Yup," I stated confidently.

"I'm not sure 'geek' is the right noun to use when describing me," he whispered into my ear as his strong hands lowered and his fingers found my clit. "Try again."

"Hmmm," I moaned. "There's dork. And dweeb. And . . ." I was becoming breathless as his fingers moved, stimulating my clit before two sank deep inside me. His other hand snaked up to my breast and began toying expertly with my nipple.

"And what, Amanda?"

"And freak, weirdo. Oh," I called out as his hands wove magic with my body. But suddenly he stopped, and I was left unsatisfied and aching for release.

"No, those will just not do," he replied casually as I felt him tugging on himself slowly, his dick poking my ass with every sensuous pull. "You'll have to do better, or I'm going to really show you a geek by jerking off when there's a naked chick with a smoking-hot body writhing around my shower."

I turned toward him, my skin emanating heat on its own, not needing the hot water of the shower to warm me. I grabbed his thick cock in my hand and began to work it, feeling the latex of the condom that stretched over him. He must have put it on before stepping into the shower. What a Boy Scout: always prepared.

God, I loved these games Kyle played. They were such a fucking turn-on. But I also knew he hated to lose. He would actually jerk off rather than fuck me if I didn't give him what he wanted.

"Okay, Mr. Sensitive, don't waste a perfectly good hard-on," I whispered seductively as my right hand continued to work him while my left reached up and wove its way into his short, dark-brown hair. "How about genius?"

His hands moved to my hips, then one skated down my pelvic bone, coming to rest on my clit. I looked up at him, and he cocked one eyebrow, encouraging me to keep going.

"And . . ." I took a deep breath in, lowering my gaze from his, "Sir," I whispered so low, it was barely audible over the running water.

My periphery picked up the slight twitch of his lips. Then he leaned down and spoke softly into my ear, "So that's the game you want to play tonight?" He sucked on my ear as

I nodded yes. "Good," he breathed. Then he abruptly pulled back from me. "Turn around," he commanded, his voice strong and deep.

I obeyed instantly, knowing that I could trust Kyle to give me what I needed.

"Keep your head pointed forward," he ordered. His hands were gone from my body, and I stood there under the water, aching with anticipation.

I heard the sound before I felt it. He delivered a sharp blow to my ass, his hand cracking over it, stinging my wet skin. I let out a startled cry followed by a deep moan.

Yes, this is what I need.

After all the emotional bullshit that had surfaced over the past hour and a half, I needed this release. It relaxed me. Soothed me.

Kyle again withdrew his hand from me and left me waiting, wanting. Finally, he delivered another slap, this time to the other butt cheek. I tilted my head back in pleasure, and it was all I could do to prevent my body from pushing back against him. But I couldn't. That wasn't how this game was played.

"You were a bad girl today, weren't you?" Kyle asked, his voice stern and authoritative.

"The *day* was bad," I murmured, incapable of articulating more as my anticipation continued to build.

Kyle didn't reply right away. Instead, he cracked me on the ass again. As he did, I felt the tension leaving. My hurt feelings began to ebb away as they were replaced with carnal desire. Sometimes a girl just needs a good, hard spanking to clear her mind. All of my focus was drawn to my surroundings as I tried to anticipate the next blow. It was utterly divine.

"Turn off the showerhead and then bend over. Put your

forearms on the shower wall for support," he instructed.

Lawyers were great at telling people what to do. This was why I adored Kyle. He could read me like a law book. He knew that I needed to relinquish control, let someone else take over so I could stop thinking for a little while. And he was so hot while he did it.

I took a small step forward and bent over at the waist. I raised my forearms and used them to brace myself. I put one arm up by my head to prevent it from colliding with the wall, while the other rested parallel to my body. In this position, my ass was thrust out toward him. He rubbed his hands roughly over it, soothing away any residual stinging.

Then his palm found my ass again, and the smarting pain rippled through me erotically. My position caused my skin to be pulled tighter, allowing the slap to reverberate through my yearning opening and sensitive clit. I moaned loudly, applying pressure with my forearms, almost pushing myself backward to cause the dull ache to stay in the lower half of my body.

His fingers pushed inside me, swirling around authoritatively, as if they belonged there. Which they did. Kyle worked me expertly, knowing my body better than anyone. After a brief moment, he withdrew his fingers and left me without his touch once again.

"I'm going to fuck you now, Amanda," he said matter-of-factly, though I knew that it was his way of telling me to brace myself.

Then, suddenly, he slammed into me, lurching me forward. I released a guttural groan of pleasure as my mind silently applauded my forethought of putting my arm up where it would protect my head. The last thing I needed was to have to explain to people how I got a giant bruise on my forehead.

He eased out of me slowly, teasing me. And then suddenly he was back, filling me again with the same forceful thrust he had employed the first time. Kyle pulled out and crashed back into me a third time before he picked up speed, his fingers digging into my hips as he held me in place and hammered into me, quick and unrelenting.

I pushed into his thrusts, bending over even more to give him unbridled access to my quivering opening. He peeled the fingers of one hand off my hip and reached around to find my clit, stimulating me in as many ways as possible.

My body was close to finding its release, and I simultaneously craved it and resented it, not fully wanting this intense pleasure to end. And as his fingers brushed against me and his cock plunged rapidly into me, my orgasm reached its apex.

I moaned loudly as he smacked me one last time, causing me to fall apart beneath his fingers and around his dick, my opening contracting as it milked him. He slammed a hand against the wall above my head as he pushed himself deeper into me, finding his own release. "Fuck," he grunted as he buried his face into my hair, his breathing jagged.

We stood there like that for a moment, trying to regain our breath. Finally, Kyle withdrew from me and opened the shower door to throw the condom into a nearby trash can. I straightened and turned the shower back on. When he resumed his place behind me, I turned to him and wrapped my arms around his neck, hugging him tightly.

"Feel better?" he asked sincerely.

"Much. Thank you."

He grunted. "My pleasure."

I giggled at his words, but I didn't let go of him.

"I picked us up some Chinese. Let's get dressed, and then we'll eat while we watch porn."

I laughed loudly, effectively releasing any trace amounts of tension left in my body. "Dream on, creeper." I smiled as I released my hold on him. We washed the sex off our bodies in silence. Then we got out of the shower, dressed quickly, grabbed our food, and stationed ourselves on Kyle's couch. He flipped through his Apple TV until he came to Netflix. I ate as he searched for a movie.

"Go to the scary ones," I prompted.

"You just need to feel all sorts of extreme emotions tonight, don't you?" he asked with a smirk.

I shrugged, not wanting to answer his question and bring back bad thoughts to my mind. "Look," I said, "that one has Megan Fox in it. So it's probably *almost* porn."

"Good call," he gasped, smiling broadly. And as the movie started and we slunk back into his couch, I was finally content.

Thank fucking God for Kyle.

chapter two

The next morning, I woke up feeling like my normal self. I had gotten home from Kyle's around midnight and had fallen into a deep, peaceful sleep. I glanced over at my clock. Nine o'clock. If I got up now, I could make the CrossFit class at ten o'clock. I briefly wondered if it would be weird to see Shane today after our heated encounter yesterday.

Fuck it. It'll only be weird if I make it weird.

So I dragged myself out of bed and headed for the bathroom.

❤

I walked confidently into the gym five minutes before class was scheduled to start. My eyes immediately fell on Shane, since he was sitting just inside the doorway on a rowing machine. He was petting a large golden retriever.

"I didn't know it was Bring Your Girlfriend to Work Day," I muttered as I passed him, not slowing to give him time to respond. I smirked, pleased with my quick wit. I didn't look directly at him as I passed, but out of the corner of my eye, I thought I saw his shoulders sag a little, as if he let out a breath he'd been holding and physically relaxed. I briefly wondered what his posture could mean when I reminded myself *again* that I didn't give a shit.

I walked over and grabbed a piece of PVC and began stretching my arms as I looked at the board that showed our workout today. Not too bad. We had to run four hundred meters and then do max reps of pull-ups. Once we'd hit max, we would run again. We had twenty minutes to do as many pull-ups as possible. Twenty minutes of Shane. I could handle that.

I looked around the room. There were only seven other members and no other trainers here. Shane continued to pet his girlfriend. Finally, he stood and made his way over to us.

"Okay, let's get started. Ten jumping jacks. Go." He took us through the warm-up and then explained the workout. Next, he set the timer on the wall and told us to line up by the ramp that led out of the back of the building. "Hold on, Amanda. Get in the back of the line so you don't get trampled when everyone blows past you," he yelled casually.

"Finally, something you know about: blowing," I answered, looking back at him over my shoulder.

Everyone laughed loudly at my remark, and I raised my eyebrows, claiming my victory.

His lips twitched as he tried to suppress a smirk. This was how we usually were. It was inappropriate banter, but it also wasn't meant to truly offend either of us. We were back on familiar ground.

"Yeah, well, from what I hear, you know a good bit about that topic yourself." His lips lifted into a smile.

Did he think a comment about my sexual prowess would embarrass me? I was almost insulted at how much he underestimated me. "Oh, baby, you have no idea," I called before turning around and readying myself for the start of the run.

"You offering to clue me in?"

His voice was husky, which threw me completely off-kilter. But I didn't dare turn around. The last thing I wanted was for Shane to know that he had rendered me speechless.

I heard him laugh behind me as he yelled, "Go."

❤

Twenty minutes later I found myself in a pool of my own sweat with my arms flopped uselessly beside me on the wall-to-wall black rubber mats of the gym floor. *That sucked way more than I anticipated.* With great effort, I lifted my hands to my face and inspected them. Calluses had formed. *Awesome.* I plopped my arms back down on the mats and closed my eyes, trying to regain feeling in my upper body.

When I opened them again, I saw Shane standing over me, smirking.

"Tough workout, huh?" he asked, clearly pleased with himself that we were all exhausted.

"Nothing you do is tough." I worked my way into a sitting position, sighing heavily from the extra exertion.

He chuckled softly before extending a hand to me. "Come on," he said. "Stand and stretch before your muscles lock up."

I hesitated, wondering if he was going to drop me on my ass if I let him help me up. I also wasn't sure I wanted his help, but that seemed petty, even for me. I glanced up at him before accepting his outstretched hand and allowing him to pull me up.

Thankfully, he didn't drop me. However, once standing,

I found myself directly in front of him with maybe only a foot between us. There was a strange pull in my core, attracting me to him as if by a magnet. A magnet I had somehow managed not to notice until now.

I became hyper aware of my body and began to worry that if something didn't pull us apart soon, I wouldn't be able to resist the urge to close the gap between us and push my breasts into his broad chest. He stared intently at me for a moment before he took a step back and cut the electricity between us.

"Hey, guys, one more thing," he yelled as he turned to the rest of the group. "Friday is Kate's birthday. We're goin' to a bar in Manayunk. I'll give you the details later in the week, but keep the night open. All are welcome." He then walked off back to where he had tethered his dog.

I briefly wondered if he and Kate were dating. Why else would he be organizing a party? Though maybe he wasn't organizing it, just passing the word on. My surly brain tried to remind me that I didn't care, but for some reason, I did care. I just wasn't sure why.

The crackle I had felt moments earlier crossed my mind. *No, no way. I don't like Shane. He is a total douche. Not to mention that he doesn't meet Rule Number Two.*

I pushed all of the nonsense from my mind, grabbed my water bottle, and walked toward the cubbies. But as I passed Shane, I felt the need to speak to him. "So, why did you bring your dog here?"

My mind rushed through possible responses:

1. The dog kept trying to run away from him, seeking a better life elsewhere, so he had to keep her close to foil her escape.

2. She was pregnant with Shane's puppies and he wanted to

prevent her from birthing them in his closet.

3. The dog had complained that he never took her anywhere anymore.

4. She kept letting all of the other dogs in the neighborhood hump her and it was making Shane jealous.

But his actual response was a letdown.

"My air conditioning is broken, and I didn't want to leave her in my house."

"But there's no air conditioning in here, either," I pointed out.

"Yeah, but we have the fans going, and the dock doors open. At least there's air circulating in here."

I nodded my head, not wanting to verbalize that he had a good point and had done the responsible thing. He clearly loved the bitch.

"Okay, well, have fun in your sweltering house. It probably reminds you of where you were born." I cocked my head to the side. "When *was* the last time you were able to visit your old dad Satan in hell?" I smiled broadly at my comment, impressed with myself, as usual.

He looked up at me as he sat beside his dog on the floor, regarding me with mild amusement. "You're a real piece of work, you know that?" he finally muttered, clearly unable to think of a snappy comeback.

"Yup," I replied perkily before turning toward my cubby to retrieve my keys.

As I walked toward the door, I looked at Shane, the smile still prominent on my face, rubbing in my victory.

"See ya later, smartass. Oh, and you'd better be at the

party on Friday," he added.

My smile fell slightly. "Why?" I asked, confused.

"Because for some reason that baffles the shit out of me, Kate really likes you. She'd enjoy having you there," he replied simply.

"I'll try to make it. See ya." As I walked out of the gym and climbed into my car, my brow furrowed. I drove home desperate to figure out why I was filled with emotion. I pulled into a parking space outside of my apartment ten minutes later, no closer to an answer. Shane's explanation made perfect sense, and I was happy that Kate enjoyed my company enough to want me at her party.

So then why the hell did I feel so disappointed?

❤

By the time Tuesday finally rolled around, I was desperately in need of a night out. I still couldn't completely shake the weird feeling I'd gotten at the gym Saturday. And I'd spent most of Monday dodging Bader and his continuous requests for me to look at the numbers on the LaPorte account again.

When Steph and I returned from lunch Tuesday and Master Bader still hadn't given it a rest, I finally took the documents from him and retreated to my office. Danielle followed behind us, and since I knew the LaPorte numbers were correct, we simply closed the door, spread the paperwork across the table and desk so it looked like we were working, and took the second half of the day to ogle the gorgeous intern through the glass wall.

Hot Rod, as we referred to him, was about six-foot-two with sexy dark hair and a naturally tan complexion. He wasn't too built, but his toned body was noticeable through the fitted suits he often wore. And he had kind of an irresistible goofy charm to him.

He was in his last semester at St. Joseph's University, and we knew his time here was limited unless he was able to get a job with the firm. Since we might only be graced with his presence for a few more weeks, we decided we would create a competition that would, one, allow us to have permanent images of Hot Rod even if he left the company, and two, provide a solid form of entertainment until that time came.

The idea was to take the best inconspicuous pictures of him. Steph volunteered to judge, as she didn't have any confidence in her ability to take pictures without Rod noticing. Danielle and I were more than happy with that, as we enjoyed a challenge—and also gawking at hot men—and would now get to have someone decide who was the better stalker.

"Okay, let's agree to the rules," Steph insisted. "Rule number one: You can't tell Rod about the competition. And number two: You can't ask him to get in any pictures. No group shots or anything tricky like that. Got it?"

Danielle and I nodded in unison.

I had been competitive ever since my middle school softball team won the championship one year, and since then I'd hated to lose. I also knew that this was a sure win. I had been strictly following a set of rules for the past four years. Danielle was out of her depth here.

"What are we being judged on?" I asked eagerly.

"Yeah," Danielle urged. "Are there certain categories? Like best crotch shot or something?"

We all laughed but quickly agreed that categories were a good idea. Steph rounded my desk to find a blank legal pad and pen and returned to the couch to make a list. "Since I'm judging, I get to make the categories. I definitely love the crotch shot one, so that's a given. Hang on for a sec."

Steph scribbled on her notepad. With her dark-rimmed glasses and red hair in a loose bun, she definitely had a hot librarian look going. Danielle and I took the opportunity to eye-fuck Hot Rod as he bent over to fix the paper jam in the copier that was right outside my office. Steph caught a glimpse of him too and immediately jotted something else down.

"I'd love to show that Hot Rod how well I drive stick," Danielle sighed.

"Okay, listen up," Steph said after another minute or so. She cleared her throat and stood to make it seem more official. "The competition is called Hot Rod Shots. There are five categories. You will text any pictures you take to my phone over the next three weeks so that you won't see the pictures the other has taken. We need to keep it fair. Then I'll choose a winner for each category. Best out of five wins."

"Okay, sounds good. Now let's hear the categories," I said.

"The five categories are as follows: Best Crotch Shot. That one was already established, and I think it speaks for itself. The type and tightness of his pants . . . how closely you zoom in . . . all of it matters, ladies. So consider that when you take the pictures. The second category is Most Seductive Expression. You might want to catch him chewing on his pen, running his tongue across his luscious pink lips like he does when he's deep in thought." She paused, clearly caught up in her own fantasy. "Wait, on second thought, can I participate and not judge?"

Danielle and I shook our heads and laughed.

Steph sighed and continued. "Best Ass Shot is next. Then Best Smile. I know that one seems kind of innocent, but we don't wanna be barbarians, for God's sake." She lowered her legal pad and looked at us to gauge our reactions so far. "And lastly, Best Hair Day. You know how sometimes Hot Rod has his hair extra messy? Well, I'm thinking a hair day that looks like he just came up for air after you've used those thick, dark locks to move his head back and forth between your thighs for twenty minutes. But I'm giving you too many ideas," she added quickly. "Just use your imagination."

"I've got this in the bag," I said confidently as I clapped my hands together once and raised them high in the air with clenched fists.

"No way," Danielle said. "I can see his desk from my office. You don't stand a chance. Plus, you're like a fucking giant compared to me. I'm practically at crotch level without even having to bend down. If that's not an advantage, I don't know what is."

"This is true. Is that why it was so easy for you to suck Eric's dick under his desk without anyone knowing?" I laughed as I said it and then added, "Actually, I kinda feel like I'm missing out a little because I've never gotten fingered or dry humped in a corporate setting before. It seems to happen all the time in books."

As always, Steph had to rein us in again. She explained there would be a concluding ceremony with a prize for the winner after the three weeks were up.

Once we all agreed on the terms, we spent what was left of the day discussing our plans for the night. We agreed to meet at Steph's house, as she would be our designated driver. She said we could leave our cars there and spend the night if we needed to. Steph's boyfriend, Dan, had just moved in, but she said he was sweet, and he definitely wouldn't mind us staying.

Danielle wouldn't tell us what was in store for the night.

She actually said that the trick to a "good night from hell" was that you didn't plan much of anything. You just let things unfold naturally. We'd start at a local bar and see where the night took us.

At four thirty, I headed toward Bader's office to drop off the "revised" LaPorte account. Not because I wanted to be berated in an English accent about how incompetent I was or how the female sex was only good for procreation and knitting. I went to Bader's because Hot Rod's desk was on the way. As I strolled toward him on my way back to my office, I held my phone out and pretended to text as I snapped a photo of him with his legs open wide, leaning back casually in his chair examining a spreadsheet. Definitely not the close-up crotch shot I had hoped for, but it would do for my first attempt. *Practice makes perfect.*

I grabbed my belongings from my office and quickly texted the picture to Steph before throwing my phone in my purse and heading toward the elevators.

❤

I sped home, eager to get the night going. Well, "sped" might actually be an understatement. I never go the speed limit. Ever. So when I say I "sped," what I meant that I used the shoulder as a fourth lane to get through traffic on I-95, and when the road finally opened up a bit, I changed lanes like Mario Andretti and floored it down the left lane. When my exit finally approached, I found myself perpendicular in front of a tractor-trailer as I cut across the highway. The driver blasted his horn loudly.

Fuck you, asshole. I got places to be.

When I opened the door to our apartment, Lily was lounging on the couch reading. *Teachers.* She had barely done anything all summer. She was always texting me stupid pictures of herself relaxing and mocking me for having what she called a real job.

I told her if she sent me one more picture of her feet from a lounge chair at the pool, I would cut her friggin' toes off one by one. She had finally gone back to work for those meetings or whatever bullshit teachers have to do in the beginning of the year, and she *still* managed to have more free time than I did.

"What's goin' on?" I asked when she didn't look up from her book when I came in.

"Nothin'. Just hanging around. I grabbed lunch with Sarah earlier and then got a pedicure. I thought about texting you a picture but decided against it." She laughed. "You can see 'em live." She lifted her foot off the couch and wiggled her freshly painted toes in the air.

Asshole. "Wait, I thought you had work?"

"Took a personal day. Yesterday was *so* boring. They talked our ears off for seven hours straight about how we aren't supposed to lecture to kids. Irony at its finest. Not to mention, we learned our theme for the year: be a hands-on teacher. I don't wanna know what that even means. I couldn't do another day of that shit without a break first."

"A personal day? The last two months have been nothing but personal days, you crazy bitch. Now get your lazy ass off the couch and get dressed. We're going out."

❤

When we arrived at Steph's at eight fifteen, we followed her onto the back deck. Danielle was already there, and she was clearly buzzed. She'd been pre-gaming for a good hour or so. A half-empty bottle of vodka was on the table, and the two of them were sitting with Steph's boyfriend, Dan.

"Funnel cake, ladies?" Dan asked as we opened the gate to the backyard. "I just made 'em."

Who makes friggin' funnel cake in their house?

"Hell yeah, I'll take some funnel cake," Lily nearly yelled as she ripped off a piece from Danielle's plate. "Can you make fried Oreos too?"

Who the hell asks questions like this?

"Damn right, I can make fried Oreos. Comin' right up." Dan left to go inside to make us some more treats.

Was this how "good nights from hell" always started?

For the next half hour, we gorged ourselves on fried desserts and vodka before deciding that it was time to head out. By nine o'clock, we had arrived at a bar about ten minutes from Steph's house, O'Leary's, which had a deck overlooking the Delaware River.

It was perfect for an August night. O'Leary's was already packed when we arrived, despite the fact that it was a weekday, because of its drink specials. On Tuesday nights, they offered a free Jell-O shot with every drink.

After about fifteen minutes, we somehow managed to find an open table out on the deck. Danielle bought us a pitcher of margaritas, and when the waitress arrived, we immediately threw back the Jell-O shots she'd brought with her.

"So Dan seems awesome," I said genuinely to Steph as I poured my drink. I had never actually met him before tonight, so I only knew what she had told us about him.

"Yeah, but he's definitely weird sometimes. I mean, who

makes fucking funnel cake at home?"

My thoughts exactly.

"He does shit like that all the time," she continued. "He likes to make dinner, and he's a good cook because that's what he went to school for, but he makes up these stupid songs while he cooks. It's so annoying. I'll be sitting there reading a magazine, and I'll hear, 'Going to put the oven on now, oven on now.'" She mocked him in a low-pitched singing voice that didn't resemble his at all.

"Dude, you're fuckin' lucky," I told her. "Let him sing if it means he cooks dinner. Nate's idea of starting dinner is sitting in his video game rocker with his Xbox controller in his hand and yelling, 'It's six o'clock. Are we gonna eat sometime or what?' Just put in some fucking earbuds if it bothers you, and let him do his thing."

Steph laughed loudly and agreed that I was probably right. "You know me, though. I find fault in almost every guy I've ever been with. You know . . . one doesn't have side steps on his truck . . . another wears the wrong shoe size. You know how I am."

"Hey, shoe size matters," Lily interjected, already starting to slur from the alcohol. She ran a hand through her wavy brown hair to pull it out of her face.

"Yeah," Danielle chimed in. "At least you have a boyfriend, Steph. I have what I'm supposed to call my 'man.'"

"What?" I laughed. "What's that mean?"

"You tell me," she said. "You know I've been seeing Brandon for like two months, right? Well, for my thirtieth birthday a few weeks ago, a bunch of my family got together for a little party at my uncle's house. I invited Brandon, and I asked how I should introduce him. I'd been meaning to have this conversation with him anyway, and I figured it was a good time for it."

Danielle poured herself another drink and wiped the table in front of her with her napkin where the margarita had spilled a little before continuing. "Well, he said he wasn't in high school, so he wasn't anyone's boyfriend. He was like, 'just tell 'em I'm your man,'" she mocked in her deepest, dopiest voice. "I mean, what the fuck? I think my exact words were, 'My man? Who the fuck says that? You may not be in high school, but until I start wearing cheap hoop earrings down to my shoulders with my name in the metal and get a fucking airbrushed T-shirt, I'm sure as shit not calling anyone *my man*.' I mean, can you believe that?"

We all burst out laughing. Danielle was the only person who could put that kind of flair on such a mundane occurrence. I loved hearing her stories.

"I gotta pee," I said. "I'll grab another pitcher on the way back." As I rose and began to make my way inside, I started to feel the alcohol in my system. My eyes focused on the wooden floorboards as I weaved around people and headed toward the restrooms. The line was surprisingly short. And if it weren't for the fact that I had dressed like a dumbass, my trip would have been brief.

As I entered the stall, I realized my mistake. *Who wears a romper to a bar?* Earlier, I had thought it was a good idea. It was white, and the material was light and loose with spaghetti straps, which I thought would be perfect for the humid night. What I hadn't considered was that going to the bathroom would be a tremendous pain in the ass, and with the amount I planned to drink, I'd be frequently inconvenienced.

I pulled the stupid thing down, but as I tried to hover above the seat, the inside of the fabric nearly touched the toilet. *Eww, no fucking way!* I had no choice but to take the whole thing off completely and squat above the toilet with basically nothing on. I wasn't even wearing a bra because the romper had one built in. *This is gonna be a long night.*

Finally, I made my way back to the bar with the pitcher in one hand and Jell-O shots in the other. But by the time I returned, there was already another pitcher on the table. I motioned to it. "I said I'd get one."

"You were taking too long." Danielle shrugged. "We got thirsty."

"This is gonna get warm before we drink it all, though." I thought for a second. "I'll get another glass. Looks like you're having a few drinks, Steph. It's still early." I looked at my phone. Ten fifteen.

I returned with a glass and poured her a drink immediately. She took it without protest. "I wanna make a toast," I slurred way too loudly, splashing liquid out of my glass and onto my hand. "To a good night from hell!" I glanced around to see a group of four good-looking guys nearby staring at me. "And to hot fucking single men at bars," I added, raising my glass in their general direction.

As I sat back down, one of the guys glided over to us, clearly taking my drunk, impromptu toast as an invitation to hit on us. "I heard you mention something about fucking hot single men a minute ago," he said with a smirk. He couldn't have been more than twenty-three at the most but looked even younger.

"I think I said '*hot fucking* single men,' actually. And what *are* you, like fifteen? Did you borrow your older brother's ID to get in here or what?" He was definitely the youngest of the group he'd come with, but he was still cute.

He furrowed his brow, confused. "Huh? Hot fucking single men? Fucking hot single men? What's the difference?" He reached his hand out to shake mine. "I'm Colin, and I'm actually twenty-two. That makes me legal. Plus, I like older women." He shrugged. "But yeah, my older brother Jason *is* over there. So you weren't too far off." He laughed and pointed to the tall one with dark buzzed hair and tattoos peeking out from under the sleeve of his black T-shirt.

"The difference," Lily said, answering his rhetorical question as she smacked her open palm on the table, causing the glasses to shake, "is that *in her version*, 'fucking' is used as an adjective. In *your* version, it's a verb. That's a big difference."

Jesus Christ, did she think now *was the time for a grammar lesson? Fucking English teachers.*

But she didn't stop. "In *yours*, it means we wanna *fuck* you." She reached out as she said the word "you" and poked Colin hard in the chest.

"Okay, then I like mine better," Colin replied with a wide, boyish grin. He really did look like a teenager.

"Oh my God, oh my God!" I yelled. "I just remembered. My fake ID is on the wall inside. They took it from me when I was twenty. It's been up on their Wall of Shame ever since. That was over eight years ago."

"Holy shit! You're almost *thirty*? That's even older than I thought."

My eyes shot daggers at Colin, but I did my best to ignore his flippant comment. "I need another drink. Then I'm going inside to get my ID back."

Colin called his brother and his friends over to join us for another round of drinks and Jell-O shots until I got enough liquid courage to venture inside to get my ID. When I downed the last of my margarita, I told the group I was heading to the Wall of Shame to get back what was rightfully mine. I had often wondered how many people had looked at my ID on that wall. I had never actually seen it myself, though, which would make finding it that much harder.

I pushed my way through the crowd toward the front doors and leaned up against an adjacent wall casually so I could examine the fake IDs plastered directly behind where the bouncer was seated. When any customer tried to get in with a fake ID, the bouncer would tack it to the wall behind him. That was how mine had ended up there.

There had to be hundreds on the wall, and I was too far away to see clearly. I would need to bring in reinforcements. So I texted the girls to come help me. I knew that the noise of the outdoor deck would make it difficult for them to hear their phones, but I was too lazy—and by this point much too drunk—to make my way back outside to get them in person.

As I waited for them to arrive, I enjoyed one of my favorite pastimes: people-watching. I had always enjoyed imagining what each person's story was and seeing how they interacted.

The crowd mostly consisted of people in their twenties and thirties.

Goddammit, Colin. There are *older people than me here.*

One couple on the dance floor caught my eye. I named them immediately. "Jamie" was grinding her ass shamelessly against "Shawn's" crotch, and I watched them move to the beat of the music as Shawn grabbed her hips. I'd often wondered how guys didn't come in their pants when this happened. Of course, maybe they did. I had no way of knowing.

With her three-inch heels, black mini-skirt, and neon

pink tube top, I imagined that Jamie was training for her new job. I looked around for a nearby pole, hoping that she would be able to complete the stripper image I'd envisioned for her, but I couldn't find one.

Then she spun around to face Shawn and draped one hand on his shoulder while the other explored his chest and stomach. They were both hot and damn good dancers, so I actually kind of enjoyed watching them. That is, until they started making out. Then they just looked like trashy teenagers who needed to be pulled apart by a chaperone at a high school dance.

These two reminded me of why I'd come up with Rule Number Three: Don't kiss in bars. It made people look classless. It was for this reason that no matter how badly I wanted a guy, I refused to be all over him in public.

Finally, Steph and the two drunks arrived to help me. We devised a plan, which involved Danielle distracting the bouncer while Steph and Lily scanned the wall for my ID. The problem was, that's as far as we got with our plan. Danielle made her way to the bouncer and immediately engaged him through conversation and her tits, while Lily and Steph moved closer to the wall of IDs behind him.

However, they were prevented from getting closer than four feet from the IDs because, though Danielle had successfully turned the bouncer away from us, he was still blocking much of the wall. Then I saw Lily reach into her purse, and she began using the camera on her phone to zoom in on the IDs. *Genius.* Within a few minutes she had found it.

Lily excitedly pointed it out to me, then stepped back. She had found it, but she wasn't about to do my dirty work for me. It was approximately three feet above the bouncer's left shoulder, and with Danielle to his right, I thought I could easily step up on the table nearby and reach up to grab it without him noticing. I handed my clutch to Steph to hold and used a chair to hoist myself up. I climbed cautiously onto the table and checked to my left. The bouncer was facing the opposite way, still preoccupied with Danielle.

Even in my drunken state, I was able to balance myself relatively well on the wobbly high-top table while I stretched up to reach my ID. I eyed it closely, remembering how often I had thought of this ID and the fun times it brought me until its life had been tragically cut short by an O'Leary bouncer one fateful night during the summer of 2010.

Just as I grabbed hold of it to pull it down, I was awoken from my nostalgic daydream to a hand latching on to my ankle. *Fuck, he saw me.* By pure instinct, I shook my leg to escape his hold. And with one quick jerk, I kicked him in the face. Accidentally, of course. But it didn't matter. I pulled the ID down between my fingers as he reached up higher, grabbing on to the top of my romper.

Then I heard a sound I recognized immediately: fabric ripping. I had no choice but to reach down and grab hold of my clothes to keep myself covered up when my strap broke. With my ID and romper gripped tightly in one hand, I was powerless to resist the bouncer's efforts. He easily brought me down off the table, holding me tightly in place with one hand and snatching the ID from my hand with the other. He tacked it to the wall again directly behind him with a threatening glare.

I squirmed and screamed for him to let me go, but my efforts were futile. I was too drunk and too concerned with keeping my romper above my boobs to escape.

"Call the cops!" he yelled to one of the other bouncers. Then he directed his booming voice at me. "You kicked me in the fucking face. You shouldn't even be in here. You're underage!" he shouted.

"No, that's not mine. Well, it *is* mine, but it's old. I mean, *I'm* old. My friend has my real ID," I said, pointing to Steph, who was still holding my clutch.

"She *is* old," I heard a deep voice confirm.

Thanks for the help, Colin, I thought as I rolled my eyes at him.

Steph handed the bouncer my license, and he let me go to examine it. "Well, I guess you're allowed to be in here," he said disapprovingly as he handed it back to me. "But the cops are on their way already. You'll have to explain all this to them when they get here."

Shit. I sat down in a chair, trying to figure out what to do next. I *had* kicked him in the face. I would probably be arrested for assault. A few minutes passed before I saw the police pull up, and the bouncer got up to meet them outside so he could talk to them. I saw him pointing to his eye, where the skin was already beginning to bruise and swell. He gestured wildly to the two officers, presumably describing the story in detail as he made me out to be a complete lunatic.

I don't know what possessed me to do this, but something inside me just took over. Adrenaline? Fear? Maybe it was just the alcohol. I wasn't sure. But I knew I had my one shot to escape. I looked at the guys. Then I looked at Steph, Lily, and Danielle. "Run," I said calmly. Then I jumped up suddenly, grabbed my ID off the wall again, and ran through the bar toward the back deck. It took a second for the group to realize what was happening, but they quickly followed.

I was so frantic, I didn't even care that I wasn't holding my romper up anymore. My left boob bounced freely as I sprinted out the back doors and onto the crowded deck. *What a dumb fucking move.* There was nowhere to go. I pulled the fabric up to cover myself and turned around to see the bouncer and two cops yelling and pushing through the crowd.

Not only would I be arrested for assault, but they would probably tack on resisting arrest as well. So I did what any normal person would do in this situation: I let go of my clothing again, gripped my fake ID and clutch tightly, and jumped off the deck into the Delaware River.

But no one followed me.

As I resurfaced and began to swim downstream toward the riverbank about fifty yards away, I noticed the police reach the girls and speak to them. But it was impossible to hear the conversation over my frantic breathing and clumsy swimming. I just hoped those bitches weren't snitches.

❥

At about one forty-five in the morning, I arrived at Steph's house by cab, drenched from head to toe. As I opened her door, I saw the three of them sitting in the living room, clearly relieved to see me.

"We tried to call you," Danielle said. "What the fuck happened to you?"

"Um, my phone doesn't work, dumbass," I said sarcastically, tossing it onto Steph's dining room table and spinning around in my wet clothing with one tit hanging out to remind them that I had just taken a midnight dip in the fucking Delaware an hour ago. I would need to get a new phone.

"*You're* the dumbass," Lily shot back. "The cops just wanted to talk to you. When they saw you reach the shore, they said that it was probably enough punishment that you swam in that filthy water. Besides, I think they were relieved that they didn't have to haul some drunk girl out of the river."

Then, without warning, Dan emerged from the kitchen with a skillet, singing, "Who wants pancakes?" to the tune of the song "I Want Candy." When he saw that I was half naked, he stopped short, spatula in hand.

I just shook my head, plopped myself down on a chair next to where he was standing, and tossed my fake ID onto the table proudly. "Here's to a good night from hell," I said, smiling as I snatched a pancake off the hot skillet with my bare hands and shoved it into my mouth.

chapter three

I sat on the black mats pretending to warm up. I had a hangover from hell, so I figured that I may as well also *be* in hell. That is why I dragged my ass to CrossFit after work Wednesday. I needed to purge my system of all of the alcohol and contaminated river water I had imbibed.

I may throw up all over the gym, but fuck it.

After what I had done last night, puking would pale in comparison.

Last night replayed in my mind. Had I really jumped off the deck of a bar? Fucking right I had, and it was awesome. I smiled slightly as the image of my three best girlfriends sitting in Steph's living room, waiting for my wet, drunk ass to show up entered my mind. It is a wonder they didn't have me committed.

I gave up the stretching and threw my body back so that I was supine on the mats, my arms splayed out. I probably looked like a chalk outline at a crime scene. I closed my eyes as I listened to the blaring music and the grunting of men who were lifting weights that were too heavy for them. I think I had almost fallen asleep when I heard his voice.

"Okay, Kate, get their stats," Shane yelled as the class before mine finished their workout.

My eyes remained closed until my body felt that familiar jolt of electricity. I opened them to find Shane staring down at me, looking amused.

"What?" I snapped, not in the mood for his shit and also somewhat annoyed at the way my body naturally responded to his.

"Rough day?" he asked, trying to suppress a laugh but failing miserably.

"Night," I mumbled, throwing my arm over my eyes to signal that I wanted him to leave me alone.

"Rough night? What did you do? Go out with your harpy friends, get annihilated, and spread cheer and mirth to fellow Pennsylvanians?"

His sarcasm didn't escape my attention. I moved my arm and struggled to sit up. "If you must know, Sir Snoops-a-lot, I did go out last night with my *awesome* friends, I perhaps got *slightly* intoxicated, and definitely spread cheer and…wait, did you say mirth? Who the fuck says that? Anyway, long story short, I had a good night from hell. Now if you'll excuse me, since you are clearly too wrapped up in my life to do your job, I'm going to go warm up." I stood with more grace than I thought possible and stalked away from him.

"A good night from hell, huh? I've had a few of those," he called after me.

"Sweetheart," I replied sweetly, "our definitions of good nights from hell are different. Mine involves a late-night swim in the Delaware River as I flee the police. Yours involves LSD and duct tape. Good night for you, hell for her." I let this sink in as I continued walking.

Think he was in my league, did he? Glad I set that straight.

The workout was over forty-five minutes later, and I was

drenched in sweat. I had no doubt that I smelled like a still. I was sure I was perspiring about eighty-five percent alcohol. Someone could probably get drunk just by licking me. *Hmm, I wonder what Kyle is up to . . .*

"Okay, guys, good work. Tell Kate your times, and don't forget, we're going out Friday in Manayunk. We're starting at the Lucky Goose at ten. We hope to see you all there."

I started hobbling toward the cubbies when Kate bounded up to me.

"Hey, Amanda, are you coming on Friday?" she asked sincerely.

"Umm . . ." I was cornered. It wasn't that I didn't want to go necessarily. I just hadn't made up my mind yet and wasn't sure I was ready to commit to going. "Yeah, I'll be there." *Coward.*

"Great. We're going to have such a good time. I'll see you Friday," she squealed as she bounced off toward the office.

"See ya," I called after her as I gathered my stuff. When I turned around, I saw Kate throw her arms around Shane. He hesitated, then drew his arms around her awkwardly.

He must not like PDA either.

And as I walked to my car, I felt that familiar pang of disappointment again. It was really getting on my nerves.

❤

Thursday, Master Bader was in a particularly foul mood and made me run the LaPorte numbers *again*. He also wanted me to research any other known assets the company had acquired in the past five years. Isn't that what we had interns like Hot Rod for? To do the bullshit so we could focus on our other clients?

So, after pretending to re-run the numbers and delegating the assets assignment where it belonged—to Hot Rod—I focused on my other responsibilities. And I actually got a lot accomplished with only minimal prompting from Steph. I also managed to get a sweet picture of Rod licking yogurt off his finger. I almost came on the spot.

At five fifteen, I packed my stuff and headed to the gym. By seven thirty, I was walking into my apartment. CrossFit had been uneventful, and Shane and I had barely interacted. I had left feeling weird, like my experience wasn't fulfilling without some kind of banter with him. Oh well, I was sure I'd get plenty of opportunities to make his life miserable tomorrow.

"Honey, I'm home," I yelled as I walked toward the kitchen. I found Lily running around like a madwoman as pots overflowed and something lay charred on the counter. I eyed her suspiciously. "What's up?"

She sighed as she turned toward me, her face flushed and her eyes misty. "I tried to cook dinner."

"And cook it you did. *Really* cooked it," I responded as I inspected the burned meat. I think it was meat. I'd have to eat it to be sure, and that was definitely *not* happening.

She slumped down in a chair, rested her elbow on the table, and propped up her head with her hand.

"Hey, Lily, what's wrong?" I asked, truly concerned.

"Who is ever going to want to be with me if I can't even cook a simple meal?"

Oh, shit, here we go. "Lily, that's silly. No one cares that you can't cook."

"How could they not care? I'm not domesticated at all. I'd make a lousy wife." She dropped her head so that her hand now covered her eyes. She'd had these brief sad bouts since spring.

Thankfully, they had started becoming fewer and farther between.

"Lily, look at me." I bent slightly at the waist to get closer to her level as she slowly lifted her head and met my eyes. "He didn't leave because you couldn't cook. And he wouldn't have stayed if you could." I uttered the words softly. I knew how she felt: lonely, depressed, and more than a little broken. She just needed to give it more time.

"I just miss him so badly sometimes. Sometimes I just think that, if I could make myself a better person, he'd come back." The tears slipped over the rims of her eyes and streaked down her cheeks. My heart felt for her in this moment. I didn't want to see her hurting.

I sighed. "Lily, you are a good person. I know you doubt that sometimes, but it's the God's honest truth. If you guys are meant to be, then you'll be. If not, you'll find the person who is meant for you." I straightened up. "Now let's trash all this crap and order a pizza."

She smiled slightly. "Okay."

"Good. Let me just throw my gym bag into my room, and then we'll decide where we want to order from. Look on TV and see if any good movies are on."

Lily nodded her head, and I spun around and made my way out of the kitchen. When I reached the doorway, she said, "Amanda?" I turned my head to look at her. "Thanks." She smiled, more genuinely this time.

"Anytime," I replied.

After dropping my bag in my room and changing my clothes, I plopped down beside Lily in the living room. I registered the movie she had chosen: *Jerry McGuire*.

I glanced over at Lily, who would clearly take a happily

ever after any way she could get it, and smiled. "This chick couldn't get any more cliché if she tried." Those types of movies were always so predictable. And the long, over-the-top speeches? It was all a little much for my taste. As I settled back into the couch, I couldn't resist rolling my eyes at the dialogue. *She owes me for this one.*

❥

Friday morning, I arrived at work to find out that Master Bader had taken the day off. *Miracles do happen.* After I finished running around the office like a kid on Christmas morning and gossiping with my coworkers about his possible reasons for being out—which ranged from his dick finally tiring of the incessant abuse and coming off midstroke to him being up all night burying bodies in his backyard—I finally settled down and did some work.

By the end of the day, I had caught myself up on three accounts, played a rousing game of office whiffle ball, and took some Pulitzer-worthy pictures of Hot Rod. At four o'clock, I declared my day finished, and I left for home, feeling like the rebel I was.

❥

It was nearly eight thirty, and I had decided on a tangerine-colored cotton jersey dress with cap sleeves for Kate's birthday extravaganza. I spun once in front of the mirror. The length was short, falling midthigh, but I liked the flirty appeal of it. It did have a plunging V-neck, which revealed some serious cleavage, but I was all about flaunting my assets.

Overall, the look I was going for tonight was cute and fun,

and this outfit definitely got that across. These people saw me drip sweat multiple times a week, so I figured casual chic was a fine option. I paired it with a chunky necklace and some flip-flops. I briefly considered a heel, but I didn't know how much bar hopping would be involved tonight, so I decided to stick with comfort.

I had desperately tried to get someone to go with me, but I'd found no takers. The girls were still recovering from Tuesday, and it was also probably a little too soon for them to want to be seen out in public with me.

I'd tried wrangling Kyle next, but he'd said that Manayunk had lost its appeal for him ten years ago. *Really? Ten years?* He was barely thirty-three.

Though I had to admit, I wasn't too thrilled about going to Manayunk either. Manayunk was a neighborhood on the outskirts of Philadelphia. It had one main street, aptly named Main Street, that was home to a ton of bars and upscale restaurants. The bars were a common hangout for college kids and people in their early twenties.

As I parked my car in a lot across from the Lucky Goose, my mind flashed back five years when I had frequented this area with Nate. We had had some good times down here. I shook my head to dissolve the nostalgia, threw my keys into my clutch, and started across the street.

The Lucky Goose was expansive, with a bar that ran about half the length of the place to the right of the entryway. The rest of the bar was open space and it was *fucking mobbed.* I started walking back, knowing that I just had to keep my eyes peeled for a large group of extremely well-built individuals. As I approached the back half of the bar, I finally saw them.

Of course they would be as far from the entrance as

humanly possible. Shane had probably led them back there, the jerk. I continued to cut through the crowd until I finally reached them.

Kate saw me immediately and came running over, clutching me in a big hug. "I'm so glad you made it," she exclaimed in my ear.

"Of course. I wouldn't miss it," I said, smiling. The truth of it was, I would have loved to have missed it, but I didn't want to disappoint Kate on her birthday. Furthermore, though I hated to admit it, I wanted to see what Shane was like outside of his natural habitat.

I quickly scanned the crowd for him, finally seeing him standing behind Justin, a huge mountain of a man who looked like he could bench press an SUV. Just as my eyes settled on Shane, his head perked up slightly, turned, and he met my gaze. We stood there for a moment, neither of us breaking the staring match we found ourselves in. I felt heat bloom low in my abdomen as I took him in.

He was wearing a red polo shirt that pulled tightly over his sculpted chest and shoulders. His jeans were loose fitting, and though I couldn't see the waist beneath his shirt, my imagination told me that the jeans sat low on his hips, offering a glimpse of the muscled lower abdomen that pointed straight down to his majestically long cock.

Okay, so maybe my imagination was running away from me a bit.

Finally, I registered that Kate was speaking to me. I cleared my throat and tried to figure out what the hell she was saying.

"And that's about it," she concluded, smiling broadly.

Well, replying to this is going to be interesting.

"Great. Thanks," I said, figuring that response would apply to nearly every situation. I really needed to start listening to people better.

She nodded and bounded off into our group. I watched her stop next to Shane and engross herself in the conversation he was having with Justin and a few other CrossFitters. Something had to be going on between them.

I decided to mingle since I rarely ever got to talk to most of these people. We were normally gasping for air too much to form words. Walking over to a few people I saw most often in class, I struck up a conversation.

Glancing down at my watch sometime later, I was shocked to see that an hour and a half had passed. I had been having such a great time, it felt like only a half hour tops had gone by. I was laughing with Cedric, Brit, Tanya, and Rob as we all imitated our respective bosses. Evidently, we all worked for total dickbags.

I was cackling hysterically at a story Cedric told about how his boss walked around for an entire day, oblivious to the fact that he had a pair of women's underwear hanging from the back of his belt like a tail, when I felt a strong hand on my bicep. I spun around, expecting someone from my gym, and then froze.

It took a moment for my brain and my mouth to get back on the same page. Eventually, I was able to mutter a single, meek word: "Nate."

"Hi, Amanda," he said, smiling. *Smiling? This asshole is smiling at me. The fucker!*

"Hi," I replied, probably looking every bit as confused as I was. "Where did you ... What are you doing here?" The group I had been talking to backed away slightly to give us more privacy. But that wasn't what I wanted. I didn't want to speak privately with Nate. I didn't want to speak to him at all. My breathing accelerated as panic rose in my body.

"I was just meeting some friends. What about you?" He casually took a sip of his beer, looking at me expectantly.

He was so calm, it made me want to gouge his eyes out and feed them to a sewer rat. The thought of eyes caused my own to slip quickly down his body. He looked good. Damn good. He actually looked exactly the same as he had when I last saw him about four years ago, except that his hair was slightly longer.

"Uh, I'm . . . here with friends too," I stammered.

"Hmm, that's nice. You're looking good, Amanda. *Really* good.*" He smirked down at me, his eyes roaming freely over my body.

His comment disarmed me, and I had no idea how to respond. *Jesus Christ, Amanda, snap out of it.* This wasn't like me. I wasn't this shy, self-conscious, pathetic girl. But right now, with Nate standing barely two feet from me, this was the girl I had become. The real me fled and was hiding behind harsh words and devastated tears from four years ago. *Well, shit.*

I was staring down at the floor, willing my sarcasm to come back to me so I could tear this asshole to shreds. And as I stood there, struggling to find words, I felt an arm wrap around my shoulders. My head jerked up when I heard his voice.

"Hey, baby, where ya been? I've been looking for you." Shane pressed a brief kiss to my temple. I nearly wiped it away on reflex. "Hi, how are you? I'm Shane, Amanda's boyfriend. And you are?"

Wait, what? My boyfriend? What is happening here? Is Shane . . . saving me? I didn't know whether to be grateful or horrified.

Nate stumbled a bit, his cool facade slipping slightly, "Uh, hi. I'm, uh, Nate. I used to date Amanda."

"Oh, small world," Shane replied, smiling, though it didn't reach his eyes. He gazed impassively at Nate. I stared at Shane like he was Bigfoot.

"Uh, yeah, well, it was good seeing you, Amanda. Nice to meet you, uh..." Nate fumbled.

"Shane. Nice to meet you too."

Nate started to reach out his hand, but when Shane made no movement in return, Nate ran the hand through his hair instead and then walked off.

"Who the hell was that prick?" Shane asked, dropping his arm from my shoulder.

"I... He was nobody. Just..." I took a deep breath and willed myself to calm the fuck down. "He's just some pompous douchebag I used to date."

"Interesting," Shane mumbled before taking a sip of his beer. "You okay? Your whole body tensed when you saw him."

I nodded slightly, my head cast down toward the floor again.

"Hey, Amanda, look at me," Shane said softly. When I didn't comply, he placed his hand beneath my chin and raised my head for me. The look on his face was one of concern. He wasn't mocking me, like I would have expected.

But somehow, the concern was worse. I didn't need his pity. Nor had I needed him to pretend to be my boyfriend. *Except...maybe I had.* No, I pushed that thought from my mind. I didn't need anyone. I had just been caught off guard. I could have handled Nate.

The real Amanda was flooding back into me with a vengeance. And right as I was about to tell Shane where he could go stick his white knight act, I stopped. He had only been trying to help. There was no need to verbally eviscerate him when it was actually Nate I wanted to yell at. I took a deep breath and let it out slowly.

"Sorry," I said finally. "I'm fine. I just didn't expect to see him. It caught me a little by surprise."

"Yeah. You need a drink?" Shane asked, a little louder than he'd probably intended. He seemed uncomfortable.

"Sure." I smiled genuinely. "I'd love one."

"What's your poison?" he called over his shoulder as he made his way toward the bar.

"Stoli and cran," I yelled after him.

He was back fairly quickly considering how packed this place was. He handed me my drink and then placed his hand on the small of my back and ushered me to a few stools that lined the wall.

"Thanks," I said sincerely, hoping it covered more than just the drink.

"No problem," he said, staring intently at me, letting me know that he understood.

I needed to lighten the mood and reassert myself in my body. "So, is that how you pick up chicks? You just saunter up to them, refer to yourself as their boyfriend, and hope it sticks?" I said lightly, my smile wide.

"It's probably more effective than your tactic of staring at the floor and letting all the color drain from your face." He smirked.

Embarrassment crept through me at his words, and I worked hard to keep my eyes trained on his. "It's the damsel in distress technique. I feel it worked quite well. Got you to buy me a drink, didn't it? Sucker," I said with a laugh that was only partially forced.

"That it did. So, are you insinuating that it was me you were trying to pick up in that situation?" He lifted an eyebrow and gawked at me in that annoying, cocky way he had.

"No, I was just trying to give you some pointers. Show you how it's done." I was a bundle of nerves and emotions.

Are we flirting right now? Do I like it? Fuck.

"Oh, was that what that was? A lesson for me. How kind of you." He rolled his eyes playfully, and I had a sudden urge to tell him the truth about Nate. I couldn't explain why, but I wanted him to know it. To know me.

But at the same time, I didn't want those things. I had made it my mission in life to never be vulnerable again, *especially* in front of Shane Reed. There was something about him that I just couldn't put my finger on. He caused me to feel a gamut of emotions, and I hated most of the ones he elicited. But I didn't hate *him*. Weird.

"Your boy and his posse moved closer."

I looked up and saw Nate and his crew congregating not ten feet away from where we sat. *He really is a piece of shit.*

I tried to seem unfazed but clearly failed, because Shane leaned into me and whispered in my ear. "Let's give him something to watch."

Before I was able to reply, Shane pulled me off my stool, positioning me so that I was standing between his legs, my back to his chest. He then slipped his arms around my waist and pressed his mouth to my ear. I had to resist the urge to nuzzle into him as his breath grazed my ear. "Watch. He's going to glance back in five, four, three, two, one . . ."

As if on cue, Nate whipped his head toward us briefly and then turned back to his friends.

"Wow, how'd you know he'd do that?" I asked, allowing

Shane to hear how impressed I was with him for the first time, well, probably ever.

"He wasn't going to be able to resist. He moved closer so that he could watch you. And when I noticed his shoulders tense, I knew he wasn't going to be able to hold off much longer."

"You're like Yoda," I mused, turning my head to look at him. Then we both burst out laughing.

That was quite a change. Shane and I playing on the same team for once, trying to take down the dark overlord of pain and misery. I felt myself relax and my mood brighten.

Shane and I continued to play the game, laughing and putting our hands freely on each other. Nate either left or moved to a different part of the bar about fifteen minutes into our charade, but by that point, I barely remembered he was there to begin with.

Finally, Shane called attention to it. "Well, I think we chased him away." I had turned toward Shane a while ago, and my hands were resting on his shoulders, though my arms were slightly extended to provide us with some distance. I cast a look behind me, acting like I hadn't noticed, though I had. Nate hadn't been standing back there for at least the last five minutes.

I begrudgingly began to slide my hands off his shoulders but suddenly stopped. I wasn't ready to lose contact with him yet. Instead, I pushed my hands back farther and clasped them behind his head, drawing him into a hug.

"Thank you," I whispered.

"For what?" he asked softly as his hands slid around my waist, returning my hug. I was suddenly overcome with the desire to feel those hands beneath my dress, trailing up and down my exposed skin.

"For saving me." I uttered the words before I could censor them. Once they left my mouth, I stilled, realizing that I was opening a door with Shane I wasn't sure I wanted to walk through.

He pulled me closer to him, and my chest pressed against his toned pecs. I instantly felt a dull ache low in my belly and took notice of the moistness in my panties for the first time. I tried to even out my breathing. Shane Reed was turning me on, and I wanted him. Badly.

But I couldn't do this. No matter how strongly my body was pulling me toward him, my mind was screaming at me to back off. I had rules for a reason, and Shane didn't meet my criteria. Trainers didn't make even close to the kind of money I made. I knew; I had Googled it. I risked too much otherwise. But I couldn't just pull away. He had done too much for me tonight. He deserved my letting him in a little.

I pulled away from him and moved to his side, resuming my seat on the stool. "I dated Nate for a year and a half right after finishing college. Long story short, we moved in together, I thought I was going to marry him one day, and then I came home to find a note telling me that he had only been *pretending* to love me and that he couldn't do it anymore. And I haven't seen him since. Until tonight, that is." I expelled the words in what felt like a single breath. It felt good to release them, like a weight had been lifted off my shoulders.

"Wow," Shane replied, his eyes wide. "What a cocksucker."

I slipped my arm around his shoulders. "My thoughts exactly," I said, laughing.

My eyes skimmed the bar and fell on Kate. She was talking with some other people from the gym, but her eyes were glued to Shane. When she saw me notice her, she quickly looked away.

It was none of my business, but I had to know. After all, I had shared personal information with him. Maybe he'd reciprocate. "So, what's the deal with you and Kate, anyway?" I asked, trying to sound nonchalant.

"What do you mean?" He seemed confused.

"Is something going on between you two?"

"No. What makes you ask that?" he questioned.

"Really? You don't see it?" I couldn't believe he was this obtuse.

"See what?"

"Nothing. Never mind." I tried to drop it, but his look told me he wasn't going to let me off the hook that easily. "I just figured that since you were throwing her this party, you guys were involved somehow." I tried to recover quickly. I didn't know how Kate would feel if I outed her penchant for staring at him.

"Well, first of all, I didn't throw this party. She wanted everyone to come out, but she felt weird asking everyone herself. Kind of like she was throwing herself a birthday party. So I said I'd spread the word. And second of all, I don't believe that's what prompted you to ask your question, so spill it."

Damn, he's good. "Well, it's just that . . ." I thought for a moment about how I could phrase this so that Kate didn't come off seeming like a stalker. "She stares at you a lot." *Epic fail.*

"She does?"

"Uh, yeah. She's doing it right now."

Shane's eyes quickly darted around the room to find Kate. As his eyes locked on hers, she quickly averted her gaze. He didn't say anything.

"I think she likes you. You should go talk to her. It'd probably make her night." The words tasted bitter leaving my mouth. The last thing I wanted was for him to leave me and go talk to her. But I didn't want to cock block him either. He had no shot with me, but he probably had a great one with her.

He shook his head. "I don't see her that way. We're friends, but she's more like a sister to me. And why are you sending me over to her? Trying to get rid of me?" Amusement played on his face, but there was something else in his eyes. Something darker. More carnal.

I shuddered involuntarily as I found myself getting lost in those eyes. My body inched closer to him: a subconscious movement caused by the magnetic pull that existed between us. My eyes moved to his lips, pink and full and so utterly kissable.

"Hey, guys, how's it going?"

The trance broke, and I looked over to see Kate.

Shane cleared his throat. "We're good. Just shootin' the shit. How about you? Having fun?" he asked, smiling broadly.

How the hell had he regained his composure so quickly? Hadn't he been lost in that moment with me? Maybe. Maybe not.

"Yeah, I'm having a great time."

Kate shot me a brief look but quickly looked away. She seemed to be trying to ignore me. Her eyes flitted over to me again but then locked on Shane. "A few of us decided to head over to Tonic. They have a DJ. Are you in?"

"Uh, sure," he said. "Coming, Amanda?"

I watched Kate's face fall slightly, but she recovered quickly and looked at me sweetly.

"No, I'm getting tired. I'm just gonna head home." *There's your birthday present, ya big baby.*

"Oh," Shane seemed momentarily at a loss for words, like he was caught between whether he should attempt to change my mind or just let it go. Ultimately, he made the right choice. "Let me walk you to your car."

"No," I replied harshly. "That's okay. I'm right across the street," I added to try to temper my initial response.

"Well, let's all walk out together, and then I can make sure your ex doesn't pop out of the bushes and kidnap you," he said, clearly only slightly kidding.

"If you must," I muttered, shaking my head for Kate's benefit. I didn't want to ruin her night and figured reverting to smartass Amanda was the best way to do that.

Shane paused and looked at me briefly, wondering where my shift in tone had come from. I didn't look back at him. Instead, I put my hand on Kate's arm and thanked her for inviting me.

"Oh, no, thank you for coming," she said, completely devoid of emotion. She made no attempt to return my touch in any way. *I guess Kate has some claws.* Maybe she should piss on him to mark her territory.

It took a few minutes to gather everyone who was left, but eventually we were making our way toward the door. I waved goodbye to no one in particular as I made my way across the street. Once I reached the sidewalk, I chanced a quick look over.

Kate was already leading everyone down the street toward their next destination. Everyone except Shane. He stood stock still, watching me all the way to my car. As I opened the door, I started to give him a slight wave, but he had already started following the crowd, his head bowed slightly downward and his hands in his pockets. He never looked back in my direction.

I climbed in my car and started her up. And as I pulled out of the parking lot, I wondered if this qualified as a good or bad night from hell.

❤

Unfortunately, my dream of Master Bader being arrested for murder or bleeding to death from a severed appendage hadn't come true after all. So when the Tuesday after Labor Day rolled around, he was back. And after being out for a day, he was more of a dick than usual. I guess he figured he was just making up for lost time when he handed me some accounts that an intern had fucked up. Now I had to do those in addition to my own responsibilities. It almost made me wish I had done more Friday so I wouldn't have to work late. Almost.

I considered delegating some of the workload to Hot Rod, as I contemplated killing two birds with one stone. I could relieve myself of some responsibility and also get a picture of Rod running his hand through his already rumpled hair as he became baffled by the numbers. He wasn't the brightest. But luckily for Rod, God had blessed him with an amazing body, so it balanced out.

But after some consideration, I decided that for once, I would actually have to just suck it up and do it myself. Master Bader hadn't told me which intern had screwed it up in the first place, so I couldn't chance having it get messed up again. Better just to do it myself and make sure it was done correctly.

Shortly after lunch, I heard Bader's voice from down the hall. "Mandi!" he yelled. "Get in here. Are you done with Pallo Tech yet?"

"I'm coming, Mr. Bader," I shouted back. *Wow, there's a sentence I didn't think I'd ever hear myself say.*

Some of the other employees also must have had their minds in the gutter, because they laughed and made obscene gestures as I passed by. This included Hot Rod, who made a motion like he was jerking off, and as I shuffled past his desk, he "finished" by shutting his eyes, opening his mouth widely like he was screaming, and drawing in a sharp breath.

God, I've been waiting to see the Hot Rod "finish" for weeks. Where was my fucking phone when I needed it?

The sexiest expression picture wouldn't have even been a competition.

♥

By six thirty, I finally saw light at the end of the tunnel. A few more hours and I would hopefully be able to get out of here for the night. Minutes later, my phone buzzed with a text from Kyle.

Hey, you wanna grab a bite . . .
then afterward I'll grab a bite of u?

I sighed with disappointment. Unfortunately, his proposition couldn't have come at a worse possible time. If I took Kyle up on his offer, I'd never have the accounts ready for tomorrow morning. But God, was it tempting to just say to hell with this whole work thing.

Fucking and food—in that order—sounded exceptionally alluring. Especially since my sexual frustration had hit a new high since Friday at the bar when Shane and I were rubbing against each other like we were trying to ignite a flame using only our bodies.

All weekend I'd avoided thoughts of Shane at all costs. I hadn't gone to CrossFit, and despite the fact that I was hornier than all hell, my vibrator stayed tucked away in my drawer. I knew if I resorted to that, I would only think of him. And I couldn't let myself do that. But Kyle could provide the sexual gratification I craved.

After some deliberation, I decided that I needed to keep my priorities straight, and I was proud of myself for it. I think.

> *Thanks for the invite. Tempting,*
> *believe me. But I'm stuck at work for a*
> *few more hours. Why don't you get some*
> *food if you're hungry, and I'll see you*
> *when I get off from work.*

He wrote back almost immediately.

OK

But nothing after that.

❤

By seven twenty, I was the only one left in the office. Even Hot Rod had left, but not before I had snapped a picture of his ass through my glass wall as he added paper to the copier. He'd been working later recently, probably hoping to make a good impression and get hired after his internship. Tonight, that had worked to my benefit as well. *I like your dedication, Rod.*

My fantasy about Rod was short-lived as I heard a voice say, "Hi." I looked over to my door, startled, and saw Kyle walking toward me with a pizza from the place down the street that made the tomato pies he knew I loved.

"What are you doing here?" I thought I'd been clear in my text that I'd need to finish working, and his text of *OK* seemed to indicate that he understood. Though I can't say I was entirely disappointed to see him standing above me in a tight white T-shirt that barely skimmed the waist of his faded ripped jeans. "I said I still needed to get some work done," I added, in an effort to convince myself as much as I was trying to convince him.

He smirked, letting his sparkling hazel eyes run down my chest and torso. Then he put the pizza down on the glass coffee table in front of the deep-brown leather couch and pulled out his phone. He pointed to part of the last sentence I had written.

"I'll see you when I get off from work," he said with a seductive hum to his voice.

I looked at him quizzically before the double meaning of what I had written sunk in. *Shit.*

"I'm here to do just that," he added playfully.

I studied his expression, hoping to get an indication of what he actually meant, but it revealed nothing. "What did you have in mind?" I was suddenly beginning to forget about my responsibilities at the office.

"Eat first," he directed, lifting a slice of pizza and touching it to my lips. "Take a bite."

Suddenly, I wasn't hungry. I wanted nothing more than to push Kyle onto the couch, strip him naked, and ride him like a drunk college girl on a mechanical bull: fast and hard and with no reservations.

But sensing his insistence, I obeyed, taking a few small bites and chewing slowly while keeping my eyes locked on his. After a few minutes, he must have felt that I'd eaten enough, because he put the pizza back into the box.

"Aren't *you* hungry?" I asked.

"Not for *that.*"

Holy shit! How could such an innocuous phrase turn me on so much more than I already was? I felt my insides clench at the prospect of what Kyle might have in mind. My abdomen tightened and my pulse increased as his eyes bore into mine for a few more moments. Then I watched as he surveyed my lips and neck until his focus dropped lower, and I thought I could actually feel his eyes caress my breasts on their journey down to my legs.

I shifted in my seat and enjoyed the fleeting feeling of the most sensitive part of me moving gently against the chair. A soft moan escaped my lips, signaling that I was ready to take whatever he was going to offer me.

Then Kyle positioned himself behind me. He hadn't touched me yet, and I craved him more because of it. I yearned for the gentle graze of his fingertips upon my tingling skin and the rough grasp of his large hand as he squeezed my heavy breast with just the right amount of force.

But he didn't give me either one. Instead, he leaned down into my ear, touching me only with his warm breath. "Get back to work," he commanded.

I shut my eyes and inhaled sharply at the sound of his voice and the feeling of the vibration on my ear. I leaned to the side, inviting him to lick my flesh and sprinkle soft kisses up and down my neck.

He traced my jawline with the edge of his nose, exhaling

softly as he moved up and down my neck. "I'm serious about working, you know?" he prompted in between bites of my earlobe. "This won't happen until you get done what you need to do. The longer you procrastinate, the longer this sexual torture will last." As he said the last sentence, he ran his fingers up my thigh and under my skirt, toying with the elastic edge of my thong.

My hips flexed upward involuntarily in response.

"And what I have planned for you *will* be sexual torture, Amanda. You can count on that." He paused for a moment, allowing me a few seconds to process his intention before speaking again. "If you continue to work, I'll continue to pleasure you. Though know that it won't be to the point of release until you're done with whatever work you need to finish for the night. If you stop working before you're done, I'll stop. In other words, keep your focus, and I'll keep mine."

I spun in my chair just enough to see Kyle's seductive expression, and I shot my own back at him. Only mine was somewhere in between complete arousal and utter frustration. I had a nagging feeling that what I felt now would be nothing compared to what Kyle had in store for me.

This could be fun. Or it could be absolutely unbearable. Though something told me it would probably be both. Without saying a word, I turned back to my computer. *Let the games begin.*

Just the thought of Kyle touching me while I worked made it even more difficult to focus. As I put my hand on the mouse to click into one of the cells of the spreadsheet I had on my screen, Kyle unbuttoned my silk blouse and reached around to cup both of my breasts in his hands through my sheer black bra. He squeezed down my full curves and tugged my nipples between his thumb and index fingers. The pain increased with each pull, causing even more wetness to pool between my thighs.

I focused on importing the numbers I had in front of me. My gratification would be delayed already, and I didn't know how much of this I could handle. There was no way I would draw this out any longer than I needed to.

As Kyle removed a hand from my breast, it felt naked without the touch of his rough palm and expert fingers. I heard a belt buckle clang and then his fly unzip, which told me that if I turned around, I would get a spectacular view of his large cock.

But I didn't dare move. I was too full of arousal and need. If I took my eyes off my computer, Kyle would stop his deliberate teasing.

I heard him groan deeply, and when he walked around to the front of my desk, he was completely nude. His dick was hard and heavy under its own weight, pulsing as he stood before me like a piece of art for me to admire. My body needed him, and I was sure he had to feel the same.

"Reach under your skirt with your left hand," he instructed. "Take your panties off and toss them to me."

I did as Kyle instructed. He held my thong in his hand for a moment, inspecting it with his fingers while keeping that intense stare on me. I felt as if his eyes could melt me.

He grabbed hold of himself toward the base of his shaft and began to pull slowly. "You're so wet," he said as he gripped his cock tighter. His eyelids fluttered with pleasure. "Touch yourself now."

Without hesitation, I used my left hand to hike my skirt up just enough to give me the access I needed. Part of me was disappointed with the fact that I would be doing this to myself when Kyle was only a few feet away and could easily give me a hand, so to speak. But I would have control over this. I could probably get myself off in mere seconds with how turned on I already was. A few quick strokes in all the right places and I'd be done. The thought was enticing.

I moved my hand in quick circles over my throbbing clit and immediately felt the stimulation I'd craved. My eyes darted to Kyle as I watched his hand move faster. His tip had become slick with pre-come, and I licked my lips at the thought of taking him in my mouth.

"Concentrate," he said, nodding toward my computer and eyeing the papers I had spread on my desk. My breathing increased, and my heart pounded in my chest as my eyes darted back anxiously to the screen. Kyle could sense how close I was to coming by the look on my face and the rapid pace of my hand. "Slow down," he commanded.

Oh, God. What a fucking asshole. I was so close, and he was going to make me do this at a torturous pace: one that would keep me completely balanced on the edge of release without allowing me to find it.

But I complied. This game was much too fun to forfeit now. Besides, I knew it would be worth it when I finally got to have Kyle inside me.

I somehow managed to take my calculator out of my desk and punch in a few numbers. As I leaned over my desk more closely, I slid two fingers inside myself and began to grind slowly against them in my chair.

Kyle again sensed my urgency. "Stop," he said brusquely. "Watch me when I come."

Oh, no fucking fair! What a clever tease.

He was going to bring me to the brink of climax and then

make me watch in frustration while he enjoyed his own? But I couldn't look away. He moaned a guttural sound as his bicep flexed with every pull. And his solid abs tightened more when he found the release that I so desperately craved. His tight fist moved in quick jerks as he held my thong at the head of his cock to catch the semen that shot in hard bursts.

Then he tossed my panties onto my desk near the papers I had laid out and walked toward me, still semi-erect. "Time to get back to work," he said with a sweet, flirtatious smirk. It hit me that he wasn't just talking about my job when he said it. He'd planned to work on me as well. "Finish what you have to do on the computer. Then we're moving to the couch."

Hell yes!

Somehow I managed to type the data into each cell and make sure the formulas were calculating correctly in Excel, all while Kyle kneeled beside me, swirling one tantalizing finger around inside me. He applied pressure to spots I didn't even know existed and moved me back and forth against his hand. With each small tap of his thumb against my clit, I ached for more. I needed a constant touch there, but he refused to provide it, only making the frustration that much more unbearable. I shut my eyes when I felt like I could explode any second and clenched myself around his finger, needing to feel a sensation of fullness.

But he knew what I was doing, and when he noticed my eyes shut, he denied all contact completely. I actually thought if I rubbed myself against the chair at the right angle, I could come from that alone.

"Uh-uh-uh," Kyle scolded playfully. "Not until you're done with your work."

"But *you* got off," I begged. "Please, Kyle." My breathing

was ragged and harsh.

"That was part of the torture, sweetheart. Well, for you, anyway. I, on the other hand, enjoyed it tremendously."

I quickly seized this moment to import the last few numbers and click Save before Kyle decided to distract me further. "Couch time," I said enthusiastically.

"What's all this?" He motioned to the papers on my desk.

"I just need to read them and sign off that the asset evaluation is correct. It won't take long."

"No," he added, running his hand across my drenched opening again, "it definitely won't take long." I understood his innuendo immediately.

"God, Kyle. Just fuck me. Please. I'll get the rest done right afterward."

"Amanda, you know that's not how this game is played. Comments like that make you seem like you want to quit. You don't wanna quit, do you?" He cocked his head to the side, already sure of my answer.

A soft "No" was all I could manage.

"Good. Now take your papers and lie down."

You don't have to tell me *twice.*

In seconds, I was positioned with my head against a throw pillow at one end of the couch. I held the papers tightly in one hand and a pen in the other. As I'd hoped, Kyle parted my legs and positioned his face between them. He raised my hips slightly to angle me just right. My opening gripped his fingers, and I writhed against his tongue as it flickered lightly across my sensitive clit.

Every so often, he would suck hungrily and then pull away when he knew I was right on the verge of orgasm. I was powerless to keep him there. Under normal circumstances, my hands would have found his head and pressed him up against me until I came apart around his soft tongue and fingers. But I was forced to flip through a pile of paperwork, plastering an increasingly sloppy signature at the bottom of some of the pages every so often.

"You almost done?" Kyle asked as he moved up my torso to bite on my nipples.

"Yeah, asshole. I'm about to finish."

Ha, you're not the only one who's skilled at puns.

Kyle rose to move toward the desk again. For a second, I thought he was getting dressed and was actually going to leave me like this. Until I heard the foil ripping open.

Thank fucking God.

I quickly signed the last two documents, not even bothering to look at them. I would have to check them tomorrow. Then Kyle stood before me again, rolling the condom down his thick length. *God, even that is hot.* Then he took the papers from my grasp and flung them to the carpet. "You're done, right?"

"Not quite," I said, making my meaning clearer as I dug my nails into his ass and pulled him eagerly toward me. He gripped the armrest of the couch for leverage and thrust himself into me. At last, I felt the fullness I'd craved. This wasn't going to take long. But ironically, after all this time of wanting this so badly, I didn't want it to end. Kyle had teased me for so long that even being on the brink of orgasm felt nearly as good as actually getting one.

He kissed me hard, and I moaned into his mouth. Then he let go of the armrest with one hand and reached down to grab his dick. He positioned his hand around its base and moved it in circles to massage me internally with his tip.

I'd never remembered being so turned on before. So close

to climaxing for this long without finding a release. Then, just when I thought he couldn't possibly do anything more to arouse me, his hand brushed against my clit in just the right way and I lost all control.

The orgasm that shot through me coursed all the way up my spine, making even the nerve endings of my head fuzz with pleasure. I never quite came down completely from the high because I had been so aroused for so long. I screamed in pleasure but could not seem to form any actual words.

"Fuck yeah, baby. I love when you get so tight like that when you're coming. Do it once more for me."

His speed increased, and he pounded harder into me, reaching a point high inside me that caused me to convulse around him again without warning.

"Yes, Kyle! Jesus Christ, this feels so fucking good."

He moved in and out of me a few more times as he tugged on my hair and groaned his release deep into my ear. When he finally pulled out of me, my body missed him. As I watched him toss the condom into my wastebasket, all I could think was that I hoped the janitor didn't clean my office tonight.

This sure as hell beat Danielle's office blowjob story, and the proof was in my trashcan.

chapter four

The next few weeks were a hazy blur of work and CrossFit. Master Bader had been even more of a prick than usual, insisting that some of us stay late just so we could get ahead on some of our accounts.

Unfortunately, even Shane had jumped on the Bader bandwagon, because he had been pushing us—*and by us, I mean me*—even harder than usual. One evening had been exceptionally challenging. I had been at work for over twelve hours and hadn't eaten much that day. So when I arrived at CrossFit and saw our workout, I knew it was going to be grueling.

Six rounds, each with five shoulder overheads, fifteen bar-facing burpees, and a hundred-meter run. We had three minutes to complete the first round, and the time dropped by five seconds each round. After my fourth round, Shane gave me a little incentive to take it up a notch.

"Tell you what, Bishop. If you can finish the next one in under two minutes and fifteen seconds, we won't hold a sixth round."

Damn it! Now I would have to do it, or I'd look weak. And I definitely didn't want to look weak in front of such a perfectly built specimen. Plus, others were counting on me.

I finished my shoulder overheads without too much of a problem. But, as always, the burpees were the most difficult. As my arms began to burn and my stamina hit the shitter, I could barely jump over my barbell. Finally, I finished my fifteen and dragged myself out the back dock door.

"Comin' up on two minutes, Amanda. Almost done."

"Thanks for the warning," I yelled back between heaving breaths as I ran. "Something tells me I'm not the first woman you've said that to."

My sexual innuendo got a chuckle from a few people, and even Shane couldn't help but laugh a little.

"Looks like Bishop was able to save you all from another round," he announced as I clocked in at two minutes and twelve seconds. "Nice job today. Listen, before you go, I just wanted to make a quick announcement. I'll be participating in a CrossFit competition this Saturday in Northeast Philly. I was hoping some of you would be able to come out and show your support. I'd truly appreciate it. If you're interested, Kate has the flyers with all the information." Shane lowered his voice to just me as I began to turn to get my things. "You coming, Amanda? I mean, you'll finally get to find out what a hard body actually looks like."

Normally, I would have spat some sarcastic jab right back at him. Like *Is that why* you're *going?* Or *Doesn't your boyfriend mind you being around so many hot men at one time?*

As if by reflex, my mouth opened to speak, but instead, all I could do was focus on the words "you coming" and imagine Shane with his shirt off, muscles rippling as he lifted weights in front of an audience.

I'm so screwed.

❤

The following day, the Hot Rod Shots competition finally came to a close, and I was desperately looking forward to having Steph announce the winner later that evening. A girls' night was long overdue.

As Rod packed up the personal belongings he had in his desk—unfortunately, the company said they couldn't find a place for him . . . *sigh*—I took my last close-up shot of his ass as I reached around his solid waist to hug him goodbye before I left for the day. I strutted confidently out of the office, admiring the picture on my phone.

Was it too late for me to pursue a career in photography?

❤

Steph and Danielle came over around eight so we could give Rod the going-away party he deserved—of course, he wasn't actually *invited* to it. We'd planned to hang out by the pool at my apartment complex after it closed. We would drink Coronas as we superficially memorialized Rod. And eventually, Steph would declare a winner and award a prize.

The evening began with a less than graceful hop over the black fence. When we'd managed to get all three of ourselves and the Coronas over the fence safely, we settled in for the night. With a toast in our chairs by the pool, we pretended we were in a Corona commercial and had just been transported to a tropical setting instead of a dimly lit apartment pool.

Then Steph rose and removed a piece of lined paper she had tucked away in her purse. "We are here tonight," She somberly began, "to pay tribute to Hot Rod."

Ha, she's even prepared a speech. This is going to better than I expected.

"But today is not one of sadness," she continued. "Rod, you may not be with us anymore, but you will always be in our hearts." She put a closed fist over her heart and closed her eyes. "And also in our camera rolls."

We all chuckled before she continued.

"Today is a day of remembrance. We are not here to focus on how Rod's time with us was tragically cut short." She shook her head and sighed, pretending to get choked up. "That's not what he would've wanted. Instead, we are here to celebrate the time that we *did* have with him. I'd like to begin by having each of us share a story about Rod that is especially memorable to us. I guess I'll begin."

Steph sat down, put her paper away, and took a gulp of her beer. "During Rod's first day, I asked him to get me the sugar out of a high cabinet in the lunchroom. I knew there wasn't any sugar up there. And I didn't even have coffee or anything to put it in. I actually feel a little guilty about it. He's so dumb," she added, like she was just noticing it for the first time. "I just asked him so I could watch his untucked polo shirt rise above the waistband of his pants while he reached above his head. Of course, that was before he realized that a polo was too casual to wear to work," she laughed, clearly caught up in her nostalgic fantasy. "Ahh, those were the good old days." She looked up at us expectantly. "Who's next?"

"I'll go," I said eagerly, grabbing another beer from the cooler. "This probably happened like four or five weeks ago, I guess. Rod and I got into the lobby elevator together one morning, and it got pretty crowded as more and more people got on. By the time the doors shut, my ass was pressed up against his crotch. I don't know what I'm more ashamed of," I said, shaking my head in feigned embarrassment. "The fact that even as people exited the elevator, I still didn't move away from him, or the fact that I didn't hit the emergency stop button when we were finally alone and fuck him senseless between the fourteenth and fifteenth floors."

The girls laughed.

"That's pretty good," Danielle said. "But not as good as mine. We had lunch together a couple of days ago. We were eating cake left over from Beth's birthday, and I felt a little icing on the corner of my lips. Before I even had a chance to grab a napkin, Rod reached over and wiped it away with his finger."

"Oh. My. God. That's totally hot." Even I was impressed.

"Wait, I'm not done. It gets better. He put his finger to my lips and let me lick the icing off."

We were speechless. All I could think to do was start a slow clap.

Man, Danielle might be more of a competitor than I originally thought.

"Now that we've taken a moment to properly remember Rod, it's time move on to the reason we are all here tonight," said Steph. "First of all, both of you did an exceptional job with your photography. It was definitely a difficult decision, which is the reason why I had to look at the pictures over and over again. Well, it was *one* of the reasons, anyway. Now it's time to examine each category and determine a winner. We'll start with Best Smile." Steph pulled out two pictures from an envelope on the glass table.

"You had them printed?" I laughed.

"Of course I had them printed." She said it like it was a stupid question.

Steph arranged them side by side in front of us. "I actually really like the angle of Danielle's," she began.

I examined it closely. It was taken slightly from the side, revealing a dimple on his right cheek.

"But the lighting and distance of Amanda's are unbeatable," Steph continued. "Hers is a close-up, and since she made use of the natural lighting during midday, his teeth look extra white. He should really be a toothpaste model."

"One for me. You're going down, Danielle!" I could really talk a lot of shit sometimes.

"Only if you're talking about me going down on Hot Rod's rod," Danielle fired back with a smirk.

"The next category we'll evaluate is Best Crotch Shot." As Steph laid the pictures on the table, I immediately knew I'd lost this one. Danielle's was a close-up of Rod in mesh shorts that he sometimes changed into at the end of the day before heading to the gym. The picture was only from his knees up to his waist. Since his white T-shirt was on the shorter side, the shape of his dick was visible through his thin navy shorts.

"Okay, Danielle obviously wins this one," I conceded. "But since you two bitches already have this picture, this one's mine." I snatched it up quickly and gave it another long once-over before tucking it into my pocket carefully.

"It's tied up," Steph reminded us.

"Let's do Best Hair Day next," Danielle requested.

Steph flipped through the envelope and placed the next two pictures on the table. They were both fairly similar, and because I had taken so many pictures of Rod over the past several weeks, it was difficult to remember which one was even mine. They both looked to have been taken on the same day, because he was in a pale-pink button-down shirt with the sleeves rolled to his elbows. His hair was also exceptionally long. Suddenly, I remembered what day it had been taken because the next morning he came in with it freshly cut, and I had been thankful that I'd taken the picture the day before.

"This one was close," Steph said. "I really had to examine them to even notice a difference. But I had to go with the picture on the left. Rod looks freshly fucked in this one. If you look very closely, you can see that the hair on the sides of his head is beaded with sweat. I think this one was taken on a hot afternoon after he'd walked back to the office from lunch."

Danielle looked at me. It was clear she didn't know whose picture was whose either.

"This one's Danielle's," Steph added when she realized we didn't know who'd won this leg of the competition.

Danielle celebrated by clinking glasses with Steph, while I moped internally.

"And now for Most Seductive Expression," Steph said excitedly as she eagerly showcased the two pictures. This time I recognized mine immediately. Rod had stooped down to pick up some files that he'd knocked over one day, and since I had made a habit of carrying my phone with me at all times, I had been lucky enough to take a quick picture of him as I walked by. As if his upward, penetrating gaze wasn't enough, he also happened to be biting on his lower lip.

"In Amanda's," Steph said, "he's on his knees. Need I say more?"

Danielle's disappointment was audible.

"It's tied up again. And last, but certainly not least, is Best Ass Shot." Steph set the picture I had sent just hours earlier on the table first. "You really played 'til you heard the whistle blow, didn't you?"

"Yeah, I'm actually surprised you were able to print it in time."

"Well, I'm nothing if not thorough," she said as she placed Danielle's picture next to mine.

I had to admit, Danielle's had a real chance. Rod's snug, dark-gray pants hugged the hard, round curves of his backside perfectly. The picture looked to have been taken from about six feet away, allowing a complete shot of his legs up to the back of his messy hair. In a way, seeing the entire length of his body actually made it more alluring.

Then I studied my picture. The loose khaki pants he had worn earlier had not fit nearly as perfectly as the ones he sported in Danielle's picture, but my shot had something Danielle's didn't: innovation. From the camera angle, it was clear that my arms had been wrapped around Rod when I had taken the picture, allowing me to snap a close-up image of the top of his firm ass without even zooming in. It was . . . artistic. It was . . . ballsy.

And after Steph lifted it up to me with a smile, I was sure it was the winner. "The competition was hard-fought, but I think even Hot Rod himself would agree that Amanda's picture was just slightly better," Steph said.

I stood to bow, and Danielle clinked the neck of her bottle against mine to congratulate me.

Then Steph handed me what felt like a wrapped picture frame. Probably a collage of my photographic talents.

I smiled proudly.

"In fact, I *know* Hot Rod would agree," she added slyly. *What? Oh, shit!*

I tore open the paper and stared wide-eyed at the framed photo. Or should I say *it* stared at *me?* No. She. Didn't. There, in my hands, was a picture of Hot Rod sitting shirtless at my desk with his hands behind his head.

My eyes shot quickly to Steph, and as if there was still any doubt as to whether she had told Rod about our little competition, I read the personalized note from him at the bottom.

Congratulations, Amanda! Though I think the Best Smile award should go to Steph.

I studied his face and was confused when I saw his soft pink lips pressed tightly into a sexy line. But my stupid grin widened when Steph snapped a picture of me, and I realized what he'd meant. The clever fucker had been talking about me.

chapter five

There were people everywhere. Who knew so many people liked CrossFit? When Shane had announced that he'd be competing this weekend and would like some support from the gym, I was instantly filled with foreign emotions.

I genuinely wanted to support him, though I wasn't sure where this desire was coming from. And as I walked around the large, open gym covered in black rubber mats and littered with weights, I knew one thing for certain: I was really starting to like Shane.

But I also knew that I had to ignore these growing feelings for him. Ever since Kate's birthday, my mind had flitted back to him. The way his arms felt when they were wrapped around my waist, the tingling sensation I had gotten when his breath tickled my ear, the comfort he had provided when I had needed it. But I had to knock it off.

I needed to stop fantasizing about him touching me, rubbing against me, trailing his lips down my naked... *Okay, enough.* I was like a fourteen-year-old boy. And while I would normally be proud of that, in this case, I wasn't. A relationship between Shane and me would never work. Nate had taught me that.

But I didn't want to be completely without him, either. I

craved some kind of contact with him, even if it wasn't intimate. So, that left me ... where?

As friends. That's where it leaves me.

Yes, friends. I could be friends with a guy who was sexy as hell. After all, I was friends with Kyle.

Okay, bad example.

Despite my resolve, I still didn't trust myself not to run out onto the mat and lick the perspiration off Shane's body as he competed, so I'd brought reinforcements. Lily was eager to join me since she had missed Kate's birthday party because her parents were in town.

She didn't want to seem totally unsupportive of the gym; however, she had plans in the evening—she wouldn't tell me what they were, sly devil—and she was only staying for a bit. So I'd invited Kyle to tag along to keep me company after Lily left.

He had needed some prompting, since watching large men grunt and lift weights wasn't exactly his cup of tea. But then I told him that there was also a female division, so he'd changed his tune quickly. He had also offered to drive, though I suspected that mostly had to do with the fact that I was directionally challenged and we probably would've ended up somewhere in Jersey rather than in Northeast Philadelphia where the competition was. Lily chose to drive herself since she had to leave early.

As soon as we arrived, we wandered around the gym looking for Team Shane. Kate had gotten purple shirts made with that moniker on them and had handed them out to all of us who intended to come out to support him. I couldn't help but feel a slight hesitation from her when she handed me mine, but I chose to believe that it was all in my imagination. Kyle, the tallest of us, scoured the gym for purple shirts.

He finally tapped me on the arm and pointed to my left. I followed his hand and saw some faces I recognized. I grabbed Lily, and we headed toward them. But as we approached, the crowd grew denser. I stepped up on my tippy-toes, trying to see what had everyone's attention. I saw a group of shirtless men waiting their turn to perform what appeared to be cluster ladders.

"What the hell are they doing?" asked Kyle.

"Cluster ladders," I replied absentmindedly as I tried to scan the group of men for Shane.

"And those are...?"

I let out a sigh before answering him. "There are, I don't know how many bars...a lot. As you move through them, the weight gets heavier. They have to squat clean them into a thruster. They keep going until they can't perform the motion."

"Okay. I'm just going to pretend I know what all of that means," he replied as he craned his neck to get a better view.

I couldn't get a clear look at the guy who was competing now, nor did I see Shane anywhere. Finally, the audience began to clap. *I guess whoever's turn it was is finished.*

Then I saw Kate walking toward the mat. She was handing someone a water bottle.

And there he was. Shane must have been the one who had just finished the cluster ladders. I put my hand on Kyle's shoulder as I tried to gain more leverage over the crowd. Shane took a step toward Kate and came into view.

Upon seeing him, my jaw dropped, and I became instantly grateful I had worn underwear. Otherwise, I was worried a wet spot would have become visible through my jeans due to my immediate arousal at seeing Shane shirtless.

In the six months I had been going to CrossFit Force, I

had never seen Shane without a shirt. Therefore it had been left up to my imagination to picture what he was working with underneath it. My imagination didn't even come close to the real thing.

Shane's abs were shredded. They literally formed a maze on his stomach. His chest was broad and puffed out with muscle. And he had what was probably the sexiest tattoo I had ever seen on a human being. I had known he had one because it ran the entire length of his right arm. However, I hadn't realized that it snaked up his shoulder and down the right side of his chest and stomach. It was a thick, black tribal that ran in intricate designs. I desperately wanted to run my tongue over its outline as my fingertips gently followed the lines his abs created.

Kate handed Shane a purple T-shirt.

Dear God, please don't put that on.

Thankfully, he just held it in his hand as he continued to drink water. I'd never wanted to be a water bottle so badly in my life, as I watched his strong, sure hands squeeze the bottle in an effort to extract fluid from it. Everything he did was erotic.

"Should we go over?" Lily asked, pulling me from my sex-fueled thoughts.

"Yeah, let's go," I murmured as I began to push through the crowd.

Shane's head turned at the shuffle in the crowd. Our eyes locked, and his face lifted slightly as he started to turn toward me. But then, as Kyle draped an arm over my shoulder in order to prevent himself from getting separated from me, Shane stopped. His features hardened before he cast his eyes toward the floor, handed the bottle back to Kate, and walked off toward the other members of CrossFit Force.

What the fuck is that about?

"Where did he go?" Kyle asked from behind me.

Kyle. Was that why Shane had walked away? Because Kyle had put his arm around me? I wondered . . .

I pointed to the rest of Team Shane and kept moving in that direction.

As we approached, I saw that everyone was crowding around Shane, high-fiving and bro-hugging him. However, he barely returned their gestures and stalked a few feet away from everyone as we strode up. I threw a glance in Shane's direction, but his back was to me.

"Did he blow it?" Lily asked Gavin, a fellow purple-shirt-wearer, loud enough that I could hear.

"Nah, he did awesome." Gavin was flexing and puffing out his chest like he had been the one competing.

"Then why does he look like someone put his dog's head in a box and mailed it to him?"

God, she's morbid. I have to start preventing her from watching movies like Se7en.

Gavin shrugged his shoulders and turned his attention to the remaining competitors who were awaiting their turn. I did the same, wondering why I had even bothered to come today.

Shane, as usual, was being a total dick. I closed my eyes briefly and shook my head, chastising myself for thinking he'd actually want me here. But when I opened them again, I found a whole new reason that I wanted to be here.

Jesus Christ!

There were gorgeous, shirtless men everywhere. My eyes scanned every last one of them as I tried to understand how I had been so blind to them all until now. I was losing it.

"If you eye-fuck them all now, there won't be any left for

later," Kyle whispered in my ear.

"I won't need to eye-fuck them later. I'll fuck one for real," I replied in awe of the sight before me. It was a horny chick's dream.

Kyle let out a loud laugh. "You're a total nympho."

I gave him a megawatt smile, signaling that I not only knew that I was, but that I was also proud of it.

"Sadly for you, I don't think many of these guys meet your requirements."

I turned to give Kyle my best pout when I heard a stern voice.

"What requirements?"

My head flew to the right, and my eyes connected with Shane's as he sauntered up to us. He only held my eyes for a second before looking down to fiddle with the T-shirt in his hands. Kate, of course, was half a step behind him.

"Hi, Amanda," she said warmly but quietly.

"Hi, Kate." There were a few seconds of awkward silence before Kyle lightly nudged me. "Oh, yeah, this is my friend Kyle. Kyle, this is Kate and Shane."

Shane gave Kyle a slight nod of acknowledgment while Kyle reached his hand out to Kate, who accepted it quickly.

"Nice to meet you both," Kyle said, though he only looked at Kate.

I couldn't help but notice that their handshake lasted a little longer than usual. My eyes darted back and forth between them, and I thought I saw Kate's posture improve slightly, but I couldn't be sure.

Well, this could be interesting.

I glanced over at Shane, who also seemed to notice the sparks flying in front of us. I raised an eyebrow at him, and his lips twitched a little. Kyle must have realized that he was still holding Kate's hand, because he suddenly broke their contact.

Clearly affected by my dear Kyle, Kate began speaking rapidly. "We're heading over to the next event. I think everybody is going to go up higher into the bleachers. They'll be able to see from there. Unless you guys want to walk over with us?" She spoke the last words hopefully and directed them completely at Kyle.

"Yeah," Kyle replied instantly. "Uh, I mean, if you want to, Amanda."

I could barely contain my grin. Kyle normally played it cool around women. Kate must have gotten under his skin.

"Yeah, that's fine. Just let me find Lily." I turned and scanned the crowd. I finally caught sight of her talking to a girl named Jocelyn. I didn't know her that well, but she and Lily were friendly. "Lily," I yelled. "Hey, Lily," I screamed after she didn't respond. Her eyes darted around before settling on me. "We're going over to the next event. You coming or staying?"

Lily looked around her. People surrounded her, packing her into her spot on the bleachers like a sardine. She finally waved her hand, signaling for us to go without her.

"Okay, let's go. She's staying."

Shane rolled his eyes and started walking away from us. If it weren't for Kyle needing a wingwoman right now, I would have told Shane to go straight to hell. But I bit my tongue for the greater good: Kyle getting laid.

The next event was on the other side of the huge gym, and it was difficult to get through the crowd. Kyle and Kate ended up falling behind a little, talking closely. Kyle had stuffed his hands into the pockets of his jeans as Kate flashed her dazzling smile repeatedly. Not wanting to walk alone, I caught up to Shane.

"So, what's your next event?"

He glanced over at me, annoyance showing on his face.

He's really asking for it.

He finally let out a sigh and responded to me. "The next one will test endurance, speed, and agility. Burpees, double unders, kettlebells . . . It's going to be tough."

"Well, for you it probably will be." I was done being nice.

"Thanks a lot," he bit out sarcastically. "So, I'm not sure how into you your boyfriend is." He threw his head in Kyle's direction. "Though I can't say I'm surprised. I only see you a few times a week, and that's more than enough for me."

Ah, sarcastic Shane, how I've missed you.

"Oh, trust me, he's been into me." Shane's jaw tightened at my response, and I felt a welling of pride that I'd succeeded in pissing him off. But that response was short-lived, as I realized that I didn't particularly like the feeling of Shane being mad at me. "He's not my boyfriend, just a good friend," I said quietly.

Shane didn't look at me, but I saw the tension leave his face, which also served to make me relax.

What the hell is this guy doing to me?

Just then, a large man came out of nowhere and bounced into me. I would have fallen sideways if it hadn't been for two strong hands that grasped my biceps firmly.

"Yo, asshole, watch where the fuck you're going."

It took me a moment to realize that it was Shane yelling.

Oh shit.

"It was an accident, asshole. Calm the hell down." The guy who had knocked into me didn't make a move toward Shane, but he wasn't backing down either.

"Don't you tell me to calm down, you piece of shit." Shane released my arms and moved into the other man's space so that the two men's faces were only inches from each other.

I grabbed Shane's arm and tried to pull him backward. He was here to compete, not get in a brawl because of me. "Shane, stop. I'm okay. It's fine. Come on, you're going to miss your heat." My voice was pleading. I didn't want to be the cause of Shane getting disqualified.

He stood there glaring at the other man for a few more seconds before he let me pull him away. The man wisely didn't say anything else as Shane backed up.

"Are you okay?" Shane asked when we had walked a few feet. He stopped, turned to face me, and put his arms back on my biceps, his thumbs circling my skin softly.

My heart thumped at the contact as a sizzle ran down my body.

"Yeah, I'm fine," I replied huskily. Our eyes locked, and he held my gaze for what felt like an eternity, though it couldn't have been more than a few seconds. "Thanks," I breathed.

"No problem." He gave my arms a slight squeeze before releasing me and resuming his walk. Then, suddenly, I felt his hand reach for mine and grasp it firmly. "Stay close to me. These people are maniacs."

And as we walked briskly toward his next event, I tried to ignore how right it felt to be holding his hand.

❤

Kyle and Kate finally caught up to me as I stood watching Shane warm up for his next event. They seemed engrossed in their conversation, which was fine with me, since I was engrossed with watching how Shane's muscles tweaked and rippled as he practiced the different movements and stretched.

And that was how the rest of the day went. Shane kept qualifying for the next round, so we followed him to each station. And though he didn't grab my hand again, he walked close to me, his biceps rubbing against my shoulders frequently. As Shane competed, Kate and Kyle talked about God knows what while I gawked at Shane. It was a perfect afternoon, actually.

At the third station, my phone vibrated in my pocket. I fished it out and looked down to see a text from Lily.

Hey, I'm taking off. Have fun ;)

I shook my head and clicked out of my messages and looked at the time. Wow, four twenty-four? We'd been here almost three and a half hours. Time flies when you're ogling.

When all was said and done, Shane came in fifth overall out of over two hundred competitors. I had to admit, I was damn proud of him. As his name was announced, I heard a large roar from the crowd and turned to see a small sea of purple shirts. Shane waved to them, but his eyes found mine. I smiled broadly at him as a shy smile crept to his lips.

After the awards, Shane hopped down from the small stage that had been erected in a corner of the gym. I was standing with the rest of CrossFit Force by this time, and the excitement among us was palpable.

Shane jogged over to us and yelled, "Okay, now we celebrate."

Everyone cheered and started talking at once, trying to decide where to go for dinner and drinks. I turned to search for Kyle and spotted him fairly easily, since he was the only one in this group not wearing purple. As I approached him, I noticed he was still speaking to Kate.

"Hey, sorry to interrupt, but I wasn't sure what you wanted to do." I willed Kyle to want to go out with the group. I was suddenly desperate to spend more time with Shane, but Kyle had driven, so it was his decision. Christ, I was pathetic.

"Oh, don't leave. The party's just getting started," Kate begged, her eyes looking up expectantly at Kyle.

"I'm up for hanging out a little while longer if you want, Amanda."

Kate's eyes darted to me, and I could see the pleading in them.

"Yeah, sounds great," I replied.

"Great," Kate squealed. She clearly hadn't intended for her voice to come out that high-pitched, because her face grew a tad crimson. "I'll just go find out where we're going."

And as she bounded off, I shot Kyle a look that let him know I expected to hear all about what was going on between the two of them. I just hoped he didn't give me a similar look back.

❤

Forty-five minutes later, I found myself sitting in a pub called Doc McGroggins. After a ton of bickering amongst our group, we had finally decided on this place, reasoning that it was close enough to the arena that we could walk, yet far enough that it wouldn't be packed with people from the competition.

With our group numbering about twenty-five, we basically took over the small place. It was a good choice, though. The bartenders were friendly, the hardwood floors and oak tables were clean, and the four flat screens that were scattered throughout were broadcasting various shows, not just sports. But I was too distracted to pay much attention to what was on them.

I was sitting at a long table with about ten people, but I found myself nestled between Kyle and Shane. I wasn't even sure how I'd ended up next to Shane. It kind of just happened as we filed in. I mean, Kyle had made some comment about me body-checking a girl from my gym who had attempted to take the seat next to Shane, but I had no recollection of that.

We ordered drinks from the cocktail waitress who came to our table, but we realized that we were all starving, so she quickly returned to take our food order. I suddenly found myself in a crisis. What the hell should I order?

I had no reservations when it came to food. As long as it was dead and had a high caloric value, I'd eat it. But I was sitting here with two of my trainers from the gym, and I was pretty sure they both adhered to the Paleo Diet; most serious CrossFitters did. I didn't want them to see how bad my eating habits were. I'd never hear the end of it.

When the server got to me, I ordered the healthiest thing I thought I'd be able to choke down. "I'll have a grilled chicken sandwich, please." I glanced over at Kyle, who raised his eyebrows at me. I shrugged nonchalantly at him and hoped he wouldn't call me out on my order. Damn him for knowing me so well.

The server then moved on to Shane, who turned slightly toward me as he glanced up at the server. "I'll take the wings."

"Twelve or twenty-four?" she asked sweetly as she rested her hand on the back of the chair and leaned slightly down toward him, pushing her breasts closer to his face.

"Better make it twenty-four."

"No problem," she said with a wink.

First of all, did she just wink? Who did that anymore? Second of all, it was obviously "no problem." They were on the fucking menu for a reason.

Shane turned back around, ignoring her eye flirting, and started up a conversation with Joe, who was sitting across from him. As they rambled on about CrossFit bullshit, I tried to get Kyle's attention, but he was too absorbed in his conversation with Kate.

What the hell did I bring him for if he isn't going to entertain me?

I looked for another conversation partner and found Emily seated across the table from me. She was nice enough, but she had divulged her entire life story to me one day at the gym during our warm-up. Like, loads of information. I had avoided her since. But I was out of options.

"So, Emily, how have you been?"

She looked up at me with sad eyes, and I knew I was totally fucked. "Well, I've been okay, I guess."

Disengage! Disengage!

But as we sat here awkwardly, her obviously waiting for me to ask her to elaborate and me clicking my heels together in the hope that I'd be transported out of here, I was left with little choice.

"Oh, really? Just okay?"

"Well, I'm thirty-two, and I'm living with my parents," she said. "I expected to be married by now. Honestly, everything just kind of went south when my cat died."

"Oh, no, when did he die?"

"When I was five."

I couldn't contain the laugh that flew out of my mouth. I

tried. Hard. And in my defense, I did a decent job of covering it up by acting like I was choking.

"Sorry," I gasped. "Wrong pipe." I hoped she hadn't noticed that I hadn't been drinking or eating anything that could have gone down the wrong pipe.

I suddenly felt a large hand smacking me on the back.

"You okay there, Bishop?"

"Fine," I croaked. When I looked at Shane, I saw humor alight in his eyes. I wondered if he had heard my conversation with Emily.

I didn't have time to analyze it further because Emily launched off into other childhood traumas, including her inability to save a baby bird who had fallen out of its nest, the time she had peed her pants in front of her entire third grade class, and when she had once earned a B- on her report card. "The teacher just didn't like me."

"What a bastard." I had to at least feign support. If she stopped talking to me, I'd have to sit there like a loser fiddling on my phone in order to pretend I was just too busy to talk to anyone. I stared daggers over at Kyle, my former best friend. He had better hope Kate put out, because it'd be a cold day in hell before I fucked him again. *Traitor.*

As Emily started in on her night terrors, I felt Shane's knee bump into mine. I shifted over slightly to give him more room. I picked up my drink and took a long, long sip before setting it back down, propping my elbows on the table and sinking my head into my hands.

Emily had just started gesturing wildly with her hands when I felt it again. Christ, his legs weren't *that* long.

I peeked over at him and saw him trying to suppress a smirk. *The bastard is listening.* Was his bumping me his way of showing moral support or him poking fun at the horrendous circumstance I had found myself in? My guess was the latter. Well, two could play at that game.

"Shane, didn't you tell me you have really bad nightmares?" The smirk instantly fell from his lips as Emily whipped her attention to him. "You do?" Emily asked him, clearly ecstatic to meet a fellow sufferer.

"Uh, no, I . . . uh . . ." I couldn't contain my grin as I watched him frantically search for words, "I mean, I've had nightmares, like everyone else. But, uh, nothing, nothing serious."

"What do you have nightmares about?" Emily questioned as she leaned slightly toward him, invading Joe's personal space, causing him to recline back in his chair.

Ha-ha, this should be interesting.

"Yeah, Shane, what are your nightmares about?" I asked, faking sincerity.

Shane glowered at me as he responded, "I usually don't remember."

Just then, the servers came out to deliver our food.

Shane took advantage of the distraction to lean closer to me. "You are a cruel, heartless woman for doing that to me."

I giggled a little at the seriousness in his voice. "I had suffered long enough. It was time to throw someone else on the grenade." I watched the server brush against Shane as she lowered his buffalo wings in front of him.

"Thank you," he said without looking up at her.

Now that I had Shane's attention, I wanted to keep it. "I thought all you CrossFit nutjobs ate according to that Caveman Diet?"

"A lot of us do."

"But you aren't right now."

"Sure I am. This is chicken."

"Yeah, chicken covered in sauce," I laughed. "Cavemen didn't have buffalo sauce, did they? And they definitely didn't have the ranch dressing you're dunking them in."

"I'm celebrating, so leave me alone," he replied as he continued to eat. "And what do you mean by 'CrossFit nutjobs'? You do CrossFit. Wouldn't that make you a nutjob too?"

"I just do it for the exercise. I haven't drunk the Kool-Aid like you other muscleheads." I bit into my sandwich, wishing I had ordered something else. "Though I am still a nutjob. Just not a CrossFit nutjob."

"Oh, okay. I'm glad you made that distinction. So why are you a nutjob?"

He was looking at me now, his eyes intent. He was actually interested in this answer, and that made me a little tense. What had been fun banter was turning more serious, and I wasn't sure how I felt about that. I wasn't sure how to respond.

"I'm not. I was just trying to make you feel better."

His brow furrowed slightly, and I couldn't shake the feeling that he had been testing me. And I had failed miserably.

"Well, isn't that just so sweet of you," he said sarcastically as he continued with his meal.

I took another bite of my sandwich and racked my brain for something clever to say. I didn't want our conversation to end like that. Why it mattered, I didn't care to analyze. It just did.

"So, what got you started with CrossFit?" I figured if anything would suck him back in, it would be the one thing that, as far as I knew, he was most passionate about.

"That's a long story," he replied, his eyes meeting mine again.

I looked at him expectantly, willing him to tell it to me.

"I played lacrosse in college..." And he was off. He explained how, after playing collegiate sports, he had missed the competitive spirit that accompanied them. He wandered around the gym, going through the motions. Then he found CrossFit and thus found his calling.

I sat there rapt in his story, admiring his devotion to his job. I hadn't even noticed how much time had passed until Kyle tapped me on the arm.

"Hey, Amanda, it's getting late. You ready to go?"

"What time is it?"

"A little after ten."

"A little after ten? What are you, ninety? It's Saturday night."

"I'm actually eighty, smartass. It's been a long day, and I'm driving to Lancaster in the morning to visit my parents."

"Yeah, Shane," Kate butted in, "I'm tired too. Are you almost ready?"

I looked back at Shane, who looked at his full beer. "I guess," he replied dryly.

Clearly Kate and Shane had also driven together.

"We really picked some duds to hang out with, huh?" I said to Shane, smiling widely so that Kate knew I was kidding. I didn't care what Kyle thought. "Wait..." A genius thought popped into my head. "Shane, did you drive or did Kate?"

"I did."

"Okay, so Kyle, why don't you take Kate home and Shane can take me home? I mean, I'm assuming you guys both live close to the gym?"

"Well, my car is actually at the gym," Kate answered.

"That works. Kyle lives ten minutes from there. What

about you, Shane?" Adrenaline was coursing through me at the prospect of possibly getting to spend more time with Shane. I knew I could never act on these impulses, but it was still fun to have them. And I knew that nothing would send my impulses into overdrive like a car ride with Shane.

"Yeah, I live close to the gym. I could give you a ride home."

Jackpot!

"Okay, well, you're sure?" Kyle asked me.

I wanted to snap at him that he had a lot of nerve acting like he gave a shit now. He'd been ignoring me for hours. But instead, I smiled sweetly.

"Yeah, I'm sure."

A wide grin broke out on his face, and I knew that he was happy to have the extra time with Kate. I was definitely going to need to pump him for information the next day.

"All right, then. I'll talk to you tomorrow?" he asked me. I nodded in reply. "Great. Ready, Kate?"

"Yup, I'm ready."

I watched as Kyle put his hand on the small of Kate's back. *He is definitely going to try to bang her.*

We watched them leave, and then Shane picked up his beer and held it up to his lips for a few seconds before taking a sip. He looked as if he were internally debating something.

"So," he finally said as he set his glass down and turned his face toward me, "what requirements were you guys talking about?"

My eyes darted to the seats across from us, thankfully finding them empty. I hadn't even registered that Joe and Emily had gotten up from the table. I looked at him blankly, trying to act like I had no idea what he was talking about. But of course I knew.

I had already had to dodge this question once today. And judging from how he didn't waste any time asking it once we were alone, he clearly wanted to know the answer. I wasn't going to be able to ignore it again. But that wouldn't stop me from trying.

When I didn't reply, he clarified. "At the competition. When I walked up to you two, Kyle was saying something about not meeting your requirements. What does that mean?"

Well, shit. How the hell was I supposed to explain this to him? I needed to calm down. This was Shane, a guy I had insulted almost daily for the past six months. There was no reason to be awkward. I just had to come out with it.

"Fucking Kyle," I said with a snort and then instantly regretted it. *Not your best opening, Amanda.* "Okay, well, the truth is, I kind of have rules about who I will and won't date."

Shane's face lit up like a Christmas tree. "You're shittin' me! You have *rules*? Let's go, out with 'em. I need to hear this."

"You don't need to hear anything," I said, pretending to be affronted. "It's personal."

"Not anymore. Spill it."

"No," I said petulantly.

"Amanda, we can do this the easy way, or we can do it the hard way. The easy way is you telling me your rules so I can berate you incessantly. The hard way is me incorporating burpees into every class you show up for. Choose wisely." He narrowed his eyes at me, challenging me to doubt him.

His burpee threat hit below the belt. A worse exercise had never been invented. I sighed heavily. "Fine, I'll tell you. But you have to swear you won't tell anyone."

"Fuck that. I'm broadcasting them on our website."

"Shane," I said warningly.

He let out a barking laugh. "I'm just teasing. I won't tell anybody. I swear."

I shook my head, not fully believing that I was actually going to tell him my rules. "Well, the first one is that..." And that's when I remembered the first rule.

How the hell was I going to tell him this?

He already made jokes about my promiscuity. Now he was going to know that he wasn't that far off base. Fuck it. I had my rules for a reason. I'd never been ashamed of them before, and I wasn't going to start now.

"If I think a guy could be relationship material, then I sleep with him by the fourth date." My eyes darted to Shane, who squirmed slightly. "I just don't want to invest a ton of time in a guy who's shitty in bed," I explained simply.

Shane smirked slightly. "Have you met a lot of guys who were relationship material?"

I knew that this was his way of asking if I'd been with a ton of guys. But I wasn't sure whether I had or not. Everyone's definition of a ton was different. "No, not too many. I mean, I don't put notches in my bedpost, so I can't give you a number. But I haven't slept with the majority of Eastern Pennsylvania or anything."

He considered my answer for a second before donning the look of a jubilant child again. "Okay, so, Rule Number Two?"

My voice grew a bit quieter. "I don't date anyone who makes less money than I do."

Shane's eyes bulged slightly at this. He had taken a sip of his beer but now refused to swallow it, causing the liquid to puff out his cheeks. He stared at me incredulously for a moment. Finally, he swallowed.

"Really? Why?"

Since Shane already kind of knew about Nate, I decided to be honest. It was better than looking like a money-hungry hussy. "Do you remember the guy from the bar at Kate's party? The one you saved me from?"

He sat up a little straighter. This was now the second time I had told him he'd saved me. And as he leaned closer to me, I knew that he liked hearing it.

"Well, the reason we didn't work out was because he was insecure about me making more money than him. So, after he bolted, I decided that I wasn't going to date men who didn't earn at least as much as I did."

"But not all men are insecure about stuff like that," he said quickly, taking me by surprise. "You shouldn't lump us all together because of one asshole."

My brain focused on his use of the word "us." Did he not want to be included in the same category as Nate because he didn't care about the female in the relationship making more money in general, or because he didn't care if *I specifically* made more? Had he thought about being in a relationship with me? I had to shut this down.

"But some are, you can't deny that. And I don't feel like sorting through them. My rule makes it a moot point. I like it that way." There was finality in my voice, though probably more than I felt.

He pondered my words for a moment and then looked as if he planned to debate with me but then thought better of it. "And Rule Number Three?"

This one was a piece of cake. "No kissing in bars. Or really any public place, for that matter. It's trashy and tacky and gross."

Shane lifted his hand in front of his mouth, trying to hide the smile that played on his lips. But as his shoulders started shaking, he quickly gave up and began to laugh, loudly and uncontrollably. He finally held a hand up, signaling a silent apology, since he still wasn't able to speak. Eventually he got it together.

"Sorry, it's just . . ." And the laughing seized him again.

"What, you jerk? It's just what?" I desperately wanted to be annoyed, but seeing his reaction made me giggle along with him.

"You're . . ." His chest heaved two more times before he was able to get the words out. "You're a sex snob." And the laughter roared again.

Sex snob? I had to admit, that shit was clever, even though I didn't find it completely accurate. "I'm not a snob."

"Yes, you are. You don't date anyone who you think isn't good enough for you."

"Why would anyone want to date someone who isn't good enough for them?"

"They wouldn't. But your reasons are totally superficial." He wasn't laughing now. Neither of us were.

"No, they aren't," I argued.

"How aren't they?"

"Superficial is when something only affects you on the outside. The shit that went down with Nate affected me much deeper than that. I'll go to almost any length to prevent feeling that way again. My rules may seem superficial, but my reasons for them aren't." My voice was even and calm, which was a damn miracle because I was anything but those two things. I didn't like having to justify myself to anyone. I was who I was, take me or leave me.

Shane was quiet for a minute, clearly trying to formulate his response carefully. When he finally spoke, his voice was soothing. "Amanda, I'm sorry if I insulted you. I was just surprised. I didn't know girls really had rules for who they'd date. I thought that kind of stuff was only in movies. I understand where you're coming from. I mean, I think you're crazy, but I get it." A sparkle came to his eyes at his last comment, and I knew that he was calling me crazy in the most affectionate way possible.

"It's fine, really." And I meant it. I knew how weird my rules sounded; that was why I rarely told anyone about them. But I knew that the rest of our evening would still be tense, each of us unsure of what the other was holding back. I needed to restore some humor to our conversation. "Besides, I kind of like the Sex Snob title. I may have to get a cape or something with that embroidered on it. Like a superhero."

Shane laughed. "And what would your superpower be?"

I thought for a moment, bringing my index finger to my chin. "I would be able to end bad relationships with a flick of my wand."

"Wand? Are you a superhero or a fairy?"

"Whatever. Sex snobs can be both."

"Oh, okay," he sarcastically conceded as he drank more of his beer. "Guess you really are a nutjob."

"Told you so," I replied with a sly smile.

We fell back into easy conversation after that. Some more CrossFit Force members joined us from the bar, and I had a spectacular time sitting there bullshitting with people I barely knew.

At around midnight, everyone who was left settled up their tabs and headed home, including Shane and me. The walk to the car was mostly quiet, as was the car ride home. I was fine with the silence, though. It felt . . . comfortable.

But my mouth could only stay closed for so long before it stiffened up and needed to be stretched. "What do you have going on the rest of the weekend?"

"Not too much. I'm going rock climbing tomorrow."

"Aren't your muscles tired? Give the poor things a break."

"Nah, it's fun. Have you ever been?" he asked as he glanced at me briefly before returning his attention to the road.

"Nope. I've always wanted to, though. It looks like a lot of fun."

"It is."

And that was it. I didn't know where to take our conversation when I was getting such little help, so I decided to try being quiet again.

I directed him to my house, and when we pulled up outside, I wasn't sure exactly what to say. I'd had a tremendous amount of fun with Shane tonight, and I didn't want it to end. But I couldn't tell him that. *What could I tell him?* Thankfully, he spoke first.

"So, do you want to go?"

"Go where?" I asked, confused.

"Rock climbing. Do you want to go with me tomorrow?"

"Oh, um, I don't know."

"Relax, Bishop. It's not a date or anything. You said you wanted to try it. Do you want to come?"

I hesitated slightly before replying, "Yeah, I would."

"Great. I'll pick you up tomorrow. Around ten?"

"Sure, that works."

"Man, I'm going to see you on my two consecutive days off. I must be a real glutton for punishment. Now get out of my car, Sex Snob. I'll see you tomorrow."

"You're such an ass," I mused as I opened the car door and got out. "Thanks for the ride." I closed the door and walked up the stairs to my apartment, and turned to see Shane still waiting at the curb.

I guess chivalry isn't dead.

Though I may not be able to say the same for myself after I tried to rock climb.

chapter six

As I entered Limitless Adventures, I started to second-guess my decision to come here. Well, actually, I didn't regret agreeing to try rock climbing. I'd always thought it sounded like fun, and it would definitely be a good workout. I think my real regret was going rock climbing for the first time with Shane.

Not only had I spent most of the drive here talking shit about how quickly I would scale the most difficult walls, I had also neglected to mention my intense fear of heights. This day could quite possibly be beyond embarrassing, but I couldn't let my hesitation show now.

The massive faux rock walls ranged from fairly straight inclines with larger handgrips to surfaces that would position the climber nearly horizontal with his back facing the ground. I had a feeling that Shane Reed would be zooming up one of those before the morning was over.

Shane checked us in and got me a waiver and rented climbing gear—though I insisted on paying my own way since this wasn't a date.

"I still can't believe you brought your own equipment," I said. "You're such a nerd."

His eyes bored into me with complete seriousness. This

wasn't just a game to him. "We'll see who the nerd is when we hit the wall. Now sign the waiver and let's get going."

"Calm down, Mr. Bossy. I have to read it first." Shane waited while I looked it over. He didn't need to fill one out because the loser already belonged to the club. "What's all this about rope burns and falling off the wall?"

"It just says if you die or whatever, they aren't liable. Trust me"—he leaned in to my ear and lowered his voice a bit—"I have a lot of experience with ropes, and I've never given anyone any abrasions."

My head shot over to look at him. *Is he serious?* His expression revealed nothing. I quickly signed the waiver and handed it to the husky gray-haired woman at the counter.

"Okay, your instructor's right over there." She pointed to a group of about ten people who were huddled in one corner of the gym. "You're the last two in that group."

"Thanks," Shane replied politely, grabbing our equipment and turning toward the group.

"Why do I need an instructor? You can teach me, can't you?"

"It's just a liability thing. You have to get properly trained by the employees. Plus, I already have to tell you how to do things correctly when I'm getting paid for it. What makes you think I wanna correct everything you do wrong in my free time too?"

I shook my head as he laughed at his own joke. "You think you're pretty funny, don't you?"

He shrugged. "I try."

It seemed like our group had been waiting for us, because as soon as we arrived, the instructor began. "Okay, my name's Rain."

Of course it is.

Rain looked to be in her early twenties. She couldn't have been more than five-foot-two, and she was sporting knee-length men's cargo shorts with a large gray T-shirt. Her pasty complexion was framed by dirty-blond dreadlocks that she had tied back in a ponytail with an industrial rubber band.

"I'll be your instructor for today," she said. "It looks like we're all here, so let's get started. I'm gonna go over some rules with you first. Climbing is not—I repeat—is not a game," she spat sternly in a voice that was much too deep for her small stature. She clearly took her job seriously and wasn't in the mood for any nonsense.

I leaned over to Shane. "You hear that? No messing around."

Shane did his best to keep a straight face while he looked ahead.

"The first rule of climbing is to trust your feet," Rain continued. "You'll hear me say that a lot to you while you're on the wall. *Trust your feet!*" she yelled sharply, making me jump. "Rock climbing is a vertical dance that requires focus. And concentration." She emphasized the last part to make her point.

"You hear that, Amanda?" Shane didn't avert his gaze from Rain as he whispered under his breath. "A *vertical* dance. Most of your experience is of the more *horizontal* nature, isn't it?"

Okay, I'll give credit where credit's due. That was a good one.

Rain's eyes darted toward us to keep us in line. She must have had a sixth sense for goofing around. "Climbing is a fantastic workout for your whole body. It forces you to use muscles most people don't make use of on a regular basis, like your wrists, forearms, and fingers."

Ha. "Well, that explains why you're so fucking good at it. You could probably free scale Mt. Rushmore with all the jerking off you probably do." I couldn't hide my smile. I was clearly too pleased with myself. "Now you can even claim it's part of your workout routine." I didn't look over at Shane because I knew I wouldn't be able to control my laughter when I saw his face, and Rain would have my head on a stick.

"Now, that being said, even those who are used to a more sedentary lifestyle should be able to climb. No matter your skill level, there is a wall for you here." Rain still hadn't cracked a smile.

Aren't hippies supposed to be happy and high all the time?

"Everyone look at the wall behind me," she continued. "Notice the different colors. The color helps you navigate the path to the top, and each color is a different level of difficulty."

Rain continued to blab on about the different types of grips and footholds. The only type that stuck out to me was when she talked about how the bigger ones were called "jugs." Shane made some comment about how he liked big jugs too and then made no secret of looking down at mine.

"It looks like most of you have brought a partner with you. That person will most likely be belaying you," Rain announced.

"You hear that, Amanda? I'll be belaying you." Shane couldn't help but look over at me with a wicked smirk as he said "belaying."

What have I gotten myself into?

I knew that term had to have some other meaning than what was running through my mind. My version involved me gripping a headboard and screaming while Shane bore down and pounded in and out of me ruthlessly. I shook my head, trying to force the image from my brain. I hoped Shane hadn't picked up on my daydreaming.

Shane laughed. *So much for that.* "Not what you're thinking. It means that I'll be at the bottom of the wall with the ropes, keeping you stabilized while you climb."

"Oh" was all I could get out. All of our sexual innuendos were getting to be a little much. And coming from me, that was really saying something.

At the sound of Rain's husky voice, any sexual thoughts quickly escaped me. "You'll find that if you're climbing with a partner of the same sex, you'll have similar climbing styles, and you can give each other some pointers. If your partner is of the opposite sex, you'll learn some techniques you've never tried before."

I felt Shane's deliberate gaze at her last comment.

Aaand the sexual tension is back.

"For those of you who are more experienced climbers, you can put on your own equipment and your partner's, and I'll just come around and check to make sure it's on correctly. If you need my help, just let me know."

Shane wasted no time stepping into his harness, and for the first time today, I noticed how delicious he looked. His black tank top hugged his hard chest tightly. My eyes caressed his thick tribal tattoo up the length of his arm again, just as I had at the CrossFit competition. And as he tightened the straps of his harness around his thighs, the bulge in his pants seemed to grow.

God, Amanda, look up, look up, look up. Look anywhere but there.

Thankfully—or not—Shane knelt down in front of me to

help me with my harness.

"Step through," he said as he shimmied the straps up my bare legs, skimming my smooth skin with his soft, strong fingertips. I couldn't be sure, but I thought he was taking more time than was necessary down there. Not that I minded. Shane Reed. On his knees. In front of me. I could feel myself get wetter with every sinful thought.

He pulled the straps tantalizingly up my thighs and over my shorts. I couldn't be sure if his touch was accidental or deliberate, but the effect was the same. Then he rose to stand in front of me to reach around my waist. My hips thrust forward as he tightened the straps with his arms looped around me. I could feel his crotch pressed up against my abdomen. My eyes were inches from his chest.

God, I wanted to lick him. I wanted *him* to lick *me*. And the tightness of the restraints around my thighs and ass was only making the pressure building low in my core that much more intense.

"How does that feel," he said as he tugged roughly on the harness.

The movement of my shorts against my already sensitive clit was nearly unbearable. I felt like he could make me come just by pulling on the straps. I cleared my throat and swallowed hard.

"Feels really good." *Jesus Christ, couldn't you think of anything else to say?*

"Good. It should feel pretty tight. You ready?"

Oh, you have no idea. "I guess so."

Shane moved away, giving me another glimpse—or thorough examination—of his dick—which looked to be larger than many of the others in the vicinity.

God, I can't believe I'm estimating the size of strangers' penises. Is this what my life has come to?

When Rain was satisfied that everyone had been properly harnessed, she demonstrated a few climbing techniques. She showed us how to regain our center of balance and reminded us to use our legs to propel ourselves up. I tried to pay attention because I didn't want to embarrass myself when I climbed.

But since Shane already knew all of the techniques, he kept his eyes glued to me. I was thankful that I was a female, because if I were a guy, I definitely would have been hard.

When Rain was done with her demonstration, Shane showed me a few warm-up stretches to do before beginning. Some involved me lying on the ground while he positioned himself over me and pushed on my legs. This did nothing to quell the sexual frustration that was slowly building inside me.

"Okay," Rain shouted. "Who's up first?"

I could tell Shane was eager to go, but he tempered his excitement and let a few of the others go first. I studied them closely as they moved up the wall, some more quickly and with greater ease than others. I tried to focus on where they struggled to learn from their mistakes.

Shane also pointed out a few tips that he thought might help me. I learned that I needed to look down as much as I needed to look up, and use my other foot for balance against the wall so I didn't swing out.

When it was Shane's turn to go, Rain hooked his ropes and harness to her. "I'll be belaying you," she said to Shane in a gruff tone, "since your partner clearly can't." Rain shot a condescending look my way.

I gawked at Shane as he scaled a more difficult section of the wall quickly and with little effort. His steps were carefully planned, and he moved with the fluid grace of someone who was obviously experienced.

I wonder how experienced he is at other things.

I enjoyed my view from below, as I was free to stare at his firm ass and flexed biceps as he moved against the wall above me. After Shane rappelled to the bottom, Rain gave him one of those manly handshakes that turned into an awkward hug.

"That's what's up, dude. Show 'em how it's done. You're next, Chicklet," she said, pointing at me.

I walked cautiously over toward the wall, and Rain attached my harness to Shane's with the ropes.

I had already decided that I was going for a medium-level section of the wall. I didn't want to look weak by going up a part that a child could climb, but I didn't want to fail if I attempted something that was too difficult.

I got about fifteen feet off the ground without much of a problem, but I soon realized that I had reached a section that didn't have much to grab on to. I looked down behind me to Shane for guidance and immediately got butterflies in my stomach at the height.

"Look to your left," Shane called up. "There's a small foot chip. Put your left foot there and press your right against the wall to anchor yourself and keep your balance. When you feel stable, push yourself up."

"Trust your feet!" Rain bellowed.

I did as Shane said, but after about five more feet, my hands were quickly beginning to tire. I looked back down again, and I was sure my fear was obvious to more than just me by this point. I had so much left to go. There was no way I would get to the top.

"My hands hurt!" I yelled. "Just let me down. I'll try an easier part."

"Oh, no. Stay up there. You're fine!"

Fucking Rain.

"Thrust your butt out," Shane yelled. "It'll give you better leverage."

"Is that what you say every time you make that request to a woman? Leverage?" I was glad to see that even in my compromised state, I hadn't lost my quick wit.

"I'm serious, Amanda. Try it."

To my surprise, it actually worked, but my hands were killing me from grabbing on to such small grips. And I was only about twenty-five feet up.

"Just bring me down," I nearly whined. "I can't do it. I feel like my fingernails are coming off. Seriously."

Shane's encouraging "You can do it" was cut off by Rain screaming, "Spit on your hands and keep going!"

Is she serious? "I'm not *spitting* on my hands!" I yelled down. I clung to the wall with all my strength while my fingertips started to turn purple.

"Let go of the wall for a minute to give your hands a rest," Shane suggested compassionately. "I'll keep you up there."

Cautiously, I let go of the wall, careful not to look down. I rubbed my hands together, stretched my fingers, and cracked my knuckles.

"Okay, good," Shane said. "Now swing back to the wall again."

As I shifted my weight to gain some momentum, I felt the straps on my legs move a little higher. For a moment, I wondered if this was what being in a sex swing was like.

Good God, I really am *sexually frustrated.*

At last, I managed to grab hold of one of the larger grips and push myself up with my legs.

That was no thanks to Rain, who was yelling comments like, "Goddammit, you can't even get up a wall? I can bench my own weight." And "Grab that jug like you mean it."

"Come on, Amanda. You're almost at the top. Even sedentary people can do this," Shane yelled through his laughter.

That last comment was enough motivation to propel me to the top. When I rang the bell, I was so relieved I'd gotten up there that I forgot my fear of heights altogether as I rappelled back down.

Shane wrapped his strong arms around me when I landed. I was surprised at how safe and secure I felt in them.

"Well, I guess you've had enough rock climbing for one day," he said, smiling. "You ready for some lunch?"

"Thank God you're done," Rain chimed in. "I've had a one-legged midget waitin' to get up that wall for the last ten minutes."

❤

Fifteen minutes later, we were seated across from one another in a booth at a nearby diner.

"So, Spiderman, did ya have a good time?" I looked up from my menu. "Seemed like you had a real bromance goin' with your boy, Rain."

"Wait. Let me get this straight." Shane chuckled softly and shook his head. "I do something well, and you still find a way to make fun of me?"

"Right."

"And a bromance with Rain? Seriously? I was afraid to get too close to her. I kept thinking a squirrel was gonna claw its way out of her dreadlocks any second and attack me."

I was pulled away from my daydream of a rodent jumping from Rain's head onto Shane's back when the waitress arrived. She was a cute girl, probably in her mid-twenties, with silky auburn hair and boobs that made men—and most women— want to squeeze them to find out if they're real. She gazed longingly at Shane as he studied his menu and ran a hand through his messy blond hair.

"What can I get for ya?" she asked with a flirtatious smile.

What is it with Shane and waitresses? Enough already.

Shane remained quiet for a few moments.

"Um," I chimed in, since Shane still hadn't decided and the waitress was clearly oblivious to my presence completely. "I'll take an iced tea and a cheesesteak with mushrooms and ketchup. Oh, and a side of fries." I must have worked up quite an appetite clinging to that wall. I was friggin' starving.

The waitress wrote my order down without a word and looked back at Shane expectantly.

"I'll just take tuna salad on a plate and a side salad without dressing."

"And to drink?"

"Water's fine. Thanks."

Seriously? I'd ordered normal food because last night Shane had gotten wings. And today he got tuna? And a salad with no dressing? *Who eats a salad with no dressing?* "Way to make me look like a pig," I said with an embarrassed laugh.

"You could never look like a pig," he said sincerely. He cleared his throat and shifted nervously in his seat. "So back to my bromance with Rain."

I could tell by the way he changed topics so quickly that he was a little self-conscious of how I might react to his first comment. And for some reason, I was eager to make him feel at ease again.

"Yeah, I've never really been a fan of dreadlocks either," I said. "Though I actually dated a white guy with dreadlocks before. Not something that I'm especially proud of. So your new relationship with Rain won't really be that unique?"

"Really?" Shane looked surprised, clearly choosing to ignore my snipe about Rain.

I felt the need to justify it. "But he was an awesome tattoo artist and had his dick pierced, so I think those two things should count for *something.*"

What that hell did you add that last part for? Shane isn't one of your girlfriends. He doesn't give a shit about your ex-boyfriend's private parts.

Shane raised an eyebrow and laughed out loud.

Something about knowing that I had made Shane laugh caused me to want to continue. I took a sip of the iced tea the waitress had just put down in front of me.

"Yeah, not exactly the highlight of my dating history. I was like sixteen, and he was twenty-one. He came into this hippie store I used to work in. I swear to God, he bought incense and scented oil. Not lying. Then he showed me his tattoo portfolio he had with him because he'd been out looking for jobs. When he walked around the store on his hands, I fell for him immediately."

I knew how ridiculous it all sounded, and Shane had burst into complete hysterics about halfway through my love-at-first-sight tale.

"He was really such a loser," I continued. "He didn't have his license, so I had to drive his stoner ass around everywhere. I *did* get free pot from him, though, and he bought my friends and me alcohol."

"Wow, this guy . . . what was his name?"

"Lip."

"Lip?"

"Yeah, well, Phillip, but everyone called him Lip."

"Well, this 'Lip' doesn't really seem like he was up to your standards."

Our conversation paused as we let the waitress put our food down. My eyes darted from my "fat girl feast" over to Shane's meal.

Oh well. I think my time for feeling shame vanished when I confessed that I'd dated an unemployed tattoo artist who wore patchouli.

"Lip and I dated before all my rules. Actually, I don't even know if you could even call it dating. We were either getting high or getting laid most of the time. Ah, those were the days." I sighed to feign my nostalgia at the memories. "I was young. My only real regret was not getting a free tattoo out of the whole deal. I was still a little nervous to let Lip tattoo me since he was doing it out of his cousin's basement. And he never got a job in a real shop the entire time I knew him."

"Wow, Bishop. Sex. Drugs. All you're missing is the rock and roll."

"That came later when I dated the bass player in a Creed cover band." I laughed. "That's actually my third regret."

"Third? What was the second?"

"That I never got to find out if the dick piercing enhanced the sex because I only slept with Lip in the back seat of my two-door car. Not enough room to try different positions. Ya know?" I could tell that I may have taken things a bit too far revealing that last part. I laughed awkwardly. "I'm actually not sure which is more embarrassing—dating a member of a Creed cover band or telling you about the piercing thing."

"It's fine," Shane assured me as he finished the last bite of his salad. "I like that about you. You're just... you're yourself. You don't really worry about what people will think." He laughed. "Even when you probably should."

"Come on, don't leave me hangin'. I can't be the only one with a story like that. What crazy girls do you have hidden in your past, Shane Reed?"

"The usual...just a few ex-girlfriends, I guess." He grinned widely. "Can't say I've ever dated a girl with a dick piercing."

"You're so funny," I said sarcastically.

"I know," he replied, smiling as he pulled his wallet from his back pocket. "You keep telling me that."

❤

I had insisted to Shane that we each pay our own way this morning, but he still stole the check as soon as the waitress laid it on the table and stalked off toward the register before I was able to protest. Even though I glared at him as we walked to the car, to which he simply laughed, I was secretly appreciative of the gentlemanly gesture. The ride home was spent in easy conversation. The kind that came naturally to close friends. It was strange.

As I said goodbye to Shane and walked up the path toward my apartment building, I began riffling through my bag, looking for my keys. While I was in there, I yanked my phone out as well. I slid my phone to wake as I climbed the stairs and noticed five text messages and two missed calls. All from Kyle.

I unlocked my door, threw my keys down on the small table in the foyer, and plopped myself down on the couch as I began to scroll through the text messages. The first one was sent at ten twenty-six a.m. I was already in the car with Shane, and it had never even occurred to me to check my phone during our outing.

Hey, just making sure you weren't beaten and buried alive in a shallow grave by that Shane guy—sorry, Kill Bill is on. Text me back.

God, why were all of my friends so morbid?

HELLO!!! Juicy details are awaiting you. Text me back.

If you're trying to punish me for leaving you with Captain Musclehead so I could get some alone time with that sexy girl you've been keeping from me, then you're not the girl I thought you were. Text me back, loser!

So, now I'm actually getting worried. Your phone is like your eleventh finger. Stop being a brat and text me back.

Amanda, what the FUCK!?! Where are you?? Don't make me call your mother. Seriously, get in touch with me.

Somewhere amid all of that, he had also called and left me voicemails. I didn't bother listening to them, electing instead to just call him and calm his overprotectiveness down.

His crazy ass answered after one ring. "Amanda, Jesus Christ, where have you been?"

"Relax, nutjob, I was out."

"Out? Out where? Guam? You could've texted me back. I was freaking out." The anxiety was seeping from Kyle's voice. *Damn, he really had been worried.*

"I'm sorry. My phone was on vibrate. I went rock climbing, and I didn't want to get reamed out by the flower children in there for my phone ringing and interrupting the mating rituals they were doing with the walls. You know, there have been other times when I haven't texted you back right away. You never skitzed out before." Part of me found it endearing that he had worried about me. Another part wished he'd stop acting like a pansy.

"I've never left you in the care of a guy I don't even know before either. I would've felt like such a dick if I had to explain to your family that you'd been murdered because I left you in a bar so I could get a piece of ass."

"So, you did get laid." It probably said a lot about me that the only thing Kyle said that had caught my attention was that very last bit. I chalked it up to sexual frustration. Being in close proximity to a man who was earth-shatteringly sexy but who having sex with was not an option had done things to me. Suddenly I found myself on familiar ground.

This was all Shane Reed's fault.

Kyle let out a loud sigh, probably regretting what he had allowed to slip out of his mouth. "You really are sex-obsessed. You know that, right?"

"Yeah, yeah, I know. Get to the good stuff."

"Well, to answer your question, no, I did not get laid. But—"

"Damn, that's really unfortunate," I couldn't help but interject. Kyle was a phenomenal lay. Kate should've climbed him like a beanstalk.

"Can I finish?"

I remained quiet, signaling to him that he could. Though I was incredibly tempted to comment that, no, he clearly couldn't "finish."

"I'm going out with her tonight," he blurted, knowing that this bit of information would tell me all that I needed to know.

"Holy shit, you really like her!"

"Yeah. I mean, so far. I don't know her that well. But I like what I know."

"Wow. Wow. *Wow.*"

"Have I rendered you speechless, Amanda?" I could hear his smirk through the phone.

I hesitated, trying to formulate words that could properly convey what I was thinking. "Wow."

Kyle laughed loudly. "I know, I know. It's been a while since I've taken anyone out on a date. I'm not sure I remember what to do."

"Wow." I was going to be monosyllabic for a while.

"Jesus Christ, enough with the wows," he said with mock exasperation. "I have dated women before. Stop acting like I just told you I saw Bigfoot."

"I'd actually have an easier time digesting the Bigfoot thing."

"Amanda." Kyle's tone was a warning. I was starting to piss him off.

God, he really *likes her.* Kyle never got agitated with me. "Should I go rent my tux for the wedding? I *am* your best man, right?" I couldn't resist.

"Okay, awesome. I'm hanging up now."

"No, no, Kyle, wait. I'm sorry. I'll be nice."

He let out another sigh but didn't hang up.

"So where are you gonna take her?" The answer to this question would tell me a lot about Kyle's feelings toward Kate.

"I made a reservation at Jones in the city."

Bam! He's totally into her.

Since we lived about forty minutes outside of the city *and* had just been there last night, I knew that Kyle must see something in Kate to drive all the way down there again. I was brimming with happiness for him. Kate was a good girl, and I desperately wanted Kyle to be with someone who would treat him right. I would hate to have to kill a bitch for hurting him.

I couldn't let him know this though. It just wasn't how I rolled.

"You're a bad friend."

"Wait...what?" Clearly, this was the last thing he expected me to say.

"You heard me. You're a bad friend."

"How does any of this make me a bad friend?" Confusion rippled through his voice.

"Because I told you months ago that I wanted to go to Jones, and you never took me. I suffer through having sex with you all of the time, and what do I get for my trouble? Nothing. But Kate doesn't even put out and she gets to go? Oh, the injustice of it all," I wailed for dramatic effect.

"Are you done?"

"I guess," I replied simply. "So, are you super nervous?"

"Nervous? No, I'm not in high school."

"Adults get nervous."

"When was the last time you got nervous?"

"I'm a bad example. Wait, no I'm not. I was nervous today when I went rock climbing."

"That's because you're a dumbass. Who goes rock climbing when they're scared of heights?"

It was frightening how well he knew me.

"Who did you go with, anyway?" he continued.

"Shane."

"Oh really?"

"Yes, really. He told me last night he was going, and I told him I always wanted to try it, so we went."

"That's it?" Kyle prodded.

"Yes, that's it. Now, back to more important things." I maneuvered the conversation back to him and Kate and what he had planned for the evening. He was clearly excited. I was happy for him. Just as we were saying our goodbyes and about to hang up, I needed to add one more thing. "Kyle?"

"Yeah?"

"I think this is going to be great. You and Kate. I have a good feeling about it."

"Thanks. I needed that."

I knew he did. That's why I said it. But that didn't stop it from being the truth. And as I hung up the phone, I thought, my little Kyle is all grown up.

❤

The rest of the day passed without anything exciting happening. Actually, the rest of the week passed like that.

Work was significantly less interesting without Hot Rod around to ogle. And everyone else seemed to be on autopilot, dragging their bones around the office like they were slowly becoming zombies.

Master Bader was his usual glowing self. After calling me into his office for some lame reason and talking my ear off about his coin collection, I was ready to blow my brains out. But when he started rambling on about his yearly trip to the Poconos for a Boy Scout reunion, I began daydreaming about blowing *his* brains out. Surely no one would miss him. Except maybe the sock next to his bed. But I'm sure even that thing would appreciate a reprieve.

The only thing I looked forward to was going to CrossFit. And though I tried to tell myself it was because I felt so good after the workouts, I knew that was a bunch of shit. I looked forward to seeing Shane more than I would have ever admitted to anyone. Why did he have to be so hot?

Though, at this point, my attraction to him was beyond just the physical. I was drawn to every aspect of him. The way he walked, talked, laughed, fucked—granted, this attraction was based solely off my dreams—the list was endless.

I definitely had a crush on Shane, but it was nothing more than that. I reminded myself of this as I sat in my car before classes that week, taking deep breaths and giving myself mental pep talks to refrain from throwing him to the floor and sitting on his face. *Definitely just a crush.*

Tuesday's class was disappointing, though. I arrived only two minutes before my class began—well, five, but the deep breathing ate away three minutes—so I didn't get to banter with Shane before class. And he made the workout so difficult, I didn't have any extra air to insult him during class either.

Then, after class ended, he was assaulted by the bimbo brigade as they asked him to feel their muscles for tightness. *Pathetic.* All I got was a quick wave as I clomped out the door.

Wednesday's class was even worse because Shane wasn't there at all. Brock was running class. I hated Brock. And not fake hated, like I did Shane. This was real bone-crushing, voodoo doll-making hate. He was a pompous little smidge of a man who thought he was cool shit with his Paleo brownies and veiny arms. He looked like he was covered in blue worms. He normally ran the afternoon classes, so I didn't have to deal with him much, even though he hung around the gym a lot.

"Where's Shane?" I asked in disgust. I've never been good at hiding my feelings. I'd work on it if I cared more. I didn't.

"He needed the night off. That okay with you?"

I just rolled my eyes in response, not wanting to speak to him any longer than was necessary. The class passed slowly, with Brock barely watching us perform the movements. I could've spent class standing on my head, spitting wooden nickels, and he wouldn't have noticed anything out of the ordinary.

About midway through class, I saw Kate walk out of the office and begin to circulate among us.

"Why didn't you run class?" I whispered as she walked past me.

"I had to get the billing sorted out." She made a face that let me know she had enjoyed doing that about as much as I enjoyed being near Brock.

I didn't ask her where Shane was. I thought that would look suspicious. God knows I didn't want Shane knowing I actually missed him. And I wouldn't put it past Kate to tell him.

When class ended, I walked past Brock. "Are you going to

be here tomorrow?" I uttered with contempt.

"No, your precious Shane will be back," he said mockingly.

"Thank God. I'd rather be trained by Richard Simmons than deal with you again."

"Ha. Training? Is that what you call it? I thought you were just here to pick up guys."

His comment riled me. I had never picked up a guy at CrossFit Force. Well, there had been that one guy, but that wasn't important now. I went through a phase of going after anyone with dimples and who sported a clear outline of their dick in workout shorts. I wasn't proud of it. I put on my best come-hither smile and batted my lashes.

"Jealous?"

"Of what," he scoffed.

I leaned in close. "Of the fact that I wouldn't even fuck you with someone else's pussy."

And with Brock speechless, I turned and left.

❤

I fared markedly better on Thursday. I arrived ten minutes early, just as the previous class was finishing up. As Kate recorded how many rounds they had completed, Shane wandered over to me.

"Bishop." He nodded his hello.

"Where the hell were you yesterday?" I was so tactful sometimes.

"Uh, at my brother's. It was his birthday."

Relief spread through me. In my mind, he had run off to a deserted island to elope with a Victoria's Secret model. But I covered my true feelings in the best way I knew how: with sarcasm.

"Well, in the future, could you possibly get an ax-murderer to cover your classes instead of Brock? He's a total douche."

"Nah, he's a good guy."

I shot Shane an icy glare.

"Or not," he laughed.

"So what have you been up to?" I asked, feigning disinterest as I stretched.

"Nothing much. Just being here, like always." His words would've suggested that he was bored with his routine, but his tone didn't. It was clear that he loved being here, doing what he did. "What about you?"

"Same old." My tone didn't carry the same enthusiasm.

"Any plans for the weekend?"

"Yeah, a group of us are going to the pool hall Saturday night. I think Kate's going. You wanna come?"

Yeah, Shane, do you wanna "come"?

"What time?"

"I don't know. I don't really excel with details. I rely on Lily to get me places on time. Kate," I called. "Did Kyle say what time everybody was meeting Saturday?"

"He said around eight."

"Around eight," I said, trying to pretend that I was the source of the information.

"I don't know," he hawed. "I was invited out with some other friends."

"What? Are you scared?" I cast a sideways look at him. I couldn't let him choose other friends over me. What if there were going to be girls there?

"Of what? A pool hall?"

"That I'll embarrass you with my mad pool skills."

"Your mad pool skills, huh? Why, Amanda, it kind of

sounds like you're challenging me."

"Oh, I'm definitely challenging."

"Yeah, you sure are. In every way imaginable." He laughed at his little joke as I narrowed my eyes at him.

"What's it going to be, Reed? You up for an ass kicking, or what?"

"In your dreams."

Well, he hit the nail on the head with that one. He and his ass had made numerous appearances in my dreams lately.

"I'll be there," he continued. "I can't resist schooling you in front of all your friends. I'll get the name of the place from Kate, since you clearly don't know anything," he said over his shoulder as he walked away.

And as he got class underway, all I could think about was how wrong he was. I definitely knew something. I was going to beat Shane Reed's ass in pool.

chapter seven

"Who are you all dressed up for, Lil?" I pulled myself away from the bathroom mirror to see her emerge from her bedroom. "We're just goin' to the pool hall."

"Nobody," she said with a sly grin as she put in her other earring. "Can't a girl just look nice?"

"Nobody, my ass. You look hot."

"Do I?" She spun around like a girl on prom night.

Lily looked great. And it wasn't just the fact that her fitted white ankle pants and small heels made her legs look even longer than they already were. She emitted an inner radiance that I hadn't seen in her in months. Her hazel eyes glowed when she smiled. She truly looked beautiful, inside and out. Of course, I'd never actually say any of *that*.

"Yeah, you totally do. If I were a guy, I'd fuck you."

She laughed loudly and put her hands over her heart. "Aww, you really know how to make a girl feel special," she said in a sweet southern accent, batting her long lashes.

"So is the new mystery man comin' tonight or what? I'm dying to meet the guy who can put a smile like that on Lily Hamilton's face. He must be *damn* good in bed."

"No, I might go out with him afterward, though. And who said I was sleeping with him?"

"Who said you weren't?"

"Let's talk about who *you* may or may not be sleeping with, shall we? A certain Shane Reed will be there tonight, right?"

"Shane?" I laughed out loud. Though I wasn't laughing internally. I had actually imagined sleeping with Shane quite a few times lately, and none of those times involved me laughing. "Nothing's going on between us. He's just a friend."

My eyes returned to the bathroom mirror as I straightened another section of my blond hair. I was afraid if Lily saw my face, my expression might reveal something I didn't want her to see. Something I didn't want to see either. But as I stared at my reflection, I had no choice.

"Yeah, a friend you'd like to fuck." She entered the bathroom and nudged me with her elbow, causing me to just miss burning the side of my forehead with the straightener. Wouldn't have been the first time.

"That's what I have Kyle for," I said simply. "Now how do I look?" I asked as I finished off my makeup with a little tinted lip gloss. I had tried to dress simply: jeans and a loose pastel pink-and-white-striped shirt that hung off my shoulder. I was going for cute but casual.

She took a step back and put a finger to her lips, squinting her eyes and studying me closely. "If I were a guy, I'd fuck you."

❤

When we arrived at the pool hall a little after eight thirty, everyone else was already there. They occupied a few tables near the back corner, and if Steph and Danielle's poor rendition of "You and Tequila" by Kenny Chesney was any indication, they were already a few pitchers of beer deep.

Since Shane didn't know either of the other two girls or Steph's boyfriend, Dan, he had probably spent most of his time there as a third wheel to Kate and Kyle, who were already all over each other. Clearly Kate didn't share my same need for Rule Number Three.

Shane's face lit up when he saw me. And though I tried my hardest to conceal it, I was sure my expression mirrored his.

"It's about time you showed up, Bishop. I was worried you might've chickened out."

"Ha!" I laughed loudly. "You *should* be worried. But not about me chickening out. About me kicking your ass and emasculating you in front of all these gorgeous women." I gestured my arms toward Kate, Lily, Danielle, and Steph.

"Okay, then," Shane said as he handed me a beer. "Let's get to it. Best of three. And I highly doubt I'll be emasculated."

I actually highly doubted that too. Shane's pecs strained against his snug dark-gray V-neck T-shirt. He stood, relaxed and confident, with one arm leaning against the worn wooden shelf that ran around the perimeter of the room and the other holding a cue stick parallel to his body.

Before I could stop myself, I found my gaze wandering from the bottoms of his perfectly fitted dark jeans all the way up to the tips of his golden hair, which I noticed was a little more tousled than usual. I paused briefly at the fly of his pants to imagine what might be underneath.

I eventually forced my attention to his face and the rugged stubble that had grown since I'd seen him last. Even if I beat Shane in every game we played, nothing could take his manliness away from him. It was an intrinsic quality that manifested itself physically.

"I'm competitive," I said, forcing myself from my indecent

daydreams. "What are the stakes?"

"Hmm... Let's make it interesting. If I win, you have to kiss me in public."

I raised my eyebrows at him.

"Relax, Bishop," he said quietly so only I could hear. "I don't wanna be your boyfriend or anything. We're not at a middle school dance. I just want the satisfaction of making you break one of your rules."

"And if I win?" I looked back at him, intrigued.

"You get to kiss me in private," he said matter-of-factly.

"Is that supposed to be a reward? I guess the only positive would be that I could deny it ever happened because there wouldn't be any witnesses."

I pretended to consider his offer, but I agreed to it the second he'd suggested it. I was confident there was no way I would have to break one of my rules, and the thought of kissing Shane in private was just too enticing to pass up.

"Fine," I said, feigning disgust. I couldn't help but notice Lily's I-told-you-so grin. "Not a word," I warned her.

Steph and Danielle were already too drunk to notice what was going on, so they continued striking their balls into each other's on the table next to ours while Dan tried to calm them down and get a real game going.

"You break. I'm not good at it." I grabbed the triangle and placed it at one end of the table. "Does it matter which balls go where?" I asked as I placed them inside the triangle. The laughter of those around me was the only response I received, so I put the balls in randomly.

As I leaned over to pull the triangle up delicately, I heard "Nice rack."

I looked up to see Shane staring at me from the opposite

end of the table.

"What?" he said with a shrug. "I've always wanted to say that."

Then he leaned down, eyeing up his shot. With one smooth movement, he slid the cue between his fingers, and the balls scattered across the table. He sank one stripe and one solid on the break. Then he walked around the table, carefully deliberating his possible shots before declaring that he would be playing stripes.

He made two more shots before missing and then motioned that it was my turn. I studied the table and moved toward the orange ball near the side pocket. The cue ball was nearly against it. I hit it in easily but missed the next one when the tip of the stick slid up over the cue ball on impact.

"Put some chalk on that," Shane said as he tossed it to me. "You don't want the tip to be too slick. You need a little friction."

Does he know how dirty that sounds?

Had he said that to get a reaction out of me, or was my mind in the gutter? Shane shot me a devilish grin.

Yup, definitely intentional.

Kyle, Kate, and Lily were clearly entertained by our exchange. The three of them laughed at Shane's comment and cheered him on when he sank three consecutive shots.

"Lily, you're supposed to be rooting for *me*," I said. "What the hell?"

"I kinda wanna see you kiss him," she answered. "Although hearing all about it later might be even better, now that I'm thinking about it."

I ignored her comment as Shane missed his next shot and I lined up for my own.

"Can I show you something?" Shane stood off to the side, slightly behind me.

"Sure," I said curiously.

He leaned down and pulled the stick back, running it against the skin between his thumb and index finger.

"Lighten your grip a little with your right hand, and don't curl your left fingers around the stick. See? Watch me."

So I did. I studied him shamelessly as he pulled on the stick steadily, smoothly with his right hand. I backed away to examine his firm ass as he leaned over the table confidently. I had the urge to reach around him and feel his hard chest and stomach. I felt the same tightening in my lower core that I'd felt so many times with this man recently. Was I seriously getting turned on watching Shane play pool? I briefly hoped I would lose the first two games just so I could kiss him right here.

But my competitive nature got the better of me. I humored Shane by using his technique for my next shot, and I high-fived Lily when the purple ball fell into the corner pocket. But my next shot was off-center, and I scratched.

Shane placed the cue ball close to the last striped one and tapped it in with the perfect amount of force.

"Eight ball, corner pocket," he said, gesturing to the pocket closest to me. He leaned down and kept his eyes on me as he pulled the stick back for his last shot. The cue ball collided with the eight and stopped in place on impact, but the eight ball continued and dropped into the corner pocket.

"You didn't expect me to go easy on you, did you?" Shane asked.

"Oh, I think I know you better than that. Besides, I like a challenge."

Shane's mouth raised into a subtle grin. "So do I."

Interesting. He won the game easily.

What the hell is he talking about?

❤

The next game was much more even. Shane made a few shots, and then I sank a few. Kate and Kyle decided to play Dan and Steph on the table next to us. And Danielle settled herself onto a stool and occupied herself with alcohol. I guess Shane and I were not as entertaining as we'd been the first round.

Even Lily seemed bored. I looked over a few times to see her face buried in her phone as she anxiously checked the time. I was sure she'd been texting the new hottie.

"I'm gonna get going," she said.

"But you're my ride home," I said. "Eight ball, side pocket. It's out of the way for Dan, and he's already driving Danielle." And I wasn't about to ruin Kyle's time with Kate by asking him to drive me. "I thought you weren't going until we were done?"

I lined my shot up and made it easily.

"I'll drive you," Shane said before Lily could open her mouth to reply. "It's no big deal."

I couldn't argue. I didn't have any other way home. Plus, I had to admit I was happy to get another ride home with Shane. And something told me I wasn't the only one trying to hide my excitement.

"Perfect," Lily said as she grabbed her bag off the chair and turned to leave.

"It's all tied up," I said as I placed the balls in the triangle.

"Not for long," Shane said with a smile. "I took it easy on you the last game."

I looked over Shane's shoulder and watched my traitorous

sex fiend of a friend head toward the exit. And that's when I saw him.

Shit, shit, shit.

I put my head down, hoping he hadn't seen me.

"Amanda."

I had no choice but to look up.

"Zach?"

I don't know why I said it like it was a question. If either of us should have been surprised to see the other, it shouldn't have been me. After all, it wasn't Zach who had said he was moving to another country.

"I can't believe you're here," Zach said as he moved closer to hug me, oblivious of Shane's presence a few feet behind him. "I figured you'd call when you came back to visit."

He was genuinely happy to see me, though I had no idea why.

"Wait, are you still living in Holland, or are you back for good?"

Kyle shook his head and smiled. At this point, nothing I did surprised him. And he knew better than to say anything. But Shane's face was priceless. He tilted his head to the side and raised an eyebrow before mouthing, *Holland?*

"Uh...yeah. I just got back, actually." *Jesus, why am I speaking in a Dutch accent? Is this even a Dutch accent? I sound like Borat.* "I didn't really like it."

"Wow, you weren't even there that long, and you already picked up an accent. Did you have to learn...wait, what do they even speak there?"

"Dutch. Well, Dutch isn't actually a different language. They speak English there. Just with a Dutch accent."

"Ha!" Danielle took another swig of her beer and held

her long brown hair up when one of the highlighted strands started to fall into her cup. "It is too another language," she slurred. "En, when did ya go ta Olland?"

"Don't listen to her," I said. "She doesn't make sense when she drinks. And she drinks all the time." *Fuck, this conversation needs to end.* "Well, it was nice seeing you, Zach."

It wasn't exactly a lie. He was quite gorgeous. It *was* nice *seeing* him. Just so long as I didn't have to talk to him. Or fuck him.

"Yeah, you too," Zach said. "We should go out sometime now that you're back from Holland."

"Yeah . . . well, I don't really think my new Dutch boyfriend would like that," I said, gesturing to Shane.

Shane's eyes widened before he recovered. "Ya, I no share."

"Oh . . . um . . . okay, then. Have a nice flight back."

Shane couldn't open his mouth fast enough once Zach was out of hearing range.

"You are *truly* one of a kind. And that's the second time I saved your ass, Bishop. Remember that when you kiss me after I win this game."

"Just shut up. Are we gonna talk all night, or are we gonna play?"

Since it was our last game, we had the group's attention again. Shane sank one ball on the break and then two more before missing his next one.

"Don't let the pressure get to ya, Amanda. You get to kiss me either way." He held his arms out wide in a way that said, *You know you want this.*

He was clearly enjoying our little competition, but I was going to enjoy it even more. I sank two balls with the ease of a professional. Shane chalked those shots up to luck. But when I had to shoot the next one left-handed and the ball dropped into the side pocket near him, a wave of panic swept across his face.

"Don't let the pressure get to ya, Shane." I was having way too much fun. "You get to kiss me either way."

"Damn," Steph said. "You go, girl."

I put some more chalk on the cue before lining up my next shot.

"Four ball, corner pocket. Then the seven in the side."

"You don't need to call anything that's not the eight," Shane said.

"Yeah, but where's the fun in that? Then I wouldn't get to see the look on your face when I do *this*," I said as the cue ball smacked into the four and spun a few feet backward, placing itself perfectly near the seven. After tapping the seven in, I glanced up to see Shane's bewildered expression. "Yeah, that's the look I was talking about."

"Holy shit!" Kyle said. "I didn't know you could play like that."

"Lily's one of the only ones who knows." I made my way around the table, sinking the last of the solids and lining up for the eight directly in front of Shane. "Excuse me," I said politely.

"By all means," he said, gesturing widely with his arms. "Please, finish me off."

Interesting choice of words.

It would take more than an innuendo to get me flustered. I kept my eyes frozen on Shane.

"I'd be happy to." I knew from the crack of the cue ball hitting the eight that I had made it. I didn't even have to look.

❤

"So, how'd you get so good at pool?" Shane asked as he opened the door to his black Mustang.

"So you admit that I'm good, then? Hold on, let me get my phone. Can you say it again? I need to record it." I couldn't hide my smile.

He walked around to the driver's-side door and slid in beside me. "Don't rub it in. But yeah, you're good. Obviously."

"My grandpop taught me to play as a kid. He had a table in his basement. My mom worked second shift, so my grandparents would watch me when she was at work. He always had his buddies over for games. Those guys were like my second family. The look on a grown man's face when a twelve-year-old girl hustles him is something you should see at least once before you die."

"Worse than mine?"

"Yeah, definitely worse than yours. Although I did enjoy watching you when you realized you were being hustled."

"That's funny," he said as he took his eyes off the road to look over at me, "because I enjoyed watching you when I realized you were hustling me."

Even in the darkness, his blue eyes seemed to glow, causing a warmth to radiate up my legs and deep into my chest.

I broke our gaze and shifted my eyes out the window. "Yeah, it definitely made for some interesting nights at the bars during college. I always had spending money, that's for sure."

"Not to mention the added bonus of it being unbelievably hot."

"Yeah," I laughed. "I guess I never thought of that before."

"So . . . You said your mom worked at night. Where was

your dad? I mean ... if you don't mind me asking."

"No, it's fine." I usually didn't talk about him to anyone other than people who were close to me. But for some reason, I felt like I could open up to Shane. "I never had a *dad*. Biological father is probably more accurate. My mom was young when she got pregnant with me. Both my parents were. My mom's parents offered to help her, but she was always the independent stubborn type." I couldn't believe how easily I could share this information with Shane. And I couldn't believe how easily he listened to it.

"Independent stubborn type, huh? Guess the apple doesn't fall far, does it?" he said with a gentle laugh.

"Yeah."

Though I had never considered how alike my mother and I were until Shane, of all people, pointed it out. I had always seen us as so different from one another. I was close to thirty, with a college degree and a high-paying job. No husband on the horizon and certainly no kids. But as much as I hated to admit that Shane was right about anything, he was. My mom and I never wanted someone to do something for us that we could do for ourselves.

"She got herself into that situation, and she wanted to be the one to make it better," I continued. "She was scared that if she lived with my grandparents, she might never leave. So she got a small apartment and dropped out of college to get a full-time job to support me. My father said he would help her, but he never lived up to his promise. He didn't give her any money. He never saw me. At least not that I remember. My grandfather was more of a dad than my own father ever was."

"Are you and your grandfather still close?"

"He died three years ago, but yeah, we were always close."

"I'm sorry to hear that. My grandfather and I were close too. He's the one who got me interested in sports. Long story short, he's the inspiration for this perfectly built man sitting beside you."

"I guess he never taught you how to be humble," I said sarcastically. I think we were both starting to feel that the mood needed to be lightened.

"Yeah, I must've missed that lesson."

Shane pulled into my apartment complex and shut off the car.

"What are you doing?" I asked.

"Walking you. I don't like the looks of that shady guy standing over there." He motioned to Mr. Harrison, my seventy-seven-year-old neighbor who was out with his beagle.

I smiled and rolled my eyes as I opened the car door. Shane ushered me to the main entrance, placing a hand on the small of my back as we strolled past the "shady" old man.

"Well, thanks for walking me," I said as I took out my keys to open the main door to the building.

"Sure, anytime. I'm a gentleman if nothing else." He turned to go but was clearly hesitating, and I knew why. "Speaking of . . . a gentleman always pays his bets." He faced me again and closed the short distance between us. "About that kiss . . ."

A surge of desire funneled its way through my body.

"Not here," I said, throwing my head in the direction of Mr. Harrison.

"This isn't exactly my idea of public."

"Yeah, well, this isn't exactly my idea of private. And I am the winner. My terms. Come inside?"

I unlocked the door, and we climbed the single flight of

stairs to my apartment in silence. I was conscious of the fact that Shane followed directly behind me, his bright eyes most likely focusing on my ass as I walked up the stairs.

In those four seconds, a million thoughts rushed through my head. *Is Lily home? Probably not. Am I just going to invite Shane in for a kiss and then tell him to leave? God, what am I thinking?*

But as I unlocked my apartment door, none of that mattered. I just wanted Shane's mouth pressed against mine. I craved his strong hands around my neck and lower back as he pulled me into him. My mind filled with images of my hands grabbing at his rough blond hair in the darkness.

I motioned for Shane to go inside and closed the door behind me.

"Lil," I called out. There was no response.

"Guess this is as private as it gets," Shane whispered as he stepped toward me. His blue stare locked on mine, and I felt him touch me before he actually did. I felt the energy that bounced between us, and as he leaned into me, my body pulled him in like a magnet.

My back pressed against the door as Shane cradled my chin gently, his cool breath finding my mouth before his lips did. I closed my eyes and tried to anticipate what this might feel like. I couldn't remember the last time I had been so anxious to kiss someone. I was back in middle school again, waiting to get to first base.

When Shane's lips finally did greet mine, the feeling was even better than I'd imagined. They were softer and warmer than I'd ever felt, and when he parted my own lips with his tongue, I was lost in the delicious sensation, in the taste of beer and mint on his hot mouth. The stubble on his face scratched softly across my sensitive skin, only making the experience that much more stimulating.

I expected him to pull away completely after a few moments, but instead, he backed off only slightly, hovering his mouth over mine, unsure of whether to go further. His fingers brushed my hair from my face, and a warmth radiated between my legs at his touch.

My breathing was already ragged, my pulse pounding in my ear since his first mention of making good on his bet. I slid my hands up his stomach and chest, relishing the feel of his muscular frame. My hands moved to the back of his head, pulling him closer, inviting him to be more aggressive.

He continued his soft, teasing licks on the inside of my mouth, exploring me slowly, and I swept my tongue across his top lip. He responded as I'd hoped, gently nibbling at my bottom lip. *God, is he a good kisser.*

We continued like this until a hesitant kiss between friends turned into something more passionate. With experienced precision, his tongue collided with mine. And when he pressed me up against the door, I could feel his erection on my lower stomach. I sensed him trying to control himself as he struggled not to roll his hips against mine.

But God, I wanted him to. The kiss wasn't enough. For either of us. We needed the friction that the other's body would provide. My hands massaged up and down Shane's back in rough, frantic movements, and he moaned into my mouth in response. He slid my shirt up just enough to tickle my skin with his fingertips. When I didn't shy away, he worked his way up my stomach slowly, deliberately teasing on his journey to my hardened nipples.

With swift dexterity, he shifted my bra just enough to

gain access to my breasts, which were heavy and full at the anticipation of his touch. I could feel the moisture between my thighs increase with every pull at my nipple, and as his tongue danced delicately down the front of my throat, I reached into the back of his jeans to grab his ass above his boxers. I needed him to rub against me, and he obeyed my silent request, his hips grinding in circles.

"Do you want me to stop?" he whispered against my ear.

God, no.

I didn't want to tell him to stop. Instead, I moaned into his neck through damp, sore lips and lifted my leg to wrap around him, finally tending to the dull ache that pulsed between my thighs. I could feel the increasing need for release building inside me with every roll and thrust.

My physical need was competing with my willpower. I knew I shouldn't do this. This wouldn't just be sex between friends. It would be something more. And I didn't want to know what that *something more* was. But with every stroke of his erection against me, it was becoming increasingly difficult to resist this.

He pinned me roughly against the door with his solid body, and I pulled him harder toward me, rubbing against him until I felt like I could come from this alone.

"Tell me to stop now if you want me to," he said.

I didn't know how long we'd been doing this, and my need for him was becoming unbearable. But as much as it excited me, it scared me just a little more.

"Stop," I breathed against him.

chapter eight

I hadn't spoken to Shane since the kiss. I hadn't contacted him, and he hadn't contacted me. I had also decided that avoiding CrossFit was a good idea. Until Wednesday. By Wednesday, I needed to see him. He had become a craving, an addiction that burrowed under my skin and gnawed at me from the inside until I gave in and sought my next fix. *Totally still just a crush.*

I trudged into CrossFit Force, and as my eyes surveyed the room, I stopped dead in my tracks, my jaw nearly hitting the floor.

"You've gotta be shittin' me," I said with a smirk to the intruder in my territory.

"Shut up," Kyle said as he turned his head away from me.

"Oh my God, it's happened. I never thought I'd see the day, but here it is. Kyle Merrick is pussy whipped."

"Shut. Up," he growled as he looked around to see who else may have heard me.

"How'd she do it? I've been putting out for years and never got you here. Goddamn, her coochie must be made of solid gold."

"Or maybe you're just not a very good lay."

"Holy shit, you're smoking crack now too?"

"Very funny. Now lower your voice."

"Why? Since when do you care what people think?" As I bent at the waist and stretched my hamstrings, I turned my head toward Kyle, awaiting my answer.

"Since my girlfriend works here and has no idea about the nature of our"—he motioned to the space between us—"relationship."

"Aww, your girlfriend," I said in a singsong voice, smiling wide. Then, I suddenly turned serious. "Have you told your mother? The shock may kill her. Come to think of it, can I tell her?"

Kyle's mother had never liked me. And the reason was totally ridiculous. You get plastered at one family gathering and steal a piñata, and suddenly you're an outcast. I mean, those kids stopped crying eventually. It was her son's idea, but I don't see her hating *him*.

"No, I haven't told her yet. I've only known Kate for two weeks."

"And you're already lying to her. The mark of any sound union."

"What do you mean? I'm not lying to her." Kyle seemed incensed at my accusation.

Damn, he's in deep.

"Don't get all huffy, princess. You not telling her about our 'relationship,' as you so eloquently called it, is a lie, no?"

"No."

I laughed aloud. "How isn't it?"

"I just haven't told her. I didn't lie about it. There's no point in bringing up ancient history."

"Ancient history!" I screeched before lowering my voice to a whisper. "You fucked me in my office like three weeks ago.

Since when does that fall into the realm of ancient history?"

"Amanda, please drop it. Don't mess this up for me."

My face fell instantly. "Do you really think I would ever do that?"

He couldn't have stung me more if he had tried. I sat down on the ground, probably looking like a pouting five-year-old, but I didn't care. Kyle was one of my best friends. How could he ever think I'd hurt him?

"Hey." He knelt beside me. "I'm sorry. No, I don't think you'd ever mess anything up for me. That was a dick thing to say. I'm just uncomfortable in this boyfriend role. I don't want to fuck it up. I really didn't mean what I said. Forgive me?"

"The golden coochie has changed you," I said dryly, trying to hide my smile. I couldn't stay mad at Kyle. He was... Kyle. And I loved him like a brother. Well, maybe not a brother. That would be weird. And illegal.

He cocked an eyebrow at me, waiting for me to answer his question.

"Yes, I forgive you," I exhaled, as if saying it had taken great energy.

"Good. Now get your ass up and explain this workout to me. I have no clue what any of that means," he said, motioning to the board that detailed our workout. "And thanks for not showing up yesterday. I had to endure my first class alone. I thought you usually came in on Tuesdays?"

"I try to get here four days a week, but there are no set days. I come in when I can." I silently prayed that Kyle didn't push me further. The truth was, I was almost always here on Tuesdays. I was usually too exhausted on Mondays, so I made the effort to be here Tuesdays to get my four days in. "You could've called me. I would've told you my schedule."

"That would've ruined the surprise."

"Some surprise. Shane usually insults me enough. I don't need you here for that."

"Hey, you said you forgave me, liar. Just so I can mentally prepare, how long do you plan on holding my comment over me?"

"Hmm, probably a really long time."

"Nice," Kyle said sarcastically, though a grin spread across his lips. He knew he deserved payback. It probably even made him feel better.

The previous class finished up and started gathering their things as Kyle and I traded gibes.

"Kyle, I recommend you find someone else to shadow. Bishop here doesn't do any of the movements correctly."

I hadn't realized Shane was next to me.

I looked back and forth between the two smiling faces on either side of me. "Two smartasses. Just what I need. I guess it's time to go out and join a real gym. This place is starting to take anyone on as a member."

"Well, yeah," Shane said. "We took you on, didn't we?"

"Maybe if you weren't such a shitty instructor, you'd have more impressive clientele."

"If I'm so shitty, how come you keep coming back?"

And there it was. The proverbial elephant had just crashed into the room. Shane still wore a smile, but his eyes were intense. We both knew what his real question was: since the kiss had gone further than initially intended, could we still be friends?

I had stopped him, so clearly I didn't want our relationship to progress beyond a certain point. But had the kiss ruined what we had?

I didn't want it to. So I reassured him in the best way I knew how. I walked close to him, putting my face inches from his.

"Because torturing you makes it all worth it." I tapped him twice on the cheek with my hand. "Now let's get this shit-show started so I can laugh at Kyle," I declared loudly as I walked away from Shane. As I found a spot on the mat, I glanced back at him. He was smiling as he ran his hand through his hair.

Guess he liked my answer.

Class only continued to get better as Kyle decided to impress everyone by putting a ton of weight on his bar for overhead squats. He immediately tipped over backward as he tried to stand, landing solidly on his ass.

Then he nearly kicked Shane in the crotch while attempting to do a pull-up using a band. As soon as he put his foot in the band, he clearly underestimated the resistance it would give, causing his foot to wrench up.

Priceless.

It wasn't that Kyle wasn't in great shape. He was. But he wasn't in CrossFit shape, and he definitely wasn't familiar with the exercises. When the workout finally ended, I looked over to see him sprawled out on the mats.

Kate looked over and shook her head. She had kept her distance from him since we'd been here, and I wasn't sure if it was because she was trying to keep their relationship on the down-low or if she was trying not to make Kyle feel pathetic in front of his girlfriend. I tended to think it was the latter.

"I…have…just one…question," Kyle forced out

between desperate gasps for air. "What the hell is a WOD?"

I giggled at the question. Shane and Kate were always referencing the WOD.

"Put more effort into your WOD."

"Reach max potential during the WOD."

It sounded kind of gross now that I thought about it.

"It stands for workout of the day."

"Oh...okay." He took another deep breath and sat up. "It just sounded like a weird thing to be yelling out every five minutes."

I laughed out loud at how alike we were. "You gonna get up at some point?"

"Just give me a second for the feeling to return to my legs."

"Oh, there's going to be feeling, all right. It's called pain. Deep, unmerciful pain."

He looked up at me in horror.

"You'll get used to it," I said with a shrug.

"To pain? I kinda doubt it," he grunted as he used his hands to push himself from the ground.

"Aren't your muscles already sore from yesterday?"

"Not really. Shane took it pretty easy on me."

"Well, it'll eventually become a perpetual soreness," I reassured him.

"Awesome."

I laughed at his sardonic tone as Kate walked up to us. I left when Kate mentioned taking an ice bath and Kyle suggested some other uses for the ice.

I walked to the mat where I had left my keys earlier—I had been too shocked by Kyle's presence to put them in a cubby. I looked around, calmly at first but then wildly as I realized they were nowhere to be found.

I ran outside to look for my car. It was still where I had left it, so no one had stolen it. Not that I expected that from a fellow gym member, but you could never tell. Some of these people were shifty. As I paced the mats, I suddenly heard a tinkling in my ear, followed by a voice.

"Lose something?"

I spun around toward Shane and grabbed my keys. "Thank God. I thought I'd lost them. Where did you find them?"

"You left them sitting on the floor. I didn't want someone picking them up."

"Thanks."

"No problem." He held my gaze, causing the memory of our kiss to flood back into my mind. I grew warmer, which I didn't think was possible since it was ninety degrees in this damn building, and my nipples puckered against my sports bra.

Goddamn, he's sexy.

"Okay, well, I'm outta here," I finally spoke, breaking our trance. "See ya tomorrow."

"See ya tomorrow," he said as he began walking away.

And as I watched the distance grow between us, I felt myself nearly overwhelmed with the feeling that I didn't particularly like Shane walking away from me.

❤

Unsettled. That was how I felt. I couldn't figure out exactly why but had a general idea. I had been feeling this way ever since leaving CrossFit last night. Since leaving Shane. But I left CrossFit four times a week. Why was last night different?

There was only one logical explanation: I was bipolar.

And now I was sitting at my desk about to Google symptoms of bipolar disorder rather than admit the truth.

It's more than a crush.

I had just lowered my head into my hands when Danielle barged in.

"Hey, I have— What's wrong? You look like someone just told you there was no Santa Claus."

I looked up at her questioningly. "I look like I'm five?"

"You know what I mean," Danielle huffed as she sat down in a chair across from me. "So, what's up?"

Part of me wanted to confide in her, to get it off my chest and out into the open. But I couldn't. I had a few more layers of denial to build first.

"Nothing. Just a bit of a headache. What are those?" I asked, gesturing to a stack of papers in her hands.

"Ugh, a new account Mr. Bader wants us to start running numbers on."

"Hey," I scolded, "that's Master Bader to you. Show some respect."

Danielle giggled as she put the papers down on my desk. Jesus Christ, there was a mountain of them. And as I quickly scanned them, I could tell there was no semblance of order to the mass before me.

"Steph has been tasked with organizing them for us. She told me to bring them in here so we could hide from Bader."

I eyed her harshly.

"Sorry, sorry. So we could hide from *Master* Bader," she corrected. "Do you know that he told me a story about how he slept in the same bed as his parents until he was fifteen? That's probably why he's so fucked up."

Steph walked in as I howled with laughter at Danielle's anecdote.

"What'd I miss?" she asked.

Danielle caught her up to speed as we sat around my desk and began sorting through the papers.

"This looks like a small account. Why are we handling this?" I asked. I wasn't trying to be conceited, but typically accounts like this went to accountants in their first couple of years with the company. I had bigger fish to fry.

"I don't know. Master Bader just told me to see that it got done," Danielle explained.

"Well, this doesn't make sense. Let me call the weasel and see what the deal is." I typed in the extension of Bader's assistant. Even though intra-office calls were easily identified because the extension the call was placed from popped up on the ID, Bader still insisted that his assistant field all his calls.

"Hi, Amanda, what can I do for you?" Sheila asked after she picked up the phone.

"Hey, Sheila. Is the Master in?" Sheila hated Bader more than anyone else, and I couldn't blame her. The rest of us could escape him, but it was her entire job to be at his beck and call. Poor girl.

"Oh, yeah, he's here," she replied dryly. "I'll patch ya through."

"Thanks, Sheila."

She transferred the call, and it rang five times before he finally answered it, out of breath. *What the hell had he been doing?* Scratch that. I didn't want to know.

"Yes."

"Mr. Bader, it's Amanda . . ."

"You're kidding," he said sarcastically.

What a prick. "Yeah, okay, well, I'm looking at this account you sent over, and I was just wondering, shouldn't one of our junior associates be handling this?"

"Why, Mandi? Are you too good for the blue-collar accounts? Or maybe you're too good to do any work at all." The condescension dripped from his voice.

Isn't that one guy I went out with a couple of times a hitman? I wonder if I still have his number.

"No, Mr. Bader, I was just wondering because I have a number of other accounts I'm working on, and I didn't want to take my focus away from them if this could be handled by someone else." I tried to withhold the hatred from my voice, but I was sure I failed miserably.

"Listen, Mandi, the perk of being a boss is that I don't have to explain myself to you. Now, if you're feeling overwhelmed, then maybe we should sit down and discuss whether this is really the right job for you."

Oh, no, this motherfucker didn't.

"No, I can manage fine. I just thought a mistake had been made."

"Well, maybe in the future you should keep your thoughts to yourself. Good day, Mandi."

I hung up the phone, stood, and began walking toward the door.

"Where are you going?" Steph asked.

"Down to the parking garage. I'm going to cut that asshole's brake line."

Steph and Danielle eyed me cautiously, the look on my face clearly showing that I meant it.

"After I get coffee," I added. "You guys want some?"

They both let out a relieved laugh and nodded.

Christ, do they really think I'm a murderer?

I returned a few minutes later to Danielle and Steph talking animatedly.

"What are you fools squealing about?"

"Girls' night," they said in unison.

"The band I love, Tomfoolery, is playing at the Whiskey Saloon on Friday," Steph said. "You in?"

"Absolutely. Who can turn down a little Tomfoolery?"

"Yeah, and the bar isn't bordering any bodies of water, so we thought it would be a safe place to take you," Danielle joked.

"Ha-ha," I replied. "Please, without me, your lives would be utterly boring."

"Very true," they agreed.

And as we got to work, I was grateful for these girls. They took my mind off my bipolar/Shane issues. At least for a little while.

❤

CrossFit was uneventful on Thursday. I texted Kyle on my way there to see if he was going to class. He replied that a full-body cast would be in order if he didn't take a day off. How dramatic.

Friday wound down quickly, and the girls and I finally organized the paperwork for the account Bader had foisted on us. No wonder he had assigned it to all three of us; whoever ran the business had awful bookkeeping skills. I breathed a deep sigh of relief when it was time to go home.

"We're meeting at your place, right? At eight?" Danielle called after me as I walked toward the elevators.

"Yup," I replied. "I can't wait."

"Me neither. Is Lily coming?"

"No, she said she already had plans. She's been very mysterious lately."

"Hmm, interesting. Should we toss her room after she leaves?"

"I'll keep it in mind," I laughed. Finally, the elevator doors opened and transported me toward freedom.

❤

The girls had arrived promptly at eight, and we had set off soon after. Steph had practically pushed us out the door, insisting that we get there early and procure a good table.

The place was still fairly empty when we arrived, since the band wasn't going on until ten. We settled at a table in a corner and up a couple of steps from the dance floor. Steph said this would give us a good vantage point while preventing us from getting bumped into all night. I didn't bother telling her that I was actually looking forward to a little bumping tonight.

Though I'd never admit it, Steph had been right. The place filled up quickly. At ten, the lights dimmed slightly as the band made their way to the stage. They had a skater vibe but were all nice to look at. And as they started playing, I decided they were nice to listen to as well. The lead singer had a smooth, melodic quality to his voice that contrasted nicely with the alternative rock sound the rest of the band had. I wouldn't be downloading their CDs anytime soon, but I saw the appeal.

"Let's dance," Steph yelled over the music.

"I'm in," Danielle agreed as she rose from her stool.

"I'm going to wait here and order us more drinks. I need to be drunker to deal with all of that." I pointed to the throbbing mass of bodies gyrating recklessly on the dance floor.

"All right. We'll let you off the hook this time because you're getting us more booze. But next time, you're coming with," Danielle threatened.

I nodded in agreement, and they took off, disappearing

into the abyss. I motioned for our waitress to come over and ordered another round, plus some shots of Jäger. I was definitely going to need more alcohol if I was going to venture out from my corner.

I downed my shot quickly when the waitress returned, then began sipping my vodka tonic. Suddenly, Danielle came running up to the table, breathless. I grabbed my purse and began to stand, thinking that someone had stolen Steph and we needed to go track her down, when Danielle finally spoke up.

"You're never going to believe who we found."

I looked behind her and finally laid eyes on Steph, who was pulling someone by the hand behind her. I leaned forward to get a better look.

Oh. My. God.

"Amanda, I believe you remember everybody's favorite intern," Steph said as she reached the table.

"I certainly do. How's it goin', Rod?" I took him in, not even bothering to hide the fact that my eyes were surveying him from top to bottom.

He pulled his hand through his hair. "Hey, Amanda. Small world, huh? I never thought I'd get the pleasure of seeing you girls again." He said the last line with drunk seduction. I was enamored.

"Oh, I think the pleasure's all ours. Thanks for the picture, by the way. I set it up next to my bed so I can stare at it as I fall asleep at night." I was coming on strong, but I didn't care. I was so pent up with sexual frustration that I needed an outlet. And Rod was definitely a viable one.

He smiled and moved closer to me. "You wanna dance?" he asked into my ear, his breath tickling me, making me wish that it had been his tongue.

"Absolutely," I responded as I turned toward him, staring into his large brown eyes.

He grabbed my hand and led me down the stairs and into the middle of the dance floor. I was surrounded by hot, sweaty bodies colliding together in time with the music. What had originally been something I wanted to avoid had now become an incredible turn-on.

I stood in front of Rod, my back to his muscled chest. I began to move, finding my rhythm with the sweet voice that floated through the bar. Rod moved closer to me but didn't put his hands on me. He just moved with me, rocking his pelvis into my ass as the music infiltrated every fiber of me.

His proximity was intoxicating, and I felt the cool moisture of my arousal seep from my body. We were close, but I craved him to be closer. I reached behind myself and placed my hands on his thighs, gathering a bit of his jeans and pulling him into me.

Finally, his hands found my hips and clamped down, as if anchoring me to him. I dipped slightly, arching my back and lifting my ass so that it rose between his legs. And as I made contact with his erection, my nipples hardened, and the dull ache in my lower abdomen grew stronger.

Oh, I need this.

Rod's hands drifted down my body. He pressed his palms into me, lowered them to my stomach, and then slid them down to my thighs as he hitched me beneath him. His upper body hovered over me, causing me to lean forward, giving him greater access to my ass.

As he ground against me, I tilted my neck. He took full advantage, running his tongue up and down the soft skin, sending tingles throughout my entire body. I reached over my head and behind me, finding his hair. I fisted my hands in the unruly strands, pulling his head even farther into my neck.

He ran his tongue along my jaw, up to my ear, and back down my neck, where he kissed and sucked at my flesh. I suddenly wished I had worn a skirt instead of my tight jeans and silk blouse. If I had, I was fairly certain I would have hitched it up right there and allowed him to take me amongst all of those other bodies. Public sex had never been so appealing.

And that was the thought that cooled me off a little. We were in public, in direct violation of Rule Number Three. I had always made exceptions to this rule in the past for dirty dancing. It was the one time that warranted sexual touching in public.

But what Rod and I were doing was getting dangerously close to copulation. As my mind reeled, Rod turned me to face him. And that's what killed it completely. I was instantly consumed with the thought that this wasn't the face I wanted to be seeing right then. It wasn't the face I wanted to be doing this with.

So, as the song ended, I leaned into Rod.

"Thanks for the dance." And I walked back to our table.

chapter nine

Shane had invited Kyle and me to his end-of-summer barbeque two weeks ago, but I'd forgotten all about it until he mentioned it again on Thursday and said that people could arrive Saturday any time after four o'clock. I must have been so busy staring at him while he talked lately that I hadn't been listening to what had been coming out of his beautiful mouth.

The weather was exceptionally hot for a September day, so I'd spent extra time trying to get my hair prepared for the humidity. I took one last look at myself in the mirror. My new teal-patterned sundress fit perfectly, showing off my now noticeably toned arms and legs. Maybe Shane would realize that I actually *did* give a shit about the workouts.

I didn't want to look like I had dressed up since it was just a barbeque, so I threw on some flip-flops for a casual look. It was only three forty-five, and I was ready to leave. This was one for *Guinness World Records,* for sure. I had been making a conscious effort to be on time lately. Even Bader had noticed.

"Mandi," he had said when I strolled in forty-five minutes before I had actually needed to be at work last week. "That's the kind of commitment I like to see."

I had stopped in my tracks on the way to my office because

I knew a story was coming.

"It reminds me of when I was a boy and I'd wake up with the cocks each morning."

"I'm sorry, Mr. Bader. I don't think I understand."

"My family had a farm in the English countryside. Petersfield. It was a lovely place. Some of my fondest memories are getting up with the rooster's crow to milk the goats."

Oh, that kind of cock. Thank the Lord.

"My favorite goat was one I called Betty. Sometimes I would drink the milk right from her. Just put my head underneath her and start sucking. Of course, at the time, I didn't appreciate it. What young boy wants to get up at five thirty in the morning to work on a farm? But now, as an old man, I naturally rise early. And I often wake with thoughts of Betty's teat in my hand again."

Ummm. "Betty sounds awesome, Mr. Bader."

I snapped out of my Bader memory and silently congratulated myself for being ready early. Again. And for once, I was smart enough to drive *myself* somewhere. I knew Kyle and Kate would be driving together. And who knew when they would be leaving to go try out Kate's new nipple clamps or whatever kinky shit Kyle had been introducing her to. I definitely didn't want to get stuck at Shane's and have to ask him for a ride home once everyone left.

Shane only lived twenty minutes away, but I wasn't exactly sure how to get to his house, so I wanted to make sure I gave myself adequate time to get there. The drive was actually pretty simple. No confusing roads or exits and next to no traffic.

As I pulled onto his street, I found myself surprised at the neighborhood. Mature trees lined the street, and children played in front of single-family homes of various sizes and styles. It was a family neighborhood. And it was really *nice*. I mean, it wasn't like I expected Shane to live in a slum where I had to be careful to not step on any used hypodermic needles on the way up the stairs to his apartment. Although I might have been less surprised by that.

God, I hope he doesn't still live with his parents.

I spotted Shane's house easily when I saw his black Mustang in the driveway. God, that car was badass. I'd never seen it in the light before. His home was simple but beautiful. A modest two-story with bright-white siding that was accented by deep-green shutters. And it had a cute front porch. I parked on the street and wandered up the brick path to his front door.

Shane answered almost right away. He wore loose khaki cargo shorts that had a worn look to them and a vintage red Phillies T-shirt. Like all his shirts, it was a little on the smaller side, allowing his biceps and chest to carve an outline in the fabric.

"You're here early," he said, surprised. He looked as if he'd put a little wax in his hair to make the perfectly haphazard strands stay in place, and his fingers pulled at the ends slightly as he ran his hand through it.

God, if I had a dollar for every time I thought of pulling Shane's hair myself lately…I'd have like…at least a few hundred dollars.

"I am?" I looked at my watch. Four ten. "I thought you said anytime after four?"

"Uh, I did. No one's here yet, but I'm sure they will be soon." Seeing Shane outside of CrossFit, cleaned up and smelling like men's body wash, brought back memories of our kiss after the pool hall. I briefly wondered why I'd agreed to come here.

Could I see Shane like this and not want to pick up where we left off? Would we be able to hang out as friends, or would things always be weird between us?

I handed him the bottle of Moscato and the strawberry shortcake I'd brought. "I'm always good for alcohol and dessert," I said.

"Thanks," he replied with a smartass smile as he took the cake and wine from me. "At least we know you're good for *something.*"

Yup, looks like we're still on familiar ground.

"Come on in," he said. "I'm just getting some food ready."

I surveyed his home as I stepped inside. "This is really nice." The downstairs was an open concept, allowing a view of the kitchen, family room, and dining area. Light hardwood floors spanned the entire area, and the view of the backyard through the sliding doors in the kitchen could be seen from the front door.

Shane just shook his head and laughed. "Did you think you'd have to step over a few hookers on your way to my front steps or something? What were you expecting?"

I forced a laugh as I remembered my thoughts of hypodermic needles.

"Not this, I guess."

The decor was simple and modern. Pale-yellow walls highlighted the sunlight that poured in through the large bay window in the front of the house. The furniture screamed good taste: all clean lines, dark woods, and bright, solid colors.

Though his house was definitely classy and well decorated, it wasn't extravagant or lavish by any means. Except for his kitchen. There had been some serious money spent in there. Bright-white cabinets surrounded stainless-steel appliances, and deep-gray granite wrapped around three walls and curved into a peninsula bar with three stools. "You have good taste," I said, clearly surprised as I studied the first floor of his home.

"Thanks. I just copied some ideas from some home magazines." He laughed modestly. "I did most of the work myself. This place was kind of a mess when I bought it. It was mostly cosmetic stuff, though. And buyers can't look past that, so I got a good deal on it. It's definitely taken some time to get it how I want it. I just finished the kitchen in the spring. It took a while because I had to gut the whole thing and start from scratch. But it definitely kept the cost down because I really only had to pay for the materials."

"Well, it looks amazing. Do you cook a lot?" I motioned to the double oven and gas range beside it.

"I try. I'm always telling my clients what to eat and how to cook, so I have to practice what I preach, I guess."

"What? You've never told *me* what to eat."

"No, not my CrossFit clients. I'm a nutritionist. Gotta have a day job too. I can't support myself bulking people up for a few hours a day." He took out a fruit platter from the refrigerator and put some chips and pretzels on another tray with some onion dip. "Help yourself."

"A nutritionist? Really? That's pretty cool, actually. That doesn't look that healthy, though," I said, pointing to the dip. I was secretly wondering if he was testing me with the fruit and the chips to see which one I'd go for.

Shane seemed to sense my hesitation. "Relax, Bishop. You can eat whatever you want. I try not to cook too healthy when I have company. I found that people are more willing to come back if I don't force-feed them wheatgrass and oats."

"Probably a good call," I said as I popped a few chips into my mouth. I couldn't help but think about this side of Shane that I had never seen before. Cook? Interior decorator? Though not traditional male skills, they were no less impressive. In fact, that made him more impressive. Shane was definitely not lacking in the manliness department, so having some domestic hobbies actually made him more attractive.

I couldn't decorate, and I definitely couldn't cook. If I wanted these things done correctly, I'd have to pay someone to do them. But Shane probably didn't have that luxury of hiring people to do those things. He had mentioned getting a good deal on the house and doing the work himself. I knew he probably needed both jobs to pay the bills.

❤

I helped Shane make some taco dip and prepare the fish and chicken for the grill. He showed me how to make the marinades for each, and I managed to follow his instructions easily. He didn't get as frustrated at me in the kitchen as he did in the gym.

Maybe I should start doing my workouts here.

"This is a lot of food," I said. "How many people are coming?"

"Maybe twelve max, but I like to make sure there's something for everyone. I have burgers and hotdogs too."

I whipped my head around. "Speaking of everyone, where's your dog? We aren't about to eat her, are we?"

Shane let out a laugh. "She's up in my room," he said. "She gets a little overwhelmed with a lot of people."

I heard the door open a few minutes later and the sound of some high-pitched squeals. "Uncle Shane!" screeched a cute little girl with dark curly hair and an olive complexion. Shane held his arms out just in time to catch her as she jumped on him. She looked to be about five or six.

"What's up, munchkin? I just saw you a few days ago. You missed me already?" He kissed her on the forehead.

"Yeah. Didn't you miss *me*?" she asked with a smile.

"Of course. You're missable though. Me, not so much."

If he only knew how wrong he was.

"Hey, look what I got you the other day." He pulled out a big, brightly colored swirly lollipop and handed it to her. "Do you know what it says?"

She studied the writing. "Yeah, it's my name. Mackenzie. Thanks, Uncle Shane. Can I go outside and play?"

"Sure, but wait for your mom or dad. You don't have your swim vest on, and the pool's open. You can go on the deck, though." Shane opened the sliding door for her, and she stepped out onto the deck that looked into the yard. Her soft curly hair blew in the breeze as she pressed her face against the rails to look out onto the green yard. It wasn't too big. Just large enough for the in-ground pool and some grass that surrounded it.

"She's adorable," I said. "And you're so good with her."

"Thanks. She's easy, though. She takes after my sister-in-law. Wait 'til you meet her brother, Henry."

"And you have a pool? I'm so jealous."

"What's up, playboy," called a high voice that sounded like it came from a boy who couldn't have been over the age of eleven. I turned to see a skinny, dark-haired pre-teen in a black T-shirt that read, "I'm not actually funny. I'm just mean, and people think I'm joking." I briefly wondered if they made one of those in Shane's size.

"Hey, you must be Henry," I said, smiling as I held out my hand to greet him.

He looked up from the handheld game he'd been playing for a moment. "And you must be Shane's new piece." His eyes darted approvingly to Shane. "Way to go, playa'. Slayin' some more hoodrats, I see."

Shane just shook his head and crossed his arms in disgust.

Henry held out his fist for a bump, but it was left lonely in the air. "Ah, I see how it is."

"You don't even know what any of that means, Henry. And tell your dad to stop letting you watch *The 40-Year-Old Virgin*. Why don't you go out on the deck and play with Kenzie?"

Henry slid open the door, plopped himself on one of the outdoor chairs, and continued with his game.

"That was . . . interesting," I said.

"Yeah, sorry about that. I don't know where he gets it."

Just then a deep voice boomed in from the front of the house. "Hey, fuckface. I brought *good* beer since you never have the kind I like."

"Oh, wait," Shane corrected himself with an embarrassed laugh. "I *do* know where he gets it. Amanda, this is my brother, Ben."

Ben looked similar to Shane, with the same messy blond hair, but he was a little bigger with less muscle. His face was also rounder and not as defined as Shane's. Ben had definitely been swimming in the shallow end of the Reed gene pool. "Oh, sorry," Ben said, putting the beer in the cooler and wiping his hands on his shorts. "I didn't know Shane had a lady friend coming over."

"Yeesss, you did... and she's not... Never mind." Shane rubbed his eyes with his left hand and shook his head. He seemed to realize that correcting Ben would be useless.

He took my hand in his warm palm and looked me up and down. "Nicely done, little brother. I approve."

"Oh good. I'm glad I have your approval."

"Well, I better get out there," Ben said, gesturing to Henry, who was standing on the deck railing with an empty flowerpot on his head. "Those little spawns of Satan are gonna tear the place apart."

"Sorry," Shane said when Ben left. "He's... well, I really don't know what he is. I didn't tell him you were my girlfriend or anything. I just told him some women he hadn't met were coming because I didn't want him to be a complete ass. Clearly he forgot most of the details of that conversation."

"It's fine, really."

"I guess you met Ben?" A sweet, calming voice wafted through the air. I turned to see a beautiful woman who looked to be in her late twenties or early thirties. She had long, silky black hair, warm dark eyes, high cheekbones, and full pink lips. Her smooth skin was the color of creamy cappuccino. "I'm Talia," she said with an accent I couldn't place. She extended a soft hand to me. "Don't mind my husband." Then she turned to Shane. "Pasta salad," she said, holding up a bowl and putting it on the counter. She put her arms around Shane and kissed him on the cheek. "I better get outside and keep an eye on Ben and Henry. Come get me if I can help at all, Shane."

"Was that the brother whose birthday was the other day?"

"Yup. That's him."

"Huh."

"Why do you say that?"

"I just figured it would be a brother who was a lot younger than you for some reason. He doesn't strike me as the type to have a family party. He seems a little, uh . . . old for that."

"We're four years apart. He just turned thirty-four. The kids like seeing me, especially Kenzie. And I know Talia has her hands full with the three of them," he laughed.

"She seems really sweet. Not to mention beautiful. I wish I had an exotic look like that. What ethnicity is she?"

"French and Portuguese mostly, I think. *Her* accent is actually real," he laughed. "Though you definitely gave her some competition last week at the pool hall."

I was eager to avoid talking about that night altogether. "How did Ben get *her*?"

Shane laughed out loud.

"Sorry, that came out wrong."

"It's fine. They aren't the typical couple, I know. It's amazing what having money does for you, though. I'm not saying that's why Talia's with him, but it definitely made it easier for Ben to get her, I'm sure." Anticipating my next question, Shane explained that Ben was a marketing executive at a major firm in Philadelphia. "He *is* really a good guy. He's just a little . . . brash at times."

❤

An hour later, a few of Shane's friends had arrived. I recognized one of the other guys as another CrossFit trainer named Jesse, but I didn't actually know him because he worked mainly in the morning. He'd come with his fiancée, Jen. They both seemed friendly, but I still felt slightly out of place until Kyle and Kate arrived.

"There's my girl," Kyle said with a smile as he threw his arm around me. Instantly, his eyes swung over to Kate as the realization of his slip-up struck him.

Kate stiffened slightly but relaxed when Kyle moved toward her, wrapping her in his strong arms and placing a sincere kiss on her temple.

Shane manned the grill with Ben by his side, as the rest of us fell into easy conversation on his back deck. When the food was ready, I found myself next to Kyle again as he handed me a piece of chicken from the large platter on Shane's countertop.

"Smooth move earlier, Ace," I whispered.

"Shut up," he said, piling his plate with two burgers, a hot dog, and baked beans. "Old habits die hard." He shook his head with a laugh and handed me a beer from the cooler before heading out to the deck to return to Kate.

Of course, Shane ate a piece of grilled fish and a salad with no dressing. Again. Though he didn't comment on my third helping of pasta salad, I felt the need to justify it by saying that carbs were important for training.

Shane let out a soft laugh.

"Oh, and so is strawberry shortcake," I added quickly in anticipation of dessert.

After everyone had eaten, Kate and I challenged Kyle and Shane to a game of ladder ball.

"I seriously don't think I've played this since college, when Lily and I went to her parents' lake house one year," I said. "I love this game."

"Me too," Shane said as we positioned ourselves at one end of the yard across from Kate and Kyle. "You're not gonna hustle me again, though, are you?"

"No, don't worry. I think you're safe. I totally suck at this game."

Over the next half hour, I managed to lose two games for us, and once I got one of the bolas wrapped around a tree about twenty feet in the air, I had officially forfeited the game. "It's starting to get dark anyway," I said.

"Yeah, that's why we're done playing," Shane said sarcastically as he tipped his head back to study the rope that had wrapped around the branch above his head.

By eight thirty, most of the people had gone. Ben's family left when Kenzie started getting tired, and Shane's friend Dave and his wife, Jill, had to leave to stop by an engagement party about a half hour away. At about nine o'clock, I saw Kyle whisper something in Kate's ear. She stood up immediately to announce their abrupt departure. I could only imagine what Kyle had said.

Knowing that Kyle and Kate were probably going to have great sex only made my sexual frustration that much worse. After the kiss with Shane and my night with Hot Rod, I was on edge. I would definitely have to find a way to relieve some of this sexual tension I was feeling soon. I briefly contemplated calling Zach but thought better of it.

Christ, I really must be horny if I'm considering Zach as a viable option.

Before I knew it, it was just Shane and me again. I didn't want to leave him with a mess, so I stuck around for a bit to help him clean up.

"So, is that all of your family who lives around here?" I asked. "I'm surprised your parents didn't come. I mean, I was actually looking forward to meeting the person who can give birth to two demons and live to tell about it."

Shane let out a small laugh as he wrapped up some of the leftover food. "I invited my mom. But she saw us both earlier in the week. She said to have a good time with people our own age. I'll see her tomorrow night when I go over there for dinner."

"Oh, what's tomorrow?"

"Sunday."

"I know, smartass. I meant why are you going over there? What's special about tomorrow?"

"Nothing. I cook dinner for her *every* Sunday."

I had the sudden urge to question him further. *Don't you think it's weird that you're thirty and you go on a date with your mom once a week? Are you her nutritionist?* The question I wanted to ask was, *Where's your dad?* But since he hadn't mentioned him, I decided against it.

"So . . . this was a great idea," I said as I put a bowl into Shane's dishwasher.

"Yeah, I always have this cookout. It's a tradition. I call it 'Sayonara Summer.' I like to do all the things you can't do when it gets colder: grilling, horseshoes, ladder ball, swimming."

"It's a great idea. I loved it. I wish I'd known you had a pool, though. I would've brought my bathing suit."

"You can still go in if you want. A bathing suit's basically like a bra and underwear anyway," he said with a shrug. "I'll finish cleaning up in here. There are a few clean towels out on the deck still. I'll put the pool lights on for you."

"Really?" I said before realizing that I had worn a lace thong and strapless bra. *Not* exactly *like my bathing suits.*

"Yeah. I'll come out in a few minutes. Enjoy yourself."

This could definitely be a horrible idea. In a pool. In my bra and underwear. With Shane Reed. *On second thought, it might be pretty freakin' fun.* At the very least, I would get to swim—which I loved—and I'd get to see Shane with his shirt off again.

The second realization was enough to convince me. "Okay. I'll see you out there in a bit, then."

I grabbed a towel on my way out the door and looked around to see how private the pool was. Though one home was in close proximity to Shane's, there was a privacy fence around the pool, and once I was in, no one would be able to see me. *Well, except for Shane, who would be out any minute.*

I quickly stripped off my dress and jumped in. The cool water was a shock to my system initially, but I adjusted quickly. The air was still humid, so it was refreshing. I dunked myself under for as long as I could stand, enjoying the cool water sweeping across my flesh. When I came up for air and wiped the water from my eyes, Shane was standing at the edge of the pool about five feet from me. He wore only his cargo shorts, his bare chest reflecting the soft lights that surrounded the pool. His eyes locked on mine, and despite my desperate need for air, I found it difficult to breathe.

Standing above me, Shane appeared even more powerful. He tossed his towel to the lounge chair and slid down his shorts, revealing his muscular thighs. My breath hitched as my eyes worked their way up to his short, tight, dark-red boxer briefs. I had no idea how Shane managed to remain unaroused. Just the sight of him made my insides clench with heated desire.

Without warning, Shane dove in within inches of me. When he emerged, I retaliated by splashing him back.

"What?" he said like he didn't do it intentionally. "You're already wet."

Oh, if he only knew how right he was. "Yeah, but no one

likes to get splashed," I said as I pulled my arm back, getting ready to skim it across the surface of the water toward him.

"Oh, no you don't," he laughed as he wrapped his arms around me, pinning my own to my sides for a moment before letting them go and sliding his hands down to my waist. Those lips that I remembered so well from a few weeks ago were only inches from my own. They seemed to beg me to kiss them. Or was it me who was begging?

Shane's breath faltered. And when I felt the tip of his erection against my pelvis, I took pleasure in knowing that he wasn't impervious to the effect I had on him. He stood, his feet firmly planted on the bottom of the pool, while I floated weightlessly in his arms, not able to touch the ground. I had to fight with my legs—which seemed to have a mind of their own—as I struggled to keep them from wrapping around Shane's waist and completely jumping him right there. I felt helpless and protected at the same time.

His blue stare seemed to show the same tentative restraint, waiting for me to make the first move. I had been the one to stop us last time. My body absolutely wanted this, but my mind warned me of why I had said no the last time.

Fuck it. My mind won last *time.*

My hands found the back of Shane's neck as my lips pressed against his cool soft mouth. In an instant we had picked up where we left off in my apartment. Our hands exploring the other's body with the rushed speed that we had lacked the last time. We both knew we needed this. Whatever *this* was. Shane unclasped my strapless bra and tossed it onto the pavement. His large hands clasped my thighs roughly, urging my legs around his waist.

God, I want this.

Swiftly, he spun us, pressing my back against the concrete edge of the pool as his hips maintained a deliberately slow, teasing grind against my sensitive clit.

"Are you sure?" Shane asked, pulling back slightly to regain his composure.

I shut my eyes and inhaled softly. "God yes" was my only response.

"Let me get a condom."

I watched as Shane climbed the steps gracefully. His masculine physique rose from the water slowly. His erection strained against his soaked boxers. My eyes didn't leave him as he reached into the pocket of his shorts and pulled a condom from his wallet. He bent slightly to strip completely, allowing me an uncensored view of his long, thick cock. He took it in his hand as he rolled the condom on. God, I wanted to be that condom, sheathing him tightly, feeling his hardness inside me.

I was lost in the sight of him as he returned to me, seductively making his way into the pool until he positioned himself against me again. I was conscious of how much I had missed him for the few moments he was gone.

Then he took himself in one hand, teasing soft circles with his tip while his other hand removed my thong. That last bit of fabric was all that stood between us, and once it had been removed, our urgent need could not be alleviated until we had our fill of one another.

Shane positioned his arm next to my head as he gripped the side of the pool for resistance before my opening found him and pulled him inside. With one sudden movement, he thrust all of himself inside me. I couldn't get enough of him, despite how large he was. My nails dug into his ass, pleading with him to go faster, harder.

This was what I needed: my back rubbing against the rough concrete, Shane's hand tugging at my taut nipples, his warm tongue caressing my cold flesh as he pushed me closer to release with every deep drive of his hips.

His low groan reverberated through my ear as he tugged my lobe with his teeth. I clenched around him, and he thrust even harder in response, sensing my need. I wasn't going to last much longer if he kept up this pace.

"Oh...God, Shane," I breathed. "I'm gonna..."

"I know...God...I know." His raspy voice interrupted my own as he worked inside me with precise movements.

I couldn't even finish my thought before the lower half of my body consumed all of my energy. Waves of pleasure coursed through me as I convulsed around him, shaking as my orgasm journeyed up my body until it found my head, making even my brain fuzz with pleasure.

He pounded harder into me as I tightened around him, and within seconds I felt him jerk deep within me. Moaning into my mouth, he kissed me roughly, letting his own release taper off as he continued to slide inside me.

The last few sensations of my own climax escaped when his finally died down. He remained, unmoving inside me, for a few moments. "Will it make it weird if I just pull away?" he asked with an awkward smile.

I couldn't help but let out a gentle laugh. "It's probably weirder that you asked about it, actually."

"Right," he said, withdrawing from me slowly and exiting the pool. He held up a towel and wrapped it around me as I emerged from the pool. "I'll be back in a minute," he said, grabbing his own towel and turning to go inside.

I dried off quickly and put my clothes back on before

Shane returned. When he came back out, he was wearing only mesh shorts. I remembered how I had imagined what it would be like to lick along the outline of his black tattoos. I sighed.

Missed opportunities. Maybe next time.

Wait, what was I saying? There wouldn't be a *next time.* This was a "need fuck." Nothing more. Surely I wouldn't *need* to fuck him again. *Would I?*

He took a seat next to me on the chaise lounge. "Do you want chicken or beef?" he asked casually.

What the hell is he talking about?

My expression must have conveyed my confusion. "Jesse and Jen's wedding is in two weeks. Kate and I were gonna go together, but she's bringing Kyle now, so I asked Jesse if I could bring a guest. I figured it would be fun for the four of us to go together."

I rolled my eyes, and a slow smile crept across my lips. "Chicken," I sighed.

chapter ten

The next two weeks were a monotonous routine of work and CrossFit workouts. Shane and I hadn't spoken about what had happened at his house, and that was just fine with me. But now, as I pulled on my dress, I found myself wondering what Shane would think of it. It was coral, the perfect color for fall, and the cap sleeves showcased my toned arms.

I ran my hands over the lace and twirled in front of the mirror, admiring how the flare caused the dress to flow from my body. My eyes traveled down my shapely calves, which were in plain sight since the dress stopped at the knee. I paired the dress with a silver stiletto that had a strap at the ankle. I would want to fuck me in this dress. But would Shane? And did I want him to? Our last sexual encounter had developed entirely from need, but was that need gone? I just wasn't sure.

I grabbed my clutch and made my way into the living room, where Lily was sitting watching *Millionaire Matchmaker* reruns.

"I'm going to go on this show," she declared without turning toward me.

"Catching millionaires has never seemed to be much of a problem for you," I said lightly.

She turned toward me with a grimace, which quickly

morphed into a wide-eyed gasp once she took in the sight of me. "Holy shit! You look hot."

"Yeah?" I looked down self-consciously, biting my lip. "Can you finish zipping me up?"

"Are you nervous?" Lily looked at me curiously as she walked over, like she couldn't quite believe what she was seeing.

"No. Why would I be nervous?" I was too defensive. I inwardly hoped she hadn't picked up on it as she finished zipping my dress and I took a few steps away from her.

"You are! Jesus, I better get a picture to document the day." As she walked back toward the couch and riffled among the junk that was piled on the coffee table, searching for her phone, I silently put a curse on her and her future offspring.

"I'm not nervous." *Deny, deny, deny.* "It's just that . . . going to this wedding seemed like an okay idea when he asked, but now I dunno. It seems . . . very . . . date*ish*." I scrambled for the right words, trying to properly convey what I was thinking without admitting too much.

I hadn't told anyone that I had slept with Shane, and while I was desperate to relieve some of the weight keeping this secret had placed on me, there was no way I was prepared to talk about it.

"Well, you *are* his date," Lily explained as if I was a moron. "So, it's really not weird that it would feel that way."

"But I'm not dating him. This isn't a date." I was adamant, trying to convince myself more than Lily.

"Christ, is this about your rules?" She took my silence as a yes. "Listen, you guys are going as friends. He wouldn't even have asked you if Kate hadn't wanted to take Kyle. So, what are you worried about? You're his date to the wedding, but you're not there *on* a date. They're totally different." Lily sat back like everything that had just come out of her mouth made perfect sense.

And I could accept her words. I just couldn't accept that they made me feel worse. She was right. Shane wouldn't have asked me if Kate hadn't bailed on him.

What is wrong with me? This revelation should make me feel better, not worse.

Lily eyed me expectantly, so I forced a smile on my face and tried to dig the sadness out of my voice. "You're totally right. I'm freaking over nothing."

I felt my face start to flush at my lie, so I quickly turned around to locate my purse so I could transfer the things I would need tonight into my clutch. Lily, thankfully, kept quiet. Once I was done, I dropped my clutch onto the dining room table and pulled my hand to my hip.

The clutch hit the table with more force than I had intended, and I could feel Lily's eyes on me, but I didn't turn around. I stood there for a few moments, just trying to get myself together. When the buzzer sounded, I nearly jumped out of my skin. I spun around, but Lily was already off the couch and speaking into the intercom.

"Who goes there?"

She is such a dork.

"Hi, uh, it's Shane?" He phrased his response like a question, clearly uncomfortable with speaking into the intercom.

"I don't know anyone by that name," Lily said flatly.

I smiled, appreciating the show she was putting on.

"Is this Lily?" Shane asked hesitantly.

"I thought you said you were Shane. Do you not know who

you are?" She was smiling now, thoroughly enjoying herself.

"No, uh, wait . . . what?"

"Well, first you said you were Shane, and then you asked if your name was Lily. Are you schizophrenic?"

Shane finally caught on to her little game. "Very funny. Are you done being an asshole?"

"I don't appreciate strange men talking about my asshole," Lily scolded.

"Lily, if you don't open this door, you're going to be doing burpees until your arms break."

With no further retorts, Lily buzzed him in and then swung the door open to wait for him. As he approached, she began catcalling. "Hey, hot stuff, bring some of that down here. Oww!"

I began laughing uncontrollably. This was out of character for Lily. She didn't know Shane as much more than her trainer, so her taunting of him could only have been for one reason. And as the heaviness lifted from my chest, I appreciated her dearly.

"You are going to pay with your life," Shane muttered to Lily before his eyes swung to me. He stilled in the doorway, his eyes widening.

"Told ya you looked hot," Lily said to me as she clapped a hand on Shane's back to break his trance. "Doesn't she, Shane?"

Shane blinked hard, as if the action caused his brain to begin working again. Then he registered that Lily had asked him a question. "Yeah. Yeah, wow, you look . . . You look beautiful."

"Thank you," I replied breathily. I cleared my throat, not wanting to sound so affected by him. But I was. He looked drop-dead sexy in a light-gray, two-button suit that was tailored to his muscled frame. He wore a simple white dress shirt, but it was paired with a silver and blue tie that made his eyes pop. If *GQ* ever teamed up with *Muscle and Fitness Magazine*, Shane would be featured on the cover. "You don't look so bad yourself."

"Thanks." Shane looked down at himself briefly, seemingly unaware of how delicious he looked. It only endeared him to me more.

"Should we go?" I asked, picking up my clutch and starting toward him.

"Yeah, definitely."

I picked up a shawl I had placed by the door so I wouldn't forget it. The weather had started to cool, and while the temperature was pleasant currently, it would probably drop when the sun set.

We walked out of my apartment building in awkward silence, Shane's hands buried in his pockets. He escorted me to the passenger's side and opened the door. I slid in and then waited for him to close the door. But he didn't. I flicked my eyes up to him and then gave him my full attention when I noticed he was staring down at me.

"I meant what I said. You look gorgeous in that dress." He grinned shyly as he closed the door and strutted around to the driver's side. I fought to suppress a smile, but I failed miserably. I was nearly beaming as he slid in beside me.

"Ready, guest?" he asked with a smirk.

"Ready as I'll ever be."

❤

It was about a twenty-five-minute drive to the Villanova Conference Center, where the ceremony and reception were being held. We passed the time with inconsequential chatter. I knew Jesse from the gym, but I didn't know him very well. Shane said that he had also met Jesse through CrossFit Force, and they had become good friends over the past year.

Shane parked the car and walked over to open my door for me. He offered his hand to help me out. It was a sweet gesture that instantly made me uncomfortable. People only did sweet things on dates, and I desperately needed him to knock it off.

When he put his hand on the small of my back, I had to consciously prevent myself from swinging toward him and punching him in the face. The electric current that radiated through my spine at his touch didn't help matters.

We entered through a pair of glass double doors that led into a large foyer. A server was waiting and directed us straight through the seating area to the lawn. As I stepped out, a gasp left my lips. The lawn was beautifully manicured and was lined with white wooden chairs. The center aisle was littered with red rose petals. My gaze followed them down the aisle to the pergola that the couple would be married under. Trees and brightly colored flowers surrounded the space, giving it an enchanted garden feel. It was gorgeous.

Shane pointed to my left, and my eyes landed on Kyle and Kate. We walked over to join them, and I settled in beside Kate.

"Isn't this incredible?" she whispered.

"It's breathtaking," I replied absently, my gaze continuing to roam over our surroundings.

"Hey, kid. Nice to see you too," Kyle said as he leaned slightly over Kate.

"Eh, yeah, whatever," I replied, waving my hand at him.

After a moment, I turned toward him and smiled broadly. "Just kidding, Kyle. It is nice to see you. Especially since you never hang out with me anymore. Thank God you joined CrossFit, or you'd be a virtual stranger." The words were out of my mouth before I could consider their effect.

Kate squirmed slightly, her smile fading. She knew that she was the reason I hadn't seen Kyle.

Nice one, Kyle mouthed at me.

I racked my brain for something to say that would fix what had just come out of my mouth. I had nothing.

"Yeah, well, too bad we can't all trade up," Shane said beside me. We all shot our attention to him quizzically. "Kyle traded up, and now I'm stuck with you," he clarified. He shot me a wink as a smirk rose to his lips.

Shane Reed to the rescue again.

Kyle began laughing, and Kate soon joined in, snickering as I scolded Shane mildly.

"You really wanna start with me tonight, Reed?" I challenged.

"I believe I already have." His eyes twinkled with mischief.

"Okay. Just remember, when you're crying into your pillow later, you started this."

He scoffed loudly. Just then, a string quartet began playing music and the crowd drifted into silence. We watched as the bride's mom and groom's parents walked down the aisle, followed by the bridesmaids in varying styles of red floor-length dresses, and finally the bride herself.

I had only met Jen once before, at Shane's barbeque. I was stricken by her beauty. She wore an A-line, satin, strapless gown with a pleated bodice that hugged her petite figure flawlessly. Her dark-brown hair was a mass of curls that cascaded down her right shoulder. She looked like the perfect picture of a bride.

And as she walked down arm-in-arm with whom I imagined to be her father, a touch of sorrow struck me as I realized that I would never have that moment with my father. And as I watched her walk toward Jesse, his dark eyes sparkling as he gazed at his soon-to-be-wife, I wondered if I'd miss out on that moment too.

I reined in my emotions and watched the rest of the service with an impassive expression on my face. I tried to focus on the happy couple, but my eyes couldn't help but drift over to the bride's parents occasionally. They sat in the front row gazing adoringly at their daughter, each dabbing their eyes every so often. They held hands throughout the ceremony, a symbol of their unwavering love and support of each other. At least, that was how I interpreted it.

The ceremony lasted about twenty minutes, and after the bridal party disappeared to take pictures, we were directed to a stone terrace for the cocktail hour.

"Should we . . . get a table?" Kate asked, her voice trailing off when she realized we weren't listening. Kyle and I were practically sprinting across the terrace. We didn't play around when it came to an open bar. We were tacky and damn proud of it.

We sidled up to the bar, and my eyes surveyed the bottles lined up behind it. It was a good selection.

"What can I get for ya?"

My eyes glanced up at the bartender before returning to the alcohol. Then realization hit me. "Oh my God. Mr. Fitzpatrick?"

"Yeah, that's me." The bartender looked at me curiously, as did Kyle.

Shane and Kate finally caught up to us, settling on either side of us.

"What'd we miss?" Shane asked as he observed the awkward three-way staring match that was going on.

"I'm sorry." I shook my head to bring my mind back to the present. "I'm Amanda Bishop. I was in your American History class at Brendall High. That must have been eleven or twelve years ago. I'm sure you don't remember me, but I loved your class. You were hysterical."

Mr. Fitzpatrick looked at me closely, as if trying very hard to place me. "I'm sorry," he said finally. "I can't seem to remember."

"It's fine. I wouldn't expect you to. It's just funny seeing you here." Though a part of me was a little sad he didn't remember. The man in front of me was older and slightly rounder now, but he had been an Adonis twelve years ago. I knew exactly what I could say to jog his memory.

Come to think of it, maybe I was happy he didn't remember me.

"Yeah, small world," he replied warmly. "So, what can I get you guys?"

We placed our orders, and Mr. Fitzpatrick busied himself making our drinks. When he returned them to us, I put five dollars on the bar, thanked him, and started to turn away. But before I got a full 180 degrees, I heard him.

"Wait. Amanda Bishop, huh? That name is starting to ring some bells."

Oh crap. I turned back around slowly, and the others did the same.

"Yes, yes, I remember. You're the girl who slipped me the note with your phone number in it on the back of your final exam. How have ya been?"

And shit just got weird.

Mr. Fitzpatrick now seemed incredibly excited to speak to me. I felt three wide-eyed people all staring at me, their mouths nearly hitting the floor. Kyle started laughing hysterically and excused himself from the group. Kate followed him, but Shane was glued to my side. And though I refused to look over at him, my periphery could make out his smirk.

"Yeah, that's me. I was ... whew, so crazy back then." *Clearly, not much has changed though.* I laughed uncomfortably as Shane nearly spit out his drink. "But I've been good. Really good. I'm a financial planner now. Are you still teaching?" I was trying to keep my voice light, but mortification made it squeaky.

"Oh, yeah, I'm still at it. Well, listen, it was great to see ya. I've gotta take care of these other folks."

"Oh, of course," I interrupted, desperate to get the hell out of there. "Enjoy your night."

"You, too. And Amanda?"

I looked at him expectantly.

"Is your phone number still the same?" The glint in his eye made it hard to tell if he was teasing me or if he was being a total creep.

"Uh, no, it isn't."

"Too bad. See ya around." And with that, Mr. Fitzpatrick moved on to other guests.

Once we were a few feet away, Shane started laughing.

"Don't," I warned.

"God, you make it too damn easy."

"I said don't." But my tone wasn't threatening as I tried to bite back a smile.

"You just gave me ammunition for years to come. You're never living that little exchange down." Shane was laughing so hard, his face was turning beet red and tears were welling up in his eyes.

"I was just a little ahead of my time is all. Now it's all the rage to bang your teacher."

"Yeah, you were a real trailblazer." His hysterics roared with that one, as he began convulsing with laughter.

We walked over to where Kyle and Kate were standing beside a stone wall that ran the perimeter of the terrace.

"Before you even start," I said to Kyle, "are you really surprised?"

Kyle pondered that for a moment. "Nope."

"Then let's drop it."

We discussed nothing much in particular for the rest of the cocktail hour. We were eventually prompted to start heading inside for the reception. When we walked past the bar, I couldn't resist throwing a quick glance at Mr. Fitzpatrick. And while I hoped I was mistaken, I thought I saw him wink at me.

"You sure you don't want to give him your address? It'll save him the trouble of following you home," Shane whispered in my ear.

Guess I wasn't mistaken.

❤

We found our seats, which were situated by one of the wet bars. Thankfully Mr. Fitzpatrick wasn't working that one. I took in the large ballroom, with an ornate chandelier hanging over a sizable parquet dance floor. There were windows lining one wall that looked out on the terrace. There were easily twenty-five tables in the room, all with white-linen-covered chairs and red bows.

Not long after we were seated, the DJ began announcing the wedding party. Everyone was cheering as the couples walked in to "Sexy Back." Finally, we were told to stand and "Give it up for Mr. and Mrs. Jesse Kline." We all clapped loudly as the couple entered, hands clasped, smiles wide. They moved toward the middle of the dance floor, where they had their first dance to some country song I had never heard before.

Then the DJ announced that the bride would dance with her father. I watched with glassy eyes as Jen's father took her hand on the dance floor. And as he embraced her right hand in his left and guided her in time to the music, I wondered if that's who had taught her to dance.

Had they practiced the comfortable hold they had on one another in their living room? Did Jen learn to dance by putting her feet on her father's while they listened to old records?

I had been to plenty of weddings in the last few years, and though I couldn't say I'd never thought about who would walk me down the aisle or what I would do instead of the father-daughter dance, I'd never felt this.

Something about this wedding struck me deeply. Like someone had jabbed a serrated knife inside my gut and twisted it over and over again. And just when I thought that was as deep as it could go, they pushed it in just a little bit farther.

This wasn't me. I wasn't the girl who cried at weddings. I didn't cry tears of joy, and I certainly didn't cry tears of sadness. But as the stinging behind my eyes made its way to the front, I knew I had to pull myself together.

"Excuse me," I said as I stood from the table. "I need a cigarette."

A cigarette? I don't even smoke.
I could have said anything.
I need to use the restroom. I have to take an important phone call. I'm a member of a secret British military group, and my helicopter's just landed outside.

But now, any hope I had of escaping without drawing attention to myself had just vanished.

I quickly exited through the double doors and made my way outside. The brisk autumn air stung my cheeks through my salty tears. But the smell of leaves and the cool oxygen hitting my lungs made it easier to breathe. I leaned against the building and fished through my clutch for something to wipe my face.

Until a deep, soothing voice interrupted my search. "Here."

I knew who had said it. But I looked up anyway to see Shane holding a box of tissues. He must have taken the whole box from the men's room on his way outside. But instead of handing me one, he cupped my burning cheek with his soft hand and swept away a stray tear with his thumb. His hand lingered longer than it needed to. But not long enough.

"Thanks," I said.

His blue stare bore through me. "Are you okay?"

I struggled to keep my voice steady, but it faltered anyway. "Yeah, sorry. I'm fine. I just needed some fresh air."

"You're clearly not fine. Let me rephrase that. It was a dumb question. What I meant to ask is, what's wrong?"

"I *am* okay. Really. Don't worry about me." I dropped my eyes toward the ground, not able to maintain eye contact.

"That's impossible . . . not to worry," he whispered. "When I saw you get up from the table like that . . . with tears in your eyes…all I did was worry." His fingertips brushed under my chin as he brought my gaze up to meet his again. "At least I know it wasn't me who pissed you off this time."

I was thankful for the small laugh that I exhaled.

"There's a smile," Shane said as he let his own creep across his face. "And you're a terrible liar, you know. Talk to me."

I inhaled a shaky breath and dabbed a tissue below my eyes, trying not to smudge my mascara, but something told me it was a little late for that. In what felt like one breath, I told Shane everything: that even if someone eventually wanted to marry me, seeing Jen's father walk her down the aisle and dance with her reminded me that I didn't have my own.

"First of all," Shane began, "why wouldn't someone want to marry you?"

"Are you kidding? I can't even get through a stranger's wedding without looking like a complete train wreck. Look at me." I kept my eyes locked on his and swallowed the growing lump in my throat.

His lips parted, and I could sense Shane wanted to say something but wasn't sure whether or not he should. "I *am* looking at you," he said as he brushed a stray hair away from my face with his cool fingertips. "You're beautiful."

The comment should have made me feel uneasy. I couldn't help but think that I should look away. But I couldn't drag my eyes from his.

"And secondly," he added, "you have a right to feel the way you do. You're missing a father you never had. It's understandable." He paused for a moment. "My father passed away when I was twelve. I know it's not the same. And it's different for a woman… I mean, at a wedding like this. I'm sure it's different. But I know what it's like to miss something. To miss *someone*."

"That's why you have dinner with your mom every Sunday. So she's not lonely?"

"She says I remind her of him. My mannerisms, my speech, little things like that. But I was so young when he died, it's hard for me to remember that stuff. But if it helps her remember … well, then, I guess it's worth it."

"Why didn't you tell me? In your car that night when I told you about *my* father?" I shook my head, confused.

"I didn't tell you then because that was *your* moment. That was *your* story. It wasn't about me. It's not about me now either. I just thought that knowing I understand a little of what you're going through might help."

And somehow it did.

"What happened? How did he die—I mean, if you don't mind my asking?"

"No, I don't mind. I guess in some ways it was sudden. We didn't expect it right at that moment, but we also weren't completely surprised by it either. He'd had diabetes since he was fourteen. My whole life he'd had problems with his circulation, and he'd had so many surgeries. He was always either recovering or getting sicker. There was never a time in my life that I can remember when he was what I'd call healthy. It wasn't his fault. But maybe that's why I've devoted my life to health. I don't know. I've never actually thought about that until just now."

I still struggled to hold back tears, but this time they weren't for myself.

"Anyway, the weeks before he died, he'd been home from the hospital. He'd been getting sicker, but he refused to go back in. It was like he knew he didn't have much longer, and he wanted to be home. One day during my Christmas break, the rest of us were out of the house, and he had a heart attack at home."

"God, I'm so sorry." It was all I could think to say. And it felt so impersonal.

"It's okay. It's been a long time. I never really know what to say when people tell me they're sorry. I mean, it's not your fault. We all lose people we love."

"Yeah, but what you went through... it's so much sadder than what happened to me. I mean, I didn't have anything to lose. I never had anything to begin with. But you had twelve years with him... enough to love him... to remember who he was, what he acted like... and then he was just... gone."

Shane took my hand in both of his and massaged the top with his thumbs. The delicate touch soothed me. "It's never easier to have nothing. I got the chance to have twelve years with him. And even though it was difficult when he died, I was always thankful that I got the chance to know him. There's truth to that old saying about how it's better to have loved and lost than never to have loved at all. That's kind of what I put in the eulogy. I mean, I was too scared to read it myself, but I wrote that—that I was happy to have had twelve years with him—and someone read it for me."

"That's amazing... that you were able to understand something like that when you were so young."

"I think the thing that upsets me most is that there were so many times when I wished for him to die. It was so hard to watch him like that for so many years—him in pain, us in pain. I just wanted it all to end. I thought it would be easier if he wasn't around. Better somehow. I feel guilty for that."

"Was it? Easier, I mean?"

"No, it wasn't. It's never easier to lose someone you love.

No matter how difficult you think it is to be with them . . . it's never easier when you're not."

❤

After a few more minutes, I had composed myself enough to go back inside. We took our seats just as the servers were delivering our salads. Kyle caught my eyes as I settled in, his eyes wide, asking me if I was okay.

I nodded and smiled. The meal was delicious, and we fell into easy conversation with our tablemates. They were all Jesse's friends from college, here with their wives or girlfriends. A rowdy group, I instantly liked them.

Once the entrees were cleared, the DJ put on Robin Thicke's "Blurred Lines" and told everyone to get out on the dance floor. Our entire table stood. Except for Shane. I looked at him. "You coming?"

"I don't dance."

I sat back down as everyone else made their way onto the floor. "Not at all?"

He shook his head.

"Why not? No one expects you to be Chris Brown out there."

"I just don't dance. I have, like, negative amounts of rhythm. You can go, though."

I settled back in my chair, knowing that I'd never leave him sitting alone. "Nah, I'd rather stay and bother you." I smiled at him with mock sweetness.

"Gee, thanks," he said sarcastically.

Shane and I sat quietly, watching the hijinks happening out on the dance floor. But eventually we found a new favorite game: making fun of all of the dancing drunk people. By the time everyone returned to the table for the cake cutting, Shane and I were in tears over some old woman who was shaking her ass like she was working a pole.

The cake cutting was ... well, a cake cutting. But dessert was set up on a huge table against one of the far walls. They had everything: cake, cookies, cupcakes, fondue, ice cream. Kyle and I were in heaven. Shane and Kate, of course, insisted they were full from dinner. *Fucking liars.*

Kyle and I returned with our plates brimming with sweets.

"Are you really going to eat all of that?" Shane asked.

I widened my eyes like a little kid on Christmas morning as I nodded.

"You better be at the gym on Monday. Come to think of it, maybe you should stay for two classes."

I put a piece of carrot cake on my spoon and rocked it like a pendulum in front of Shane's mouth. "Come on, Shane. You know you want some. And it even has carrots in it. It's practically like eating a vegetable. Totally Paleo friendly."

"Get that away from me."

I put the spoon in my mouth, "Fine. Just sit there and suffer, then."

After the dessert, the party kicked into overdrive. The lights were dimmed so much, they were practically off, and strobe lights flashed. Our table was empty save for Shane and me. We resumed our game. Suddenly I heard a voice behind us.

"Yo, buddy. I thought that was you over here."

I looked up to see a guy standing behind Shane, the man's hand resting on Shane's shoulder. He was handsome, lean body and square jaw, with dark hair slicked back into a sophisticated style. He directed his words at Shane, but his eyes were on me.

"Hey, Sebastian. I didn't know you were here." Shane's face was difficult to read, but it didn't look like he was all that happy to see Sebastian.

"Yeah, I got here late. Completely missed the cocktail hour." Sebastian's eyes had still not wavered from me. "Who's your date? I didn't know you were seeing anyone."

"Oh sorry, Sebastian, this is Amanda. Amanda, Sebastian." I could tell by Shane's body language that he would have preferred ripping out his fingernails than introducing me to Sebastian. Sebastian, however, seemed clueless, and he took the empty seat on the other side of Shane, leaning over him to shake my hand.

"It's a pleasure."

"Nice to meet you, Sebastian."

Shane hadn't responded to Sebastian's first round of questions, but that didn't deter him. "So, how long have you guys been together?"

"We're not together," Shane grumbled. "We're just here as friends."

"Oh, is that so?" Sebastian's eyes sparkled. "Well, your loss, Shane."

"Not really," Shane stated.

My gaze swung to his face.

He is not going to start this shit now. Is he?

"What do you mean?" Sebastian asked, clearly confused by Shane's rudeness.

"She's a sex snob. So it's not really my loss."

Oh, he was going to start shit all right. When was he going to learn that he couldn't win these games with me?

I plastered a bright smile on my face and gazed adoringly at Sebastian. "Last time I checked, just because a girl isn't interested in dating you doesn't mean she's a sex snob. Some people have standards."

Out of the corner of my eye, I saw Shane's jaw tighten. Sebastian erupted into a laugh, and I instantly regretted my words. My goal had been to put Shane in his place, not embarrass him in front of a guy he clearly didn't care for.

Suddenly, Shane scoffed. "You have standards? Last time I checked, you'd slept with enough guys in the past year to field a football team."

I narrowed my eyes at Shane, all remorse vanishing. I leaned in toward him, my lips turning up slightly, "A baseball team would probably be more accurate."

Shane withdrew from me, sitting back farther in his chair. *Game, set, match.*

"Well, you two are interesting friends," Sebastian chimed in. "So, Amanda, would you like to dance?"

My eyes darted to Shane, but he refused to look at me. I didn't want to dance with Sebastian. Shane clearly didn't like him, and that was enough warning for me. But Shane had started this little war, and I was damn sure going to make sure I won it.

"Sure, I'd love to."

Sebastian stood and offered his hand to me. I put my hand in his, and we made our way to the dance floor. Maroon Five's "Love Somebody" was playing, though it had been altered to have more of a techno vibe to it. Sebastian wasted no time pulling me into him, grinding against me like he was trying to mark me with his scent. I nearly pushed him away when I saw Shane watching us. So, instead, I turned around and pushed my ass into Sebastian. If Shane was going to stare at us, I would make sure I put on a worthy show to watch.

As that song ended, the DJ announced that he was going to slow the music down for a minute. I was ready to return to my seat, but Sebastian pulled me to him. I put my arms around his neck but braced my forearms against his shoulders to prevent him from getting too close to me. I had a very good douche-meter, and Sebastian was making it twirl nearly out of control.

A song that I actually loved came on, though I was surprised to hear it at a wedding. It was "Somebody's Heartbreak" by Hunter Hayes. Despite my excitement over the song, I was less than thrilled with my partner. I darted my head around, trying not to focus on the predatory look on Sebastian's face. A familiar voice brought my attention back.

"Can I cut in?" Shane was glaring at Sebastian, who returned an equally icy look.

"Sure," Sebastian said curtly before turning to me. "I'll be back for you." *Ugh, another creepy wink.*

Shane moved closer to me and placed his hands gently on my hips as I brought my hands to his shoulders.

"I thought you didn't dance?"

"I don't," he replied without looking at me.

"But you are right now." I wanted to know why, but he wasn't going to make it easy.

"Guess I am."

I stopped moving. "Fine, I'm going back to the table." But as I made a move to step away, Shane's grip tightened, his eyes locking with mine. I instinctively moved back toward him as he wrapped his arms around my waist, pulling me tighter to him.

I pushed my arms over his shoulders and around his neck, enjoying the warmth I felt in his embrace. We swayed gently in time with the music, our bodies naturally finding a rhythm with one another.

"I didn't like watching you dance with him," Shane said into my ear, finally answering my unspoken question.

"Why not?" My voice was husky, my body already responding, knowing that I was going to like this answer before I even heard it.

"He's not good enough for you." Shane pulled back slightly so he could look into my eyes. "And I didn't like his hands on you, trying to touch you in places I've already been. Places I want to be again."

I involuntarily gasped at his words. I definitely had places I wanted his hands to be again. My body was on fire as my clit throbbed at his words.

Shane continued to hold my gaze, and I couldn't have looked away if I had tried. Our mouths inched closer, the movement so slow that most people probably wouldn't have even noticed.

The song ended and was replaced by some upbeat techno crap, but it didn't matter. Shane and I kept our original pace, holding each other closely, our breath intermingling and sending shivers down my spine. Just as our lips were about to experience the contact we both craved, I pulled back.

"Let's get out of here," I breathed.

Taking my hand, Shane pulled me away from the dance floor. We returned to our table briefly to retrieve my clutch and his jacket and then headed for the exit without saying a word to anyone. It was chilly outside, and my thoughts briefly ran to the shawl I had left in Shane's car. As if reading my mind, Shane draped his jacket over my shoulders before reclaiming my hand and pulling me toward his car.

Once settled inside his Mustang, my brain fought to catch up to what my body had agreed to. I wasn't sure how I was feeling. All of the emotions within me were conflicting. I wanted to sleep with Shane again. Who wouldn't? He was friggin' gorgeous. And I already knew that he was a great lay. This should have been an easy decision for me.

But it wasn't.

Because I knew that this time would mean more. The smoldering look Shane had given me, and that I had returned, wasn't the look you gave someone who was just a convenient fuck.

I had been sleeping with Kyle for years, and never once had we looked at each other the way Shane and I just had. It was passion, desire, lust, need, want, and adoration all rolled into one. I suddenly knew that I couldn't agree to this. Tonight would change my relationship with Shane, and I didn't want that. Except...

"Where to?" Shane asked.

I looked around. If we turned right here, we'd be heading toward my house. That was the way I should tell him to go. I could break it to him gently and then go upstairs and pretend that the last half hour hadn't happened. That was the right decision to make.

"Stay straight."

Except, maybe I did want it.

❤

We walked up to Shane's front door and I stood close behind him as he opened it. He stepped back so that I could enter first. He threw his keys down on the table beside the door before taking my clutch from my hand and placing it next to his keys. He then took the jacket from my shoulders and placed it on the knob at the base of the banister that led upstairs. Then, without saying a word, he grabbed my hand and led me up the steps.

He took me into a room that was clearly his bedroom. The walls were a light gray, which contrasted with his dark furniture. It screamed masculinity. He lightly pulled me in front of him, placing his fingertips on my hips and slowly turning me around so that I was facing away from him. He pressed his chest tightly against my back, bringing his mouth to my neck. He ran his lips along the tender flesh there, but he didn't kiss me.

"You look so beautiful in this dress. But as soon as I saw you in it, all I could think about is how much more beautiful you'd be out of it."

My body instantly responded to his words as I felt the slickness grow between my legs. I lolled my head back slightly, bringing me into more contact with his body. His fingers left my hips and slowly trailed up my sides, moving to my back, settling on the zipper of my dress.

He moved my hair to the side as he pulled my zipper down seductively slowly. Once I felt his hands graze the skin at the apex of my ass, I shuddered with excitement. He caressed my back gently before moving his hands up to my shoulders and pushing the sleeves off my body, causing the dress to cascade to the floor and pool around my feet.

Shane loosened his tie and threw it to the floor before returning his hands to me. One rested on my tight stomach while the other drifted to my thigh, where it skimmed down the front, then up the back, cupping my ass. Then he started the torturously blissful movement again.

He was unrushed, so unlike the last time we had sex. He was making it clear that this was different. This wasn't going to be quick and needy. It was going to be slow and meaningful. And in this moment, that's exactly what I wanted.

I turned my head back so my temple nearly rested on his shoulder as I looked up at him. He took advantage of my neck being so wide open for him to rain down soft kisses and nips to my neck and shoulder blade. But finally, his eyes found mine. He lifted his hand from my thigh and used it to run his thumb along my jawline while his other fingers tangled in my hair.

We stayed like that, our lips inches away from each other again, our eyes searching the other for words we were too afraid to say out loud, until the magnetic pull between us became too much to resist.

He lowered his lips gently to mine, the kiss starting out as everything else had: delicate and purposeful. But as my lips parted to grant his tongue entry, the passion overtook us. I spun around so that my chest was flush against his, my nipples straining against the nude lace bra that harnessed them. Our lips never broke contact as I ripped open his shirt, sending buttons flying through the air.

I twisted my hands in his hair as he pulled the shirt off and let it drop to the floor. He reached behind me and pulled my ass roughly so that my pelvis pushed against him, thrusting his erection into my core before backing away slightly so I could undo his belt and push down his pants. He skillfully kicked off his shoes and socks and stepped out of his pants as I did the same with my dress.

We made our way to the bed, where he lowered my body before climbing atop me. He straddled my waist, his knees resting on either side of my ribcage as he reached his arm beneath me to pull me up higher onto the bed, his bicep flexing deliciously.

Shane pulled back, breaking our kiss so that he could pull his undershirt over his head. I touched my lips, relishing how swollen they were from his rough kiss.

He trailed a hand from my neck, between my breasts, down my stomach, and to the waistband of my thong. I ran my hand over the lines of his tattoo, wishing I could reach and outline it with my tongue as his hand roamed my body.

He reached behind me, prompting me to arch my back so that he could unclasp my bra, which he then pulled from my body and cast to the floor. He clasped my hands in his and pinned them above my head as his mouth lowered to my breast and sucked and licked it in ways that sent pleasure coursing through my veins. Then, moving to my other breast, he lavished it with similar attention.

It was all too much. I needed him to fill me. To take aim at the dull ache that had settled between my thighs and obliterate it.

"Shane," I moaned. "Please, Shane."

Hearing the desperation in my voice, Shane released my hands and pulled his boxers down. His hands then moved to the lace fabric of my thong and slowly lowered it halfway down my legs before pulling my legs up so he could slide the material over the stilettos that still adorned my feet without him having to move away from me.

With my legs resting on his shoulders, he turned his head and kissed my ankle and then trailed his tongue up the inside of my leg until he reached his destination. He spread me wide as he kissed and licked my clit, causing me to thrash and buck my upper body around the bed in brutal ecstasy.

But he held my hips firm as he continued the assault with his tongue. Shane released one of my hips and lowered his fingers to my opening, thrusting two fingers deep inside me as his tongue circled my clit. The sensation was overwhelming as my body built toward climax.

"Shane," I moaned again.

"What do you need, baby? Tell me what you need." His voice was hushed as his tongue resumed its trip up my body.

"I need you. I need you inside me. Oh, please," I begged.

Shane quickly leaned toward his nightstand and opened the drawer, pulling out a foil wrapper. I took it from his hands, tore it open with my mouth, and then spread the latex over his steely length. He then positioned his cock at my opening, pushing the head slightly into me.

"Is this what you need?"

He continued this teasing until I responded. "Yes. God, yes, that's what I need."

Shane lowered his hands to the bed and then thrust fully into me, causing rivaling feelings of pain and pleasure to ripple through my body. I stretched to accommodate him as I felt the slight pulse of his cock, causing me to grow even wetter, enveloping him and allowing him to slide inside me without resistance.

He pulled almost completely out of me before slamming back inside. My hips lifted to meet him, opening myself up to him, taking him deeply into myself. We again found our rhythm. He worked in and out of me, giving me so much pleasure that my whole body felt like it had ceased to continue functioning, choosing instead to focus on the pure eroticism of this moment.

He must have been able to feel when I was close to finding my release, because his thumb moved to my clit and began stroking it in time with his thrusts. The sensation propelled me higher, my body climbing with every brush of Shane's finger.

Our breathing grew ragged as my heart struggled to pump blood to everywhere that needed it, everywhere that Shane was stimulating. We were primal in this moment, our bodies reacting to one another instinctually.

"Are you there, Amanda? Come with me, baby."

His words caused me to shatter. An orgasm ripped through my body more violently than any other of my life. I yelled my pleasure as I felt Shane thrust twice more before a deep groan escaped from him as he found his own release. I milked the come from his cock as the pulsation from my orgasm clenched around him.

Once our orgasms calmed, Shane placed a chaste kiss on my lips before rolling next to me and pulling me to him. I rested my head on his arm and let him envelop me in his warmth. And against my better judgment, I allowed myself to drift off to sleep.

chapter eleven

The sound of a lawnmower woke me from my deep slumber. I picked up my phone off the nightstand to look at the time.

Who mows their lawn at seven forty-two in the morning? On a Sunday? In October?

No one even had a lawn at my apartment complex. It was then that I remembered where I was. *I'm at Shane's.* It's not like I had a reason *not* to remember where I was. I hadn't been drunk. It was just a moment of temporary sleep-induced amnesia. I mean, the night had been nothing short of memorable. But all I wanted to do was forget the feel of Shane's warm hands brushing across my flesh, the smell of aftershave mingling with hints of his cologne, and the taste of his sweet, minty tongue upon mine.

But I couldn't. Last night had meant something. So I had to do what I do best: avoid the situation.

As I rose quietly from the bed, careful not to wake Shane while I got dressed, I couldn't help but ignore the strange parallels to my night with Zach. Shane's gorgeous, just-fucked hair hung against his face. The V extending from his solid chest and defined abs could be seen peeking out just above where the crisp white sheet draped sensually across his hipbone. He was beautiful. There he slept peacefully, blissfully unaware of my thoughts about last night.

As I dropped my phone into my clutch and did my best to zip my dress up on my own, part of me had the urge to leave a note.

Shane wouldn't believe I'm moving to Bulgaria, would he?

❤

Thirty minutes later, I found myself sitting on the swing of an elementary school playground down the street from Shane's house while I waited for Lily to pick me up. I was busy fielding the multiple texts from Kyle about my quick exit last night when an elderly woman said hello to me, commenting on what a beautiful day it was as she cleaned up after her shih tzu.

It didn't take me long to realize how ridiculous I must have looked. Instead of on my head, my hair belonged in one of the nearby trees for birds to lay eggs in. Remnants of last night's makeup lingered on my face, ruined from all my crying, fucking, and sleeping. There I sat, a nearly thirty-year-old woman in a partially zipped dress texting on playground equipment. I nodded a polite "hello" in return.

You're not the only one who feels like they have some shit to clean up, lady.

At last, I spotted Lily's blue Elantra pulling into the lot. The wood chips bit into my feet as I made my way to her passenger-side door.

"You've got some serious details to share," she said. "Where we headed? Church? I bet you're in need of some absolution after this interesting walk of shame you're doing. You look a little formal, though, don't you think?"

"Don't start," I said flatly as I put my bare feet on Lily's dashboard like a redneck teenager. I turned on the radio to search for some country music. *Might as well complete the image.* "I've already taken a ton of shit from Kyle. I had a bunch of texts and a voicemail from him because I left the wedding early last night."

"I don't get up before noon on a Sunday to pick your dumb ass up and then get shot down when I ask for some sort of explanation. Come on, spill it."

"I spent the night at Shane's after the wedding."

"Well, no shit. I'm not a complete moron. I didn't think you slept on the fucking merry-go-round last night. Though it wouldn't have been the first time," she added with a laugh. "Why the hell am I picking you up at a playground and not at Shane's? Come to think of it, why am I picking you up at *all*?" I could feel her intense gaze on the side of my face, but my eyes remained down as I picked at my nail polish. "Oh, and how was the sex? God . . . please tell me it was hot!"

"What question do you want me to answer first?"

"Um . . ." She thought for a moment. "The one about the sex."

"Yeah," I replied in an annoyed monotone, "it was hot."

"Well, then, why did you run away?" she repeated.

I shook my head slightly. "Good fucking question."

❤

Somehow, over the next few days, I managed to dodge most of Lily's questions about Shane. My main tactic was asking her about her own sex life. She usually just replied that she didn't have one and ended the interrogation suspiciously quickly.

Kyle, however, wasn't as easy to trick, as he would have been more than happy to talk about all the great sex he was having. I just tried to avoid any texts that pertained to all things Shane.

I also dove headfirst into work. I continued getting there early each day, and I worked late to avoid CrossFit all week. Though I used that as my excuse, it clearly wasn't my *reason*. It would only be a matter of time before someone called me out on it.

By Wednesday I had a text from Shane.

Didn't I recommend you come to the gym every day this week to work off all those desserts you ate??? That was code for: Why did you do the walk of shame from my house like a sorority girl without saying goodbye? Why haven't you called? And oh yeah, did that night mean anything to you, because it sure as hell meant something to me?

Been working late. Sorry.

That was my only response. *God, I really hate being a bitch.*

On Thursday night, Lily finally called my bluff. Though, something told me she hadn't *just* realized the whole "working late" thing was a bunch of bullshit.

"Okay," Lily said as soon as I entered the apartment at nine fifteen. "Enough with the overachiever act. What's going on with you and Shane?"

Well, damn. I'd been called many things, but an

"overachiever" had certainly never been one of them. *She's definitely on to me.*

"Nothing's going on," I said, grabbing a slice of room-temperature pizza from the box on the counter. The pitch of my voice was much too high to be believable.

"Prove it, then."

❤

Lily and I pulled up outside of CrossFit Force Friday with ten minutes to spare before the six o'clock class started. I had my phone in my hand, frantically typing, trying to make it appear as though I was much too busy to actually go inside. Lily turned off the car, shifted in her seat, and began to stare me down. I did what I had done to all of my other problems recently: I ignored her.

Finally, she'd had enough. She reached for the phone and tried to pry it from my hand. I clutched it tightly, refusing to let it go. Our wrestling match caught the attention of the other gym members who were walking into class.

After about two minutes of yelling, cursing, and damn near beating the shit out of each other, we heard a tap on the passenger window. We froze like teenagers caught sneaking into our room after a long night of debauchery.

Almost in slow motion, we turned our heads to the source of the noise. *Fuck. My. Life.* Staring back at us, his face impassive, was Shane.

"You ladies want to take this inside?"

I quickly averted my gaze to the floor mats in Lily's car.

Lily looked at me briefly before yelling so that she could be heard through the window, "Yeah, we'll be right in."

Shane stood there for a moment longer, but I was too much of a coward to look up at him. Then, he finally straightened up and headed back into the gym.

Lily sat back in her seat and sighed, clearly thinking about what she wanted to say. When her voice came, it was firm but tinged with sympathy. "Amanda, listen. We both know I'm no relationship expert, but I'm also not blind. Something *is* going on between you and Shane, and you can't run from it. It isn't fair to him."

I was startled by her words. Not fair to *him*? I thought she was supposed to be on my side?

"Who's running? I'm here, aren't I?" My voice was cold, but I didn't care.

Lily looked at me. "Then I'll see you inside." She pulled the keys from the ignition, grabbed her water bottle, and made her way into the gym.

I threw my head back and took advantage of my solitude to loudly groan into my hands. This was a complete and utter mess. *I* was a mess. And I didn't know how to fix it. This was why I had my rules. They saved me from ridiculous drama like this. So I'd fucked Shane. Big fucking deal. And so what that it was amazing, and tender, and different from every other encounter I had ever had?

I quickly wiped a lone tear that trickled down my cheek.

"Yeah," I said aloud. "So what?"

❤

I walked into the gym just as the warm-up was beginning. I saw Lily standing beside Kyle toward the right side of the gym.

Of course he's here too. I guess everyone wants a front-row seat to see the disaster my life has become.

I tightened my jaw and stiffened my spine as I walked to the left. My anger at them was ill-placed and irrational. I replayed my new mantra in my head as I felt their eyes follow me: *So what?*

We went through the warm-up as usual. Not so usual was that Shane never approached me. Never even came within five feet of me. It only fueled the anger that was building. He took us through the moves for the workout. We started with twenty minutes of front and back squats with weight. Shane continued to avoid me. For the intense part of our workout, we had to do sumo deadlift high pulls, followed by ring dips and pull-ups.

"We're going to come around and have each of you do one rep of the SDLHPs so we can check your form," Shane announced.

Kate took the right side of the gym, forcing Shane to observe the people on my side. He went down the row, giving corrections or praise. But when he got to me, he was silent. I performed the movement anyway. When he still didn't say anything, I cast my eyes up toward him. His face was still impassive, but his eyes were blazing. He simply nodded his head before moving on to the next person.

My heart began thundering in my chest.

Who the hell do all of them think they are? Lily . . . Kyle . . . Shane?

I could see the judgment in all of their eyes every time they looked at me. They judged me for doing what I had always done; for being who I had always been. I'd told Shane where I stood from the beginning. He was the one who crossed the line in the sand. Not me. It was his fault our friendship was broken. But I was the one taking the blame.

Well, they want to see some emotion out of me? Here it is.

However, it wasn't the emotion they had counted on. It was rage.

When Shane said "Go," I threw myself into the workout. We had fifteen minutes to complete three rounds, and I bore all of my feelings into it. I finished with four minutes left, and only a couple of muscleheads were done before me. I waited until the fifteen minutes were up, standing with my hands on my hips and glaring at the floor. Then, I took apart my bar and began stomping toward the door.

Just as I was cursing myself for driving with Lily, I felt a strong hand clasp my bicep.

"We need to talk," Shane grumbled as he pushed me toward the office.

Once inside, my brain caught up to what was happening, and I wrenched my arm from Shane's grasp. My rage hadn't died down. I still had every bit of it.

"What the fuck do you think you're doing? Don't you ever put your hands on me."

"Oh, that's rich. That wasn't what you said on Saturday."

"Well, I'm saying it now."

"I should've known. First you let that asshole Sebastian put his hands all over you, and then you're begging me to take you to my place. I should've let him have you. The two of you are exactly the fucking same. You're just out for a good time and don't care who you hurt in the process. 'Use 'em and lose 'em.' That's his motto. Seems pretty fitting for you too."

I opened my mouth to retort but quickly closed it as I watched him run his hand roughly through his hair. He looked exasperated. And hurt. My anger cooled at the sight of him. It was then that realization hit me.

My anger had been a mask, a way to cover the truth. It had been easier to endure the past six days deep in denial than to confront the reality of the situation. And when forced to confront it, it had been easier to direct my anger at everyone else rather than where it belonged.

And as I watched his eyes search mine for the truth, I knew what I had done. I had hurt a man I cared for deeply. I had given him a piece of me only to instantly rescind it. I deserved his judgment. I deserved every negative emotion he felt toward me.

But knowing all of that wouldn't change anything. I had used my rules as a fortress against pain and betrayal for years. They were all I knew. So I buried myself behind them again.

"What do you want, Shane?" My voice was calm but firm. I was resigned to what I had to do.

He scoffed. "What do *I* want? I thought it was what *we* wanted."

"You thought wrong. *We* clearly don't want the same things." My words held a detachment that surprised even me. I was being cruel, but it was better to warn him off now than hurt him later.

He winced slightly at my words but recovered quickly, tension returning to his jaw. "What do *you* want?"

My initial reaction was to be childish and tell him that I had asked him first. But I owed him this. And I also figured that it would be easier to lie *before* I heard what he had to say. "I want to be your friend. I thought I was clear about that. I told you my rules, Shane. I never lied to you." *Except right now, that is.* "You knew where I stood."

He thought for a moment before starting toward me, closing the gap between us in milliseconds. "After everything we shared, everything we *felt*—and don't give me some bullshit about you not feeling anything. I know you did. After all of that, you're really going to use your rules to push me away?" His voice was pleading, and it nearly broke me.

Nearly.

I couldn't continue this for much longer. I already felt the stinging behind my eyes, warning me that tears were imminent. I had to end this. "I don't need to push away something I never wanted." My stomach dropped at the words, sickening me for letting them out of my mouth. Part of me wished that he could see through them. That he would know how untrue they were. But he didn't.

His eyes widened and he reeled back like I'd slapped him. But the shock of what I said was almost instantly replaced. Now, Shane was pissed. "So you didn't want what happened Saturday?"

"I wanted the sex. And I still want your friendship, though I know that's impossible now." My voice was completely devoid of emotion, but my body was racked with it.

"I don't . . . I don't even know what to say to that."

"Shane, I . . ." I made a step toward him, lifted my hand as if to touch him and briefly let my sadness show. But he tensed at my approach, and I halted. I dropped my head. As my brain desperately tried to find the right words to say, all that came to mind was the note Nate had left me. I lifted my head as tears swam in my eyes. But I didn't care if Shane saw them. I wanted him to know my remorse. My regret that I wasn't a better person. "I can't pretend to feel something I don't."

My rules had backfired. Instead of keeping me safe from guys like Nate, they had turned me into him. Now the only thing left to do was run like he had.

So I did.

♥

I fled from Shane's office, briefly looking to my right on my way toward the exit. My eyes zeroed in on Kyle, Kate, and Lily standing about ten feet from the office, seemingly to form a barrier that prevented the other members from eavesdropping on Shane and me. Despite seeing concern in their eyes, I didn't slow down. I threw open the door and stalked toward Lily's car.

Lily followed right behind, and I immediately jumped into the car when she unlocked the door, pulling my knees up against my chest to hug them. Lily glanced over at me but said nothing as she started the car and backed out of the space.

I stared out the windshield, wondering what the hell I had just done. The things I had said would cause Shane to want nothing to do with me ever again. And while my mind tried to convince my heart that this was all for the best, my heart just wasn't having it.

So, as we pulled away from CrossFit Force—away from Shane—I lost myself to the emotional torrent that had been building since Saturday.

I sobbed for everything I had willingly allowed myself to lose, all because I was too scared to keep it.

chapter twelve

After my "breakup" with Shane, the only thing that seemed clear to me was that I couldn't go back to CrossFit. I couldn't see his broken expression every time I worked out, so I did the only thing a normal, completely sane human being would do: I joined another gym.

Though I was still paying my membership fee at CrossFit, I was happy to pay any amount of money to avoid another encounter like the one in Shane's office. Over the course of the next two weeks, I tried to familiarize myself with Everyday Fitness, my new gym. Strangely enough, it felt like I was cheating on CrossFit.

The hardcore industrial feel I was used to was replaced with a commercial, franchised, hoity-toity atmosphere. However, the one benefit to Everyday Fitness was that it gave me time to people-watch. At CrossFit, I had been too busy actually exercising to take in my surroundings.

I felt oddly out of place in my T-shirt and mesh shorts at Everyday Fitness. Most of the women there sported brand-name coordinated workout gear, and some even wore makeup. I guess they were trying to impress the greased-up meatheads who strutted around with their chests out and abs clenched. Many of them didn't even use spotters when they benched massive amounts of weight.

Since I didn't have a trainer to motivate/yell at me, I stayed mainly to the treadmill, bike, and a few of the weight machines. On Wednesday, I had finally hit my stride on the treadmill as I approached the thirty-minute mark. Suddenly, I heard such overly exaggerated grunting, I momentarily thought that maybe Zach had been banging one of the heavily made-up bimbos on the rowing machine nearby.

I turned toward the sound and saw one of the leathery jocks pushing hundreds of pounds above his head. He clearly struggled to put the weight up once, but thankfully—for me—he decided to go for a second time . . . without a spotter. Just as the bar reached its highest point, he sneezed, causing the bar to come crashing down on his bulky chest.

Unfortunately, that was as exciting as Everyday Fitness ever got, and I had a feeling that the "everyday" part would soon turn to "hardly ever."

❤

By Friday, I was exhausted: physically, emotionally, mentally. The more I worked, the less I thought about Shane. So I'd been working a *lot*. I'd also been going to my new gym every day to make Lily and Kyle think I liked it there, so they'd stop worrying. But I didn't like it, and they didn't stop worrying.

By eight thirty, I was on the couch in my pajamas, lost in Breyer's ice cream and DVRed episodes of *Sons of Anarchy*.

"Why are you already in your pajamas eating an entire carton of ice cream?" The voice startled me.

Oh shit!

I was busted. Lily was supposed to be out for the night,

but there she stood, towering over me, her hazel eyes passing judgment on me and my carton of vanilla. "Um...because it's America's favorite. It says so. See?" I pointed to the side of the carton. "And why are you home? I'm trying to watch Jax in peace." I motioned with my spoon, signaling it was time for her to leave me alone.

"Don't be a smartass. I just got back from CrossFit. I'm going out in a bit." Her eyes narrowed and she visibly softened, a look of concern spreading across her face. "But by the looks of you, I actually don't think I'm going anywhere. I've let this go on long enough...you, avoiding Shane...avoiding me... avoiding your own feelings. Let me take a shower. I'll be out in ten minutes. You better be ready to talk then." She turned to make her way down the hall. "And you better save me some of that ice cream," she yelled as she shut the bathroom door.

I slid a few more spoonfuls of Breyer's down my throat as I fantasized about Jax. *Holy hell, is he hot! What will we do with the car seats when I give birth to all of his babies? They certainly won't fit on the back of his motorcycle.*

I knew what I was doing: I was avoiding. I would be forced to face my feelings once Lily returned, so I basked in my last few minutes of denial. Besides, I had gotten damn good at avoiding my feelings the past few weeks.

Why stop now? Practice makes perfect, right?

"So," Lily said, drying her hair with a towel with one hand as she handed me a bottle of wine and a corkscrew with her other hand, "may as well complete the cliché. It looks like Lifetime's filming a made-for-TV movie in our living room." She pointed to my disheveled appearance and the nearly empty container of ice cream. "I'll get us some glasses."

"You don't have to stay here with me, you know. Didn't

you have a date or something?"

"Or something," she said with a shrug. "But you're more important." The glass nearly spilled as she handed it to me.

"Jeez, full much?"

"Something tells me you're gonna need it. You'll be thanking me later."

I raised my eyebrows to let her know that I probably wouldn't. "So...what *is* this? What are we doing here?" I gestured back and forth between us with my free hand. "We're just supposed to have some girl chat and everything'll be okay? This isn't some romantic comedy. I don't know what I'm supposed to tell you that's gonna be so eye-opening." My tone was sarcastic, and I shook my head, letting her know that I was already annoyed.

"Just be honest with me." She let out her breath. "But it's more important that you're honest with yourself."

"I'm gonna need to drink this before *that* conversation can happen," I said, holding up my glass.

"That's fine," she said with a smile as she grabbed the ice cream off the coffee table and settled back into the fluffy gray cushions. "I got all night. Take all the time you need."

I rolled my eyes and downed the rest of my wine in gulps. There was no reason to drag this out any longer than necessary.

Lily sipped on her wine slowly, eating a spoonful of ice cream every now and then as she waited patiently for me to begin.

"It's like...that one night...after the wedding," I nearly whispered. "It's like it was too much and not enough at the same time. I don't even know how to explain it." I closed my eyes and breathed in deeply, trying to maintain my composure. "But we won't work!" I blurted out suddenly. "Shane and me..."

It'll be the same shit I went through with Nate all over again."

Lily took my glass from my hands and refilled it. "What makes you say *that*?"

It was a simple question. But for some reason, I struggled to answer it. In my heart, I knew Shane was nothing like Nate. Unfortunately, the same could not be said about me. I had lied to Shane. I had hurt him for no reason. "Rule Number Two," I answered, as if that was a sufficient explanation.

"God, you and your fucking rules," she groaned. "Enough with that bullshit already."

"It's not bullshit. We both know I have a reason for my rules."

"Yeah, you do. It's called fear. You're scared of what'll happen if you open yourself up to someone. Your rules are just some stupid-ass excuse for you to avoid feeling anything for anyone."

"You don't know what you're talking about." And she didn't. My rules hadn't prevented me from feeling something for Shane. All I'd done the past two weeks was feel.

"Yeah? Rule Number One: Always sleep with someone by the fourth date." Her voice was even. "That way sex doesn't have to mean anything. God forbid you wait 'til you actually give a shit about the person before you sleep with him."

I stayed silent, unable to find the right words to properly defend myself.

"Rule Number Two—"

"Rule Number Two is valid, and you know it."

"Rule Number Two," she repeated sternly. "Don't date anyone who makes less money than you. Go ahead and rule out half the fucking male population with that one, why don't you." Her voice grew louder as she spoke. "Nate was an insecure asshole. That's why he left you. It had nothing to do with how much money you made. If it wasn't the money, it would have been something else." Her voice softened. "Shane isn't Nate," she added. I recognized the emotion on her face: disappointment. "And Rule Number Three might be the most ridiculous one yet. Don't kiss in bars? What kind of rule is that anyway?"

"A good one. And I've recently changed it to include not kissing *anywhere* in public. It's disgusting."

"No, it's not," she said firmly. "I'll tell you what it is, though. Showing affection publicly is open . . . and honest. It lets people know that you care about someone. But if other people know you care, then *you* have to acknowledge you care. All of your rules . . . you just made them up to protect yourself. You know what your father did to your mom. And you know what Nate did to you. But they're not representative of *all* men." She paused as if she'd just realized something. "It's ironic, don't you think? That by trying to protect yourself, all you do is hurt yourself instead?"

"Seriously, Lily? You've got a lot of nerve sitting here on your fucking soapbox preaching to me about relationships. Did you forget how you fucked up your whole life last spring?" I knew I was hitting below the belt, but it was fight or flight. And I had fled enough lately.

Surprisingly Lily didn't fight back. "That's exactly why I'm telling you this. I made a big fucking mistake. It's *my* fault I'm alone right now. And I don't want the same thing to happen to you." She reached out to grab my hand, effectively relieving some of my anger. "If I learned one thing from what happened to me, it's that you need to give people a chance . . . to be what they want to be to you. You didn't even give Shane a *chance* to break your heart." There was pain in her eyes as she said it. I knew as well as she did that she wasn't just talking about Shane and me. "And you sure as hell didn't give him a chance to heal it."

Air filled my lungs deeply before I let out a long sigh. "So you're saying people deserve a second chance?" My tone was cynical.

"Some people do. But *everyone* at least deserves a first."

chapter thirteen

A week passed, and while Lily's words still rang in my head, I didn't think they applied to my situation. It's not that Shane didn't deserve a chance. He did. But I didn't. I had put so much stock in the idea that no guy would be able to deal with his girlfriend or wife making more money than him.

However, the truth was that *I* wouldn't be able to deal with it. I would be living my life waiting for the resentment to kick in. I would always be waiting for him to run like Nate had.

So the only thing I could do was try to get back to my old self. But that was easier said than done. Deep down, I wasn't sure I could relate to my old self anymore. Things were... *different. I* was different. And this change caused a heaviness to settle in my chest, an oppressive weight that told me just how much I didn't like who I was right now.

I was in limbo, confronted with a fork in the road and I had to choose a direction. But the roads laid out before me had no distinguishing characteristics. I figured it was because I had no clue what the hell I wanted anymore. Both choices were gray and dull, void of vibrancy and thrill. *God, I am totally lost.*

This feeling was new. Not because I hadn't been lost before. I probably had been for years. But it was cloaked in life. A desire to experience and enjoy everything I could made it seem as though I had purpose and direction. But having a good time can only be an end goal for so long. Eventually, you have to become a big girl and choose more meaningful aspirations.

I clearly wasn't ready to be a big girl.

So, when Lily suggested a night out on Friday, I jumped at the chance. I had been working, going to the "Gym for Future Stepford Wives" and then going home to bed every day for weeks. It was time to go out and drink until I forgot how miserable I was. Lily told me to spread the word to Danielle and Steph and she'd talk to Kyle. I wasn't sure how I felt about Kyle coming, since he'd undoubtedly bring Kate, but I had to suck it up. Kyle was my friend, and I needed to start acting like it.

We decided to meet up at the High Noon Saloon, a bar with peanut shells on the floor and wood paneling on the walls. The rustic feel was comforting in a down-home sort of way. And they served moonshine, which was definitely a win in my book.

Lily and I were the first ones there—due to my new insistence about being punctual—so we staked out a spot near a pool table. There were three high-tops that were far enough from each other to give us some space but close enough that we could all talk without shouting.

Steph and Danielle showed up soon after with Dan and Brandon. We all fell into easy conversation about Master Bader and his . . . idiosyncrasies. He had actually been fairly tolerable lately. The only explanation we could come up with was that he was ill. That, or he had finally graduated from peeping in windows to kidnapping people and making *them* listen to all of his awful stories.

Kyle and Kate showed up almost forty-five minutes after the rest of us. From the uncomfortable look on Kate's face, I guessed that she had tried to resist coming here tonight, and that was probably what had delayed them.

I watched them closely as they approached and said my hellos, and then they sat at one of the high-tops. There was none of the usual affection between them. No physical contact, not even any eye contact. There was an evident awkwardness radiating off them that instantly made me feel guilty.

Kyle had clearly insisted on coming, feeling a need to be here for me, and thus putting me before her. But he was wrong to do that. He should have done what any sane person in love would do. He should've chosen Kate.

As I began wondering how many people I was going to inconvenience with my drama, Danielle pulled a stool close to me and sat down.

"So, you're either going to love me or hate me, but I have a surprise for you," she said in a hushed voice so that only I could hear her.

I eyed her warily. "What is it?"

"Oh, you'll know it when you see it," she said with a smirk as she raised her glass to her lips.

"Is there a timeframe for this surprise? I want to make sure I'm paying attention."

"Oh, you don't have to worry about that. Besides, I think I just saw it walk in." She quickly stood and moved away from me, not wanting to be too close in case my reaction wasn't what she was hoping for.

My eyes darted toward the entrance and what, or rather *who*, I saw made my face break into a wide smile. *That crazy bitch.* As he strode toward me, I quickly turned to find Danielle.

I just shook my head at her as she beamed at me. This was just the surprise I needed.

"Amanda, long time no see."

"Rod, likewise."

"So, what's been going on? Danielle called me out of the blue yesterday and told me that you guys were all going out and that you specifically requested my presence."

"Oh, she did, did she?" I shot another look at Danielle, narrowing my eyes in a look of mock threat. "Well, I'm glad you could make it."

"Yeah." He gazed into my eyes, adding meaning to his words. "Me too."

A heat spread over my skin as I remembered why we called him Hot Rod. Not that I had *really* forgotten, but it was still nice to freshen up the mental image I had of him.

"So, you look like you need another drink. What are you having?" He rubbed his hands together, as if his words suggested a challenge.

I puckered my lips as I thought about whether I was game. I was. "I'll have a dirty martini with moonshine and a shot of Patron."

Rod's smile widened. "Good choice. I'll be right back."

I watched him make his way through the growing crowd. Thankfully, he was taller than most men and I was able to follow him with relative ease.

I bet that rock-hard ass will be just the distraction I'm looking for.

I was so caught up in my visual molestation of Hot Rod, I didn't even notice the couple that sat down at the table with Kyle and Kate. But as they settled in, I felt it. The magnetic pull that I hadn't felt in what seemed like years was back. And it made all of my emotional baggage come flooding back in. The misery, the sadness, the heaviness: it was all there. And as my eyes dragged toward the intruders, I already knew who I'd see.

"Shane."

The name left my lips in a whisper that only I heard. But with it went all of the air in my lungs. And as my eyes fell on him, I saw that his eyes were already trained on me, the tension he had carried in his jaw the last time I saw him still there.

Tension I put there.

My eyes were locked on his. That is, until I saw a hand run through his hair. A hand that wasn't his. My eyes flew over to the woman sitting beside him. I appraised her as I would an intruder: with immense hate and disgust.

She was pretty, though. I could give the bitch that much. She was model-thin, with silky brown hair and perfect features. *Fuck, she's beautiful.* Even I wanted to bang her, and I hadn't swung that way since a late-night dare in a frat house when I was a junior in college. Those had been such simpler times.

I quickly realized that I was staring and averted my eyes to my right, where Lily was sitting. I gave her an accusing stare. How could she do this to me? Why didn't she tell me he was going to be here? But as I took in her wide-eyed expression, I realized that she was as surprised as I was that he was here— and with a fucking *date* no less.

As rational thought began to return to me, I realized that Kate would have been the one who had invited Shane. I wondered if he knew I would be here. *Is that why he brought her? To throw it in my face how easily he'd moved on? Well, two could play that game.*

I sought Hot Rod among the crowd, but I didn't see him. I

consciously avoided looking toward Shane, though I did want to steal a look at Kyle. I knew that one look was all I'd need to figure out if he knew Kate had invited Shane or if he was as surprised as the rest of us.

When my eyes found Kyle, he was looking in my direction, but he quickly diverted his attention toward the ground. *Bastard.*

I opened my clutch and withdrew my phone. I went into my text messages and clicked on Kyle's name. Rod returned just as I finished typing out my message.

You're an asshole.

I hit Send and threw the phone back into my bag, which I tossed down on the table. I took my drinks from Rod.

"Sorry that took so long. The bar is friggin' packed," Rod explained.

"No worries." The corner of my eye caught Kyle reaching into his pocket to pull out his phone. He started to stand but stopped as I looked at Rod, said "Cheers," and threw back the Patron. Kyle sat back down and looked away.

Rod and I began talking about . . . nothing really. He told me about having no luck finding a job, I talked about what he was missing at the office, blah, blah, blah.

I tried extremely hard to maintain focus on Rod, but my periphery wandered to Shane constantly. I documented every shift he made, my body seeming to predict his movements and directing my eyes toward him so that I'd catch it all. And every time I looked at him, he was looking back, either gazing at me or glaring at Rod.

The looks were bad enough, but it was the touching

between Shane and his whore that really wore me down. Every time her hand grazed his arm, or he smiled warmly at her, or their shoulders rubbed together, it felt like I had been punched square in the gut. But when that sly temptress leaned in and gave Shane a light kiss on the cheek, I lost it.

"I have to go to the restroom," I said abruptly, interrupting some story Rod was telling.

I hadn't even realized that I was staring at Shane and his wench until Rod turned to see what I was looking at.

"You need anything?" Rod asked, still looking over his shoulder at Shane.

"Yeah, another round. You can add it to my tab," I said absently as I strode off toward the bathroom.

"That's okay, I got it," Rod replied as he walked off toward the bar.

I barely reached the bathroom in time, practically hyperventilating when I rushed through the door and firmly planted my palms on the sink. I stood there, my jagged, shaky breaths leaving me as I tried to put my thoughts in some semblance of coherence.

Okay, so Shane was here on a date. But I was sort of here with a date myself, so I had no right to be angry. Though I hadn't invited Rod, that was neither here nor there. Shane had to know that I'd be here. He invited that estrogen Rockette here to get a rise out of me, and I'd played right into his hands.

I had to go back out there and regain some power. If I had to fuck Rod on top of Shane's table, I would show him that he wasn't affecting me.

You can do this, Amanda. You're tough as friggin' nails. Start acting like it.

I looked at my reflection in the mirror, took a second

to run my hands through my hair, and then made my way toward the door. I had finally instilled in myself the necessary confidence to endure the rest of the night, only to have it drain from me as soon as I walked out of the bathroom.

Leaning against the opposite wall, looking sexy as hell in a tight gray polo shirt that stretched over his chest deliciously and a pair of faded jeans that hung just right off his hips, was Shane.

I stopped abruptly, causing the restroom door to smack my ass as it closed, making me jump slightly toward him. We stood there, silently staring at one another for a moment. Shane moved first. But he didn't move toward our seats. Instead, without so much as a word, he grabbed my bicep firmly and led me quickly through a side exit at the end of the small hallway.

I was too surprised to verbally respond or rail against him, so my legs moved in time with his. Once he pushed the door open, his two powerful hands grabbed my waist and slid me across the brick wall. Shane bent quickly and put a board in the door to prevent it from closing and locking us out. Then he turned his attention back to me, putting his palms against the wall on either side of my head, caging me in with his body.

I loved it.

But I'd never let him know it.

"What?" I snapped, trying to hide the fact that my heart was beating damn near out of my chest.

Shane leaned closer to me, his mouth precariously close to my jaw. His breath tickled my skin as he spoke. "You tell me what, Amanda. What are we doing?" His voice was raw and deep, the most beautiful sound I'd heard in weeks.

"Looks like we're both on dates." My voice was flippant, and I applauded myself for hiding the effect he had on me.

He tensed as he brought his body closer to mine. "I'm not on a date, Amanda. Jill's just a friend."

"Oh, yeah? Could've fooled me. You two look awfully close." I regretted the words, but I couldn't resist saying them. I wanted to know who she was to him. For my sanity, I needed to know.

"I've known her for years. There's never been anything romantic between us. I just…when Kate told me you'd be here, I had to come." His eyes drifted to my lips seductively. "But I needed some moral support. That's all she is. Now, do you really want to waste time talking about her when we could be talking about us?"

He pulled his head back so that he could look into my eyes, our noses just inches apart. The position we found ourselves in was intimate, and it scared the hell out of me.

"There's no *us* to talk about."

"Oh, no? Because I can't keep my eyes off you. No matter how much I try, my attention drifts to you. And whenever I look at you, you know what I see?"

I shook my head.

"I see you looking back. Admit it. You have no interest in that jackass you're with. The only thing in that bar that holds any interest for you is me."

Shuddering at his words, I felt the familiar throb at the apex of my thighs as I willed my body to refrain from arching toward him. He would provide the physical contact I craved. I couldn't help but imagine closing the distance between us and pushing my mouth to his. I wanted to feel the soft caress of his tongue, the light nip of his teeth, the friction of his lips.

Then, as if Shane could read my thoughts, sense my body begging for his, he enveloped my mouth in a passionate kiss that I felt all the way down to my knees.

In one deliberate movement, he seemed to consume all of me. With Shane's hard body pressing mine against the wall and his solid hand cradling the back of my neck, I couldn't escape even if I'd wanted to. And I sure as hell didn't want to. At least my *body* didn't. It responded to him instantly, involuntarily despite my best efforts. My lips remained parted, inviting his tongue to intrude and causing a familiar feeling to flutter deep inside my core at his touch. Lower, my wetness began to increase as my hard nipples rasped against his solid pecs.

My body willed my mind to succumb to my desire for Shane. And as he deepened the kiss, crushing his mouth to mine, my body won out. I fisted my hands in his hair and pulled him closer, our lips fervent against one another.

Despite my best efforts, a moan escaped me, a sound of complete and utter need. Not need just for the physicality of our relationship but for all of it. For the electricity that hummed between us. For the way our bodies fit together like we were two pieces of the same puzzle. For the way I knew he cared about me. For the way he wanted me. Wanted me . . . Shane . . . wanted me.

It was this thought that caused my arms to drop from his hair and go rigid at my sides. Shane wanted me in ways that I could never reciprocate. Our bodies may fit together, but our lives didn't. A relationship between us would never last, and we'd both be left broken at the end of it. And as I slowed our kiss, I knew that whatever this was, it wouldn't last.

I knew that as soon as the kiss was over, I'd run again. And as he reluctantly pulled away, I think Shane knew it too.

"Look me in the eyes, Amanda." His voice was commanding as he pleaded with me. "Look me in the eyes and tell me you didn't feel that. Tell me you didn't feel what I felt when I kissed you."

As if by some miracle, I willed my eyes to lock on his.

"I've always had an interest in you, Shane. But it's purely physical. Nothing more." The words poured from my mouth in a weak effort to convince both Shane and myself that they were true.

They weren't.

And Shane called my bluff. "Stop this. Please, Amanda, just stop this bullshit." He drew his body closer again, his chest grazing mine. "When I'm near you, I . . . I don't even know how to explain it. It's like I'm drawn to you. No matter how much I tell myself to stay away, I can't. I know you feel it too." Shane dropped his other hand from the wall and used it to cup my cheek as his voice softened. "Whatever concerns you have, baby, we can work on them. But don't run away from this. It's worth fighting for. This is me fighting for you. Please . . . just fight back."

Lily said that some people deserved a second chance. Here was mine. All I had to do was say I'd fight. To tell him that I felt the connection that bound us. Because those things were the truth. But even though he was giving me a second chance, that didn't mean I deserved it. I knew I didn't. It also didn't mean I wanted it. There were certain things I wouldn't leave to chance. My happiness was one of them.

"Are you really so desperate that you have to do all this to persuade a girl to be with you?"

These were the second-most-awful words I had ever spoken to Shane. And as he shrank back from me, I knew that the devil was building another circle of hell just for me.

I took immediate advantage of Shane's withdrawal and

threw open the door. As I hustled down the hall and back into the bar, only one thing was clear to me: I definitely wouldn't be getting a third chance.

❤

I wasted no time returning to my table and to Rod. I picked up my shot and lifted it to the air at him before throwing it back. As the heat burned down my throat, I felt slightly better. I'd rather feel the burn of alcohol than the pain of what I'd just done. I chugged my martini before looking up at Rod, who was matching me drink for drink.

"You wanna dance?" I asked him.

"After my last experience dancing with you, how could I ever say no?"

I grabbed his hand and led him to the dance floor, but not before noticing that Shane had returned to his table. I felt his stare as I led Rod into the crowd of rowdy drunks and pressed myself against him. The closeness reminded me of what had just happened outside, but I immediately pushed the thought down, trying to turn my mind off and let my body take over. This became easier as the alcohol hit my system, causing a haze to settle over me.

After a few more drinks and a lot more dancing, sensation flooded my body. My brain had effectively been shut down for the evening, and my body tried to soak up all the pleasure it could.

There was a point when Lily came over to me, but I barely remember our conversation. Something about me not wanting to do this and being sorry. The specifics were lost, but I knew I eventually told her to go home. Or maybe she told me to go home. *Whichever.*

My encounter with Kyle was a tad clearer, mostly because Rod had to pull me off him. I screamed at him that I hated him and never wanted to talk to him again. I might have also called him Benedict Arnold.

I don't know when Shane left. I was too wrapped up in my world of purposeful ignorance to keep track of him. But I did know that I needed to completely eradicate the *thought* of Shane as much as I had his physical presence.

That was my plan when I leaned into Rod and whispered in his ear, "Let's go back to your place."

I just wished I could remember if it worked.

❤

I woke up the next morning with a blistering headache and felt a warm body against my back. But I knew it wasn't the one body I wanted there. My mind, even in its disabled state, remembered back to my night with Zach and how I had thought it was such a shame I didn't black out anymore. Well, I'd found the solution to that problem: moonshine and tequila.

As I tried to sit up, I let out a loud groan and flopped back down. I hadn't felt this bad since, well . . . maybe ever. My head lolled to the left and looked at Rod.

Shit, did I sleep with him?

I took a quick inventory. I was in my underwear, not naked, so that was a plus. I also didn't *feel* like I'd had sex. I doubt that I would've felt nothing the morning after sleeping with Rod. Swollen lips or some sore muscles should've been in order. I'd always experienced those things in my fantasies of him.

"Hi."

The voice startled me. I wasn't aware he'd woken up. "Hi."

"Some night," he said as he rubbed his face with his hand.

"Yeah. I just wish I could remember more of it."

"No, it's probably better that you don't."

"That bad, huh?" I asked with apprehension on my face.

"Oh, yeah. You really let some of your friends have it. Major damage control is going to be in order for you today."

I sighed. I had done too much damage. There was no controlling it now. "Did we...?"

Rod smiled lazily. "I prefer my sexual partners conscious. So, no."

Hallelujah for decent men.

"You want breakfast, or do you want me to just call a cab so we can go pick up our cars?"

I appreciated this question. He didn't say it in a way that hindered me from choosing staying for breakfast, but he also acknowledged last night for what it was. Or what it was intended to be at least. He was like the male version of me.

"I think I'd rather just go get our cars. But thanks for the offer."

"Sure thing. Get dressed and I'll call."

Rod quickly pulled on the jeans he'd worn last night, opened a drawer, pulled out a T-shirt, and pulled it over his head. Once he left the room, I got out of the bed. It's not that I was shy about Rod seeing me in my underwear, but something about it just didn't feel quite right. I shimmied into my tight jeans and yanked my blue cashmere sweater over my head before following Rod into the living room.

The cab arrived about ten minutes later, and I was thankful that we'd at least been smart enough not to drive the previous night. Once we settled into the cab, Rod looked over at me.

"So, who was that guy?"

"What guy?"

"The one you spent the night in a staring contest with. You know, the blond Incredible Hulk."

I nearly laughed at Rod's description. Even though Rod was taller than Shane, Shane was much more built.

"Oh, him. He's just some guy." It hurt me to refer to Shane so casually, but I didn't know what else to say.

"Riiiight."

I let out a deep breath. "We were kind of involved. He wanted more, and I didn't."

"You sure?"

I looked at Rod quizzically. "About what?"

"That you don't want more."

I turned my gaze out the window. "Yeah, I'm sure."

We spent the rest of the ride in silence. When we reached High Noon, I insisted on paying the cab fare since Rod had paid for most of our drinks the previous evening. As the cab pulled away, Rod and I stood there awkwardly for a minute.

"Well," I finally said, "I guess, thanks?"

Rod burst out laughing, and I joined in, the weirdness disintegrating between us.

"My pleasure."

We each began walking toward our cars, which were only about six spaces from each other.

"I hope I have that someday," Rod said as I was unlocking my door.

I turned to see his car door open and his arms resting on the roof.

"Have what?"

"Someone who looks at me the way he looks at you." He

smiled shyly. "See ya around, Amanda."

I returned his smile. "Bye, Rod."

He got in his car and pulled away, and as I watched him drive off, I wished to myself that he did have that someday.

And that when he found it, he knew well enough to appreciate it.

chapter fourteen

My hands stayed glued to my car's steering wheel as I sat in the parking lot.

I didn't even want to start it. I had no idea where I'd be driving. I was tired of running. But I couldn't go home. Not yet, at least. Having my roommate berate me unmercifully was not the secret hangover cure I needed. I couldn't bear to hear Lily preach to me about her own mistakes as if they applied to my situation. The issue with Shane was different.

I let my forehead drop to the center of the steering wheel. And as my head lightly pounded against the horn, causing brief honks to sound, I echoed the noise internally with screams of frustration.

I just needed some time. Time to get my head on straight and reassert the fact that I had done the right thing. And there was only one place where I could do that. I settled back in my seat and turned my key in the ignition.

I began the drive to Angela Bishop's house. Also known as my mother's.

I wasn't sure why I had the urge to go there. Maybe because I knew it was the only place where I wouldn't be judged. I hadn't actually stayed the night at my mother's since college. We weren't exactly close, only talking on the phone a few times a month and seeing each other even less often. Our conversations were usually stilted, showing just how little we had in common. Besides, we both worked a lot.

She owned a pet-sitting business and was constantly staying at other people's houses while they were on vacation. If luck was on my side, that would be the case today and I could spend the rest of my Saturday there in solitude.

♥

Twenty-five minutes later, I pulled up to the small brick Cape Cod, and I immediately spotted her white Toyota Yaris in the gravel driveway. *So much for luck.* As I breezed by the car, I paused momentarily to examine the sight. The back seat was folded down, and a maroon sleeping bag covered the entire back. A few jackets, a case of water, and a box of Famous Amos cookies decorated the inside.

I briefly wondered whether I should knock on the front door of the house or the driver's side of the Yaris, because I wasn't sure which one she actually lived in.

After I took inventory of her car, I made my way up the brick path and rang the doorbell. When I didn't hear it, I knocked. She was probably still asleep since it was only eleven o'clock. Still early in Angela time. I was surprised when I heard a singsong-y "Come in" float through the house and out the open windows. I pushed down on the brass handle and threw my shoulder into the forest-green door. I was more than surprised when it didn't stick, and I nearly tumbled onto the living room.

"You got your door fixed," I yelled. "And why are you just telling people to come in? I could've been a murderer or a rapist or something."

"You think murderers and rapists knock first, honey? That's sweet. It's good to see you." She strolled out of the dining room and gave me a peck on the cheek. I appreciated that she didn't ask me what I was doing here, even though I was clearly still in last night's clothing and hadn't showered.

"Besides, I figured the knock was Will. He just left a few minutes ago. I thought maybe he'd come back for seconds."

"Will?"

"I met him the other day at my Boomerang for Beginners class in the park. He's British," she said, clearly impressed with her conquest. "You know, a British accent makes a man much hotter. It takes a guy who's a soft six up to a hard eight with just a few flicks of the tongue."

I hoped to God the tongue comment was in reference to Will's speech and not his oral sex skills.

She raised her thin eyebrows in a way that made what she was about to say even more awkward. "And Will's definitely a *hard* eight if you know what I mean."

"Mom, please. I really don't need to hear this." I shook my head and squeezed my eyes shut like I was trying to physically shake the image from my brain. It didn't work.

"I'm glad you're here," she added. "You can critique my new belly dancing routine later." If there was one thing my mom was good for, it was a random change in subject. And I was definitely thankful for it.

A look around the house reminded me why I didn't come here more often. Seating was limited to just a small plaid loveseat that was covered with half-folded clothing in the corner.

"You're building a boat?" I asked, pointing to the partially built fishing boat in the middle of the living room, propped up on wooden chocks. I actually didn't know why I'd said it as a question. I couldn't say that I was surprised. "You don't fish—wait, do you?" I realized I had no idea.

She moved a few boxes from in front of the couch and motioned for me to sit. "No, but I've been watching those shows where all those crab fisherman make hundreds of thousands of dollars for one fishing season. I bet I could do that."

She pulled a blue sweatshirt with a picture of a husky on it over her head and adjusted her blond ponytail. I noticed a few streaks of gray near her ears and some subtle wrinkles behind her glasses that hadn't been there the last time I'd seen her. Guess it had been longer than I thought.

"You can't catch crabs in this boat," I replied in reference to her latest business venture. "I don't even know how you're gonna get it out of the house when you're done. It won't fit through any of the doors or windows. By the way," I added. gesturing to the sweatshirt she'd just put on, "why *are* your windows open? It's late October. It's freakin' freezing in here."

"That's what's wrong with people today. They don't get enough fresh air."

Yeah, that's *what's wrong with people. Maybe the fresh air will solve my problems with Shane.*

"You need fresh air for the soul," she continued. "Nature rejuvenates you. Come eat, honey. I was making a smoothie when you came in." She picked up a few bills that had blown off the wooden dining room table by a gust of wind.

"I'm really not that hungry. Pretty hungover, actually."

"Even better, then. This'll clean you right out," she said as she handed me a glass that looked like it contained a cross between a baby's diaper and my vomit after a hot date with Midori Sour in high school.

"What's in this? Wait, I don't think I wanna know." I put it to my nose and was surprised that it actually didn't smell half bad.

"It's wheatgrass, plain Greek yogurt, and some other ingredients I'll keep secret because they'll just gross you out. Just drink it. It'll make you feel better."

The fact that she revealed wheatgrass and plain yogurt as the appetizing parts made me fear what else the concoction contained, but I chugged it nonetheless. *Anything to make me feel better.* My eyes caught movement by the refrigerator. "Jesus Christ!" I yelled, jumping back into the butcher's block kitchen island. "What the fuck is that? Why is there a chicken in your house?"

"That's Rosie. She's a bantam hen. I got some chickens a few months ago so I could have fresh eggs. This was before I became a vegan, of course." She picked up Rosie, and the small, colorful bird struggled to free herself of my mom's grasp. "They create a lot of dust, though. That's one of the reasons I have the windows open. They go outside to eat," she said as she shooed the bird out the back door. "And inside to shit, I guess." She laughed as she nodded toward the bird poop by my foot.

"When did you become a vegan?" *Should I be worried that was my only comment regarding the chickens?* "You just ate yogurt. That's not vegan."

"I'm working up to it slowly." She shrugged. "You should really try it. Have you ever watched that documentary about how animals are killed for food? It's so sad. I can't eat meat after seeing that." She knelt down with a paper towel to clean up after Rosie. "I did have a craving for hotdogs the other day, though. I stopped at the store and ate two when I got home. They were so good."

I had to stop myself from informing her that two hotdogs did not qualify as "working up to it slowly," but I knew my efforts would be futile.

"I'd rather butcher a cow myself than give up steak," I laughed. "Wait, Mom, what's in your hair?" I reached to touch a bumpy silicone tie in her hair.

"It's a cock ring," she said simply.

Oh. My. Fucking. God!

"I couldn't find a hair tie this morning. Mike left it here a few weeks ago." She shrugged. "Problem solved."

"Ahhhhh!" I yelled to drown out the sound of her voice as I covered my ears.

"Oh, Amanda, calm down. I'm nearly fifty, not nearly *dead*. And I'm not married. What do you want from me? I need to get laid just as much as you do."

"Mom, please just stop." My words flew out of my mouth at a rapid pace. "For the love of God!"

"Oh, all right, all right," she whined with a tinge of disappointment in her voice. Clearly she would have liked to have elaborated on her night with Mike.

My body shook with disgust. "I need to take a shower . . . especially now. And I'm gonna take a nap. Do you still have some of my old clothes here?"

She put a finger to her lips, clearly trying to remember something. "Um . . . I think I still have your high school gym uniform. The rest I gave away to Purple Heart."

"Why would you keep just my gym uniform?"

"Honey, they're veterans. They don't wanna wear your disgusting old gym uniform. Go take a shower. You look like you could use it. I'll come check on you in a little while."

Some "not tested on animals" body wash, one twelve-year-old gym uniform, and a half hour later, I was resting comfortably in my old room. I studied the posters that still hung on the wall: Boyz II Men and Leonardo DiCaprio posing like he was the king of the world—I still had fantasies of pressing my palm against the inside of a steamy car while he ravaged me.

Strangely enough, that wasn't the only thing that hadn't changed. Sure, I had a high-paying job and an apartment. But the last time I had slept in here, I had envisioned that my future would involve marriage . . . maybe even a few kids. That had been at least six years ago, and here I was, still waiting for my future to begin.

I was lost in self-pity when my mom entered. "Knock, knock," she said quietly. "Feeling better?" She plopped herself on the edge of the twin bed, rubbed her hands together, and hovered them inches above my face.

"Mom?" I blinked into her palms. "Should I even ask what you're doing?"

"Shh, it's Reiki. It's a Japanese stress-reduction technique. I've been taking classes at the Center for Alternative Healing. There's a life force energy that flows through all of us. If it's low, we feel stressed. If it's high, we're happier. Yours is very low."

I shook my head, but part of me knew she was right. My plummeting "life force energy" had been obvious to people other than me lately.

"Reiki treats the whole person: mind, body, emotions, spirit," she added soothingly.

As strange as it sounded, I did feel a sense of calm, and eventually I must have drifted off to sleep.

❤

I awoke to my own screams, and when I opened my eyes, Rosie's face was inches from mine, her dirty feet firmly planted on my chest. By reflex, I jumped up, effectively throwing Rosie's feathery body to the floor. She squawked in response, and I felt a little remorseful for how I'd treated her. I internally scolded myself for feeling that way. *She's just a chicken.*

It felt like I had only slept a few minutes, but the clock told me I had been asleep for over two hours.

"What's wrong, honey?" My mom rushed in just like she had when I'd been five and used to have nightmares that the house had caught on fire.

I had moved to stare at my pale reflection in my bedroom mirror, my bright-green eyes dulled by the past few weeks' events. Slowly, my mom appeared behind me and began to stroke my hair. "I have to stay at a dog's house tonight, but you can stay here as long as you like." She gave me a quick squeeze around my shoulders. "Oh, will you feed the chickens for me in an hour or so? I won't be back for a few days. Their food's in the garage."

I looked past my own reflection into my mother's green gaze, and I felt the little color I had left in my face leave completely. Looking at my mom made me realize that my future *had* started. It just wasn't the one I had pictured. I didn't want this: sleeping with random men and buying into every fad that came down the pike in the hope that it would give my life some meaning. I didn't want to be my mother.

"What's the matter, Amanda? You look like you've just seen a ghost."

I spun around, searching frantically for my shoes. "I think I have," I said as I headed for the stairs.

But my mom's comment effectively stopped me in my tracks when I reached the front door. "You have to stop running, Amanda," she yelled down the stairs. "You're always running from something."

"You're right, Mom. I *am* always running from something. But this time," I said, looking up the stairs at her slender frame, "I'm going to run toward it."

❤

I practically sprinted to my car. I couldn't get out of here fast enough. Or maybe it wasn't that I was eager to get *away* from something so much as I was eager to get to something. Or someone.

My visit to my mom's had finally made me certain of what I wanted: Shane. Whatever it would take to get him back, I was willing to do it. And as I raced down the highway even faster than my standard police-magnet speed, I hoped...I prayed that I hadn't ruined our relationship irreparably.

It had taken only a few short hours at my mother's house to find the clarity that I'd been missing for the past five or six years. Who knew that her ridiculous free-spirited lifestyle could have such a profound effect on me?

Shane had shared his true feelings for me, and I hadn't been kind with my responses. My words and actions had been chosen intentionally to push him away. And it had worked. I was nothing if not thorough. By the time I'd finally realized my mistake, I feared Shane had already had enough of my rejection. Of my selfishness.

What I feared most was that he'd finally had enough of *me*.

I had no idea what I'd even say when I saw him. It all felt

so ridiculous, so over-the-top. Would I just show up at his house and confess that I had been an asshole? Tell him that I needed him more than I needed my next breath? That during the last few weeks, I'd felt like I was drowning, and I needed him to rescue me?

Probably not.

That all seemed way too corny to vocalize, despite the fact that it was exactly how I felt. My best bet was just to wing it.

I was counting on the fact that Shane would be at his house, but when I got there and didn't see his Mustang in the driveway, I headed toward the only other place I hoped he'd be: CrossFit.

Relief flooded through me when I spotted his car in the CrossFit parking lot. But my relief was quickly replaced by an emotion I didn't know very well: embarrassment.

I may have a habit of putting myself in situations that could be deemed embarrassing by others, but surprisingly, I rarely felt embarrassed. However, I had a creeping suspicion that embarrassment and I were about to become damn good friends.

I pulled into a spot about fifteen feet away from the front of the gym, but for some reason, I couldn't bring myself to go inside. Shane probably had a class, and I couldn't just barge in like a lunatic and declare that I was falling in love with him.

Could I?

I briefly considered texting him and telling him to come outside and talk to me for a few minutes, until I remembered that he wouldn't have his phone on him if he was instructing a class. I looked down at the clock on my car radio: four forty-two. Class would be finishing up soon anyway.

But patience had never been one of my many virtues, so it

was time for Plan C.

I opened my door, hung myself halfway out, and pounded on the horn.

What is it with me and horns today?

I stood just outside my car, screaming between each blaring beep. "Shaaaane!" *Beeeep!* "Shaaaane!" *Beeeep!* "Shaaaane!" *Beeeep!* "Come outsiiiide!"

I kept up my obnoxious courting ritual for a few minutes until Shane emerged with an audience who must have followed him out to see what all the commotion was. Lily and Kate stood with several other CrossFit members, all of whom were clearly already amused. They seemed to be waiting to see what I would do next. They weren't the only ones. I really had no idea what I planned to do from here.

I remained behind my open door, feeling protected by the barrier it created between Shane and me. Though his solid arms were crossed in front of his hard chest, he seemed more confused than upset or irritated with me.

Thankfully, Shane spoke before I did. "What the hell are you doing, Amanda?" My name sounded both foreign and intimate as it rolled off his tongue.

Good question. How did I answer that? I had no idea what I should say. I'd never been known for having a way with words. I couldn't give some long, drawn-out speech like characters did in the books and movies when they professed their love so eloquently that it could not possibly go unrequited.

This wasn't *The Notebook*, for Christ's sake. I was standing in a parking lot in a high school gym uniform that was over a decade old. *Not exactly the most romantic scene anyone's ever witnessed.*

It would probably be best to keep whatever I said short and

sweet. I squinted and held up my hand to block the afternoon sun as I struggled to read Shane's expression. He remained stoic, patiently waiting for my answer. For the first time since last night, I allowed myself to remember our conversation outside the bar—when Shane had told me he was fighting for me.

"I'm fighting back," I yelled.

"What?" he asked, shaking his head and running his fingers through his unruly hair. "I don't get it."

"Last night," I began, "you said you were fighting for me." My voice grew calmer, quieter, as I hoped he wouldn't deliver to me the same rejection I had so harshly thrown at him time and time again. "You asked me to fight back," I reminded him. "Well, this is me fighting." I closed my car door and threw my open arms in the air, essentially letting him see me for the first time in well...ever.

"I don't get it," he repeated. "Last night you left like you always do. You told me you didn't have feelings for me. You were pretty clear about that." I could see the pain in his eyes as he spoke.

Like fans at a tennis match, our spectators' eyes bounced back and forth between us. And I hoped the dark clouds that had been settling over us weren't an omen of how this conversation would end.

I stepped a few more feet toward Shane, but something inside me prevented me from getting too close. So I stopped in front of the hood of my car. I needed the buffer that the ten feet of distance between us provided. I needed a buffer for what I was about to reveal.

The drops of rain that began to fall on my face would effectively hide the tears when they managed to work their way past the corners of my eyes. I knew I had to be honest with him.

"I can't pretend to feel something I don't," I shouted as the steadily increasing rain began to drown out my quivering voice. The last time I had said those same words to Shane, they had devastated him. They had broken him to pieces. And they had done the same to me. But now I was using those words to bring us together. "I can't pretend to feel *nothing* for you." I wiped away the rain that had gotten in my eyes because I couldn't take them off Shane. I inhaled sharply, preparing for what I was about to say. "I can't pretend I'm not falling in love with you."

Smiles spread across the onlookers' faces, and Shane's posture softened noticeably. He uncrossed his arms, dropped his gaze to the pavement, and rubbed his forehead, clearly contemplating what to say next. "I still don't understand. How do I know you're serious?" he finally asked as his gaze again met mine. There was hesitation in his voice, but his eyes held hope: hope that I would say whatever it was he needed to hear.

I tilted my head up toward the sky, and I couldn't avoid acknowledging the cliché. "It's like . . . I didn't even notice how sunny it was until it started raining." I returned my eyes to his, and I saw that he'd stepped from under the gym awning into the rain with me. "These last few weeks without you . . . I'm just tired of it pouring." I raised my arms in a shrug before letting them fall back to my sides. "I'm fucking soaked." I laughed nervously as I tugged on my gold gym uniform, which was clinging to me and practically see-through from the rain. "I miss the sun, Shane. I miss *you*."

I could see him wondering what to say from here. "What changed?" he asked incredulously. "Why would your feelings suddenly be any different?" He needed clarification, proof that I meant what I'd said.

I thought for a moment before settling on my answer. "I can't live with chickens, Shane!" I yelled frantically through the downpour, as if that justified my sudden change of heart.

"I don't even think I wanna know what you're talking about." Shane's eyebrows furrowed in confusion, and he shook his head as he turned away from me toward the building and our crowd of unwanted spectators.

"My mom," I blurted out to Shane's back, hoping that my words would stop him from walking away. "She never trusted anyone after my father left her. She didn't wanna feel that pain again. She's almost fifty now, she's barely ever home, and she puts sex toys in her hair." Unable to get my point across, I groaned in frustration until I found the right words. "She's lonely." I could hear my voice shaking. "Because she never gave anyone a chance again. She lives with chickens. You told me I was like her," I yelled as tears started to mix with the rainwater on my cheeks. "I'm not," I added quietly. "Like her, I mean. At least, I don't wanna be." I took a deep breath. "Don't you see, Shane? I never even gave you a *chance* to break my heart."

I glanced over Shane's shoulder toward Lily, knowing that my comment would elicit a response from her. She didn't disappoint. "That's *my* line," she said to Kate, smiling proudly.

"I'm giving you that chance now . . ." I continued, "to break my heart . . . to be my wildest dream or my biggest mistake . . . to be whatever it is you're supposed to be to me." I could taste my tears when I swallowed the lump in my throat. "I can't live with chickens, Shane," I repeated softly. For the first time, I felt as if a weight had actually been lifted *off* me at CrossFit.

I didn't know what Shane's reaction would be because

he still hadn't turned back to face me, but I felt better just knowing that I'd said what I needed to say. That this time, if I was left alone, it wouldn't be because I had been the one to leave.

It felt like I waited an eternity for Shane to turn around. And when he finally did, I could tell that his smile had probably been there through most of my chicken speech. "I knew I could get ya to fight a little harder, Bishop," he said with a wink. Leave it to Shane to ruin a perfectly romantic moment with a smartass comment.

And just like that, we were back on solid ground.

"And by the way," he added, looking over his shoulder at our audience. "I told her I'd get her to break her rules."

What? Now I was the one who was confused. "Rules plural? I think you only made me break Rule Number Two, if I'm correct." I smirked at him, urging him to elaborate.

"You didn't sleep with me until our fifth date. That breaks Rule Number One, I believe."

"First of all, you're the only guy who would brag about getting laid after a longer period of time. And second of all, that's impossible because we didn't go on any dates."

"Um...yeah we did," he corrected. "Our first date was Kate's birthday. I invited you, and you came, so it counts as a date. Our second date was the CrossFit competition. I drove you home. Date." He shrugged.

I rolled my eyes. "You're really grasping at straws. You know that, right?"

"Date number three was rock climbing. It's a date because I paid for your lunch. And date number four was obviously the pool hall when you referred to me as your boyfriend. I even kissed you against your door. And you loved it, if I recall." His tongue swept across his wet lips at the memory.

Well, I can't argue about loving it.

"Four dates. The barbeque was our fifth when we had sex in my pool."

"Seriously?" Lily yelled. "That's totally hot! You didn't tell me that."

"Okay," I conceded, interrupting Lily's outburst. "I'll admit that maybe you made me break two of my rules. But there's no way in hell you'll be responsible for breaking my third."

"Oh yeah?" he said, his blue eyes sparkling seductively.

"Yeah." I stepped toward him, and my hands found the back of his neck in a heartbeat, grasping his wet hair. "Because I'm breaking that one myself," I whispered against his lips before I pressed my own against them. Shane cradled me in his arms as our tongues tangled slowly. This was what the future was supposed to taste like.

Surprisingly, I'd forgotten there was even an audience watching until we heard some clapping and "woo-hoos."

"You're fucking crazy, you know that?" Shane whispered after he pulled away just enough to lean his forehead against mine.

"The rain metaphor was a little over-the-top, wasn't it?" I asked with a smirk.

"Maybe just a little," he said as he nibbled my bottom lip, "but I loved every second of it. Now let's get you out of these wet clothes."

"Mmm," I groaned into his mouth. "My thoughts exactly."

❤

After we managed to pull ourselves apart, Shane yelled, "Class dismissed" and slid into my car beside me. "My place?" he asked with a deep rasp to his already sultry voice. "It's closer." His breath tickled my neck as he spoke against it between nibbles of my flesh. Then he traced a hand up the inside of my thigh as he worked his way underneath my shorts.

"I already broke Rule Number Three. Let's just screw in the parking lot," I said, only half kidding.

"Mmm, that *would* be easy since you have no underwear on," he panted as he discovered my bareness when his fingers gently teased my entrance. "My place," he repeated. "Drive quickly, but be careful. The weather's bad." The combination of his urgency and protectiveness only made him hotter. Good thing my shorts were already wet from the rain. It made the slippery arousal between my thighs less noticeable. "Do you have any idea what I've thought of doing to you for the past few weeks?"

Um, yeah. Probably the same things I've *pictured you doing to me for the past few weeks.*

But I still wanted to hear it. "No. Tell me." God, this was so fucking hot: Shane talking dirty to me in the passenger's seat while I drove at a high rate of speed. Okay, maybe that last part wasn't all that out of the ordinary, but usually I didn't have a hot guy's fingers threatening to invade me with every brush against my skin.

"I've imagined my tongue licking down the length of your body," he said as his soft lips sent shivers against my neck.

I moved my hair out of the way and stretched my head to the side to give him better access.

"I've pictured myself pulling on your hard nipples."

My insides clenched at his words as his fingers slid up my

shirt and under my bra.

"Like this," he said, tugging on the hard peaks.

I flexed my hips upward at his touch, my clit silently begging for his attention again. "I couldn't stop myself from thinking about making you come with my mouth...with my fingers," he said as he moved his hand under my shorts again and slid one finger deep inside me, stroking my front wall with his fingertip.

"Oh God, Shane," I moaned. He had never said anything like this before. Never been so sexually forward with me. But our relationship was certainly different now.

I could definitely get used to this.

"And I couldn't stop myself from getting this hard when I thought of you." Shane took my hand and placed it on his dick, which was bulging against his boxer briefs and mesh shorts. I thought briefly about pulling off to the shoulder and dry fucking him on the side of the road, but I somehow managed to resist. Instead, I slid my hand lightly up and down his length, not wanting to get him too close to climax.

"I did that to myself so many times," he groaned against my neck, "pretending it was you. Mmm... God, what I would've given to be inside you then, to feel you around me when I came."

I pulled into his driveway just in time, because his words had almost been my undoing. "I want that too. God, Shane, you have no idea."

Quickly, we exited the car. Shane fiddled with his keys while I stared conspicuously at the outline of his hard cock against his shorts. When the door opened, he motioned me through, and I received a hard smack on the ass. "I want you on my bed. Naked. Now." For once, I had nothing smart to say back to his demand. Because . . . well, frankly, I wanted that too.

The next few moments filled me with anticipation as we ascended the stairs, but for the first time, the anticipation didn't feel solely sexual.

I anticipated the feelings that I would finally allow myself to experience with this man. I welcomed them.

When we entered his room, Shane spun me roughly to face him and slid my uniform shirt over my head, kissing down my stomach and slipping my shorts off with one hand.

He remained kneeling in front of me, and I pulled his shirt off, tossing it to the floor beside us before reaching up and unclasping my bra. I gazed down at the top of his head and ran my fingers eagerly through his messy, damp hair.

I could feel the slickness working its way down my thighs as Shane massaged my clit with his thumb while his fingers toyed at my entrance. His slow, teasing strokes made me ache for his mouth to finish what his hand had started. As if responding to my thoughts, Shane kissed up from the inside of my knee slowly until his lips gave me the stimulation I craved.

"Jesus, Shane," I said with a heavy breath. "Mmm, you have no idea how good this feels."

His response was a low groan against my throbbing clit as he guided his smooth, wet tongue inside me. With soft, gentle licks, he brought me closer and closer to orgasm, and I pressed his head against me, watching him move back and forth eagerly as he hummed into me.

His movements grew quicker at my heated response until two fingers plunged deep inside and pushed me over the edge. I couldn't help but call out his name in labored breaths as my legs nearly buckled beneath me.

His welcome assault slowed gradually as my orgasm

tapered off around his fingers and soft tongue. With gentle kisses, he made his way up my stomach and breasts until his mouth found mine again, and he crashed against me onto the bed.

He shimmied frantically out of his shorts and boxers, allowing his hard cock to spring free. For a few moments, he ground against my entrance, working me quickly toward another orgasm. And after weeks of imagining it, my tongue finally traced along the thick tribal design on his skin.

I wanted to beg him to push himself roughly inside me, to feel him fill me both physically and emotionally as we rocked our bodies in time with one another. Unable to wait any longer, I guided his tip to where I needed it most, but he paused almost immediately, probably knowing that if he started, he wouldn't be able to stop.

"Let me get a condom," he whispered.

I couldn't get enough of him, and I didn't want to wait one more second to feel the connection I'd been waiting so long to feel.

"You don't need one," I assured him as I arched my back and thrust my hips toward his. And he really *didn't* need one. I'd been on the pill for years. And more importantly, I trusted him.

At my words, Shane thrust himself deep inside me.

And there it was: the feeling that had been lacking inside me for so long. The feeling of being completely connected to someone. Being one with them.

"Shane," I whispered against his swollen lips as he kissed me softly, one firm hand resting on my hips and the other gently cradling my chin. "I want this to last."

His deep-blue eyes met mine, and the true meaning of my

words sank in with his reply.

"It will," he spoke softly as his hand swept delicately across my face. "I promise . . . it'll last."

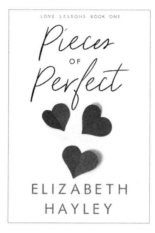

also by

e l i z a b e t h   h a y l e y

Love Lessons:
Pieces of Perfect
Picking Up the Pieces
Perfectly Ever After

❤

Sex Snob
(A Love Lessons Novel)

Misadventures:
Misadventures with My Roommate
Misadventures with a Country Boy
Misadventures in a Threesome
Misadventures with a Twin
Misadventures with a Sexpert

acknowledgments

Our husbands: Thank you for putting up with us. It's a tough job, but somebody's gotta do it. Thank you for believing in us and for encouraging us to "do what we do." Special shout-out to "Hayley's" husband Nick ("The Real Elizabeth Hayley" lol): We can't thank you enough for promoting our books when we didn't.

Fans/Readers: Thank you for your support, for all of your suggestions, and for giving us a reason to keep pursuing our dream.

To all the bloggers and other authors who've helped us out, you all are simply the best. Thanks for spreading the word and getting our work out there to readers (since we are evidently challenged in that regard).

Trish, you smut-loving bitch...what would we do without you? You told us which scenes were hot, what parts of the book needed work, and you assured us that Amanda is a relatable and likable character.

Alison Bliss: Thanks for showing us the way. Yoda you are. You're definitely the best Texan in Indiana! When are you coming to Philly so we can hang out, by the way?

Melissa: Thank you for all of your marketing advice, for pimping us as much as you can, and for believing that our

books are good enough to actually sell.

Beta Readers: Lauren, Brenda, Jessica, and Sim: Thanks for taking time out of your lives to help us make our book better. Your damn near immediate feedback and thorough critique were exactly what we needed. You girls are the best! Hope you're all gearing up to beta read our next one.

"Elizabeth": Thank you for joining CrossFit and getting some inspiration for this book. Thank you for being the first one to write a scene and for making me laugh so freakin' hard when I read it for the first time. You created Amanda! Writing together has brought us so much closer. You always know exactly what to say and how to say it—in life and in writing. You are my twin (if I were blond and about five inches taller). ~ "Hayley"

"Hayley": For once, I don't think I can find the words to express myself. But I'll try anyway. Thank you for writing with me. Thank you for helping me reach goals and dreams I would never have accomplished alone. Thank you for being there for me in every way. Thank you for being my soul sister in writing. But mostly, thank you for being you. ~ "Elizabeth"

about

elizabeth hayley

Elizabeth Hayley is actually "Elizabeth" and "Hayley," two friends who love reading romance novels to obsessive levels. This mutual love prompted them to put their English degrees to good use by penning their own. The product is *Pieces of Perfect*, their debut novel. They learned a ton about one another through the process, like how they clearly share a brain and have a persistent need to text each other constantly (much to their husbands' chagrin).

They live with their husbands and kids in a Philadelphia suburb. Thankfully, their children are still too young to read.

Visit them at AuthorElizabethHayley.com